PRAISE FOR JOE HART

Where They Lie

"The tragic crash of a small plane sets an Oregon social worker on the trail of even greater tragedies behind it . . . A well-paced exposé of dark family secrets." —*Kirkus Reviews*

"The plot takes many twists and turns and keeps readers guessing until the surprising end. For fans of Harlan Coben, Riley Sager, and Linwood Barclay." —*Library Journal*

Or Else

2023 Edgar Award Winner for Best Paperback Original

"Hart remains a suspense writer to watch." —*Publishers Weekly*

"Or Else is a thriller/suspense tour de force. Joe Hart has knocked it out of the park with a start-to-finish roller coaster ride of perfectly executed twists and expertly timed chills. Deep character development and rich narrative seals Or Else's place as the not-to-be-missed domestic thriller/suspense of the year." —Steven Konkoly, author of the Ryan Decker series and *Deep Sleep*

"The perfect thriller for a rainy afternoon, Or Else draws you into a web of small-town secrets, lies, and intrigue and doesn't let you go. Hart's well-rendered setting and characters resonate like people and places you've known. Loved every minute of this absolute page-turner!" —D. M. Pulley, bestselling author of *The Dead Key*

"Joe Hart has written compelling stories before, but it's in Or Else that he shows off just how good he is. This book checks all the boxes for me: a (seemingly) quiet, small-town drama—filled with those little quirks and secrets nobody wants to talk about—that quickly blossoms into something big, sinister, and menacing. Hart doesn't pull any punches on some serious issues, either: love, infidelity, family conflict . . . there's plenty to think about right up to the explosive ending. This is the thriller you'll be recommending for the foreseeable future."

—Matthew Iden,
author of the Marty Singer series and *The Winter Over*

Obscura

"Joe Hart is a tremendous talent, and with Obscura, he has taken his storytelling to the next level. This is a genius work of science fiction, brimming with thrills, scares, and most importantly, heart. I devoured this book, and you will too." —Blake Crouch,
New York Times–bestselling author of *Dark Matter* and the Wayward Pines series

"Outstanding . . . Fans of Blake Crouch's Wayward Pines series, with its combination of mystery, horror, and science fiction, will find this right up their alley." —*Publishers Weekly* (starred review)

"This gripping book will be a must-read for fans of SF-based mysteries such as John Scalzi's Lock In and Kristine Kathryn Rusch's Retrieval Artist series, as well as aficionados of stories about science gone wrong, too far, or both." —*Library Journal* (starred review)

"The pacing is excellent from beginning to end." —*Los Angeles Times*

"Those seeking an off-planet sci-fi thriller with a haunting plotline will devour Joe Hart's Obscura, which reads quick and is jam-packed with terrifying surprises." —The Real Book Spy

"For the reader who likes hard science fiction with some mystery and suspense thrown in, Obscura should hit the spot. It's not merely sci-fi, but a thriller wrapped in the deadly solitude of space with a determined heroine who refuses to give up." —*New York Journal of Books*

ALSO BY JOE HART

The Dominion Trilogy

The Last Girl
The Final Trade
The First City

The Liam Dempsey Mysteries

The River Is Dark
The Night Is Deep

Nora McTavish

Where They Lie
Never Come Back
Now We Run

Novels

Lineage
Singularity
EverFall
The Waiting
Widow Town
Cruel World
Obscura
I'll Bring You Back
We Sang in the Dark
Or Else

Novellas

Leave the Living
A Hole We Crawl Into
Short Story Collections
Midnight Paths: A Collection of Dark Horror
Something Came Through: And Other Stories

Short Stories

"Outpost"
"And the Sea Called Her Name"
"The Exorcism of Sara May"

Comics

The Last Sacrifice

WYNDCLYFFE

A NOVEL

JOE HART

Podium

Cover design by James Iacobelli

ISBN: 978-1-0394-9002-4

Published in 2025 by Podium Publishing
www.podiumentertainment.com

Podium

For Jade.

Always.

WYNDCLYFFE

PART 1

INANIS

PROLOGUE

She woke with a deep inhale, breathing in the dappled moonlight of the room and thought, *Something's wrong.*

Allison rubbed her eyes, making sure she was awake and not still wrapped in the undercurrent of dreams. She'd experienced this waking notion before, only to surface moments later in the real world, leaving the thin veil of sleep trailing behind like a shed skin.

She was definitely awake. She sat up and put her feet on the floor, the coolness of the wood planks sudden and shocking. Had it been the grandfather clock that woke her? Its longest tolling had drawn her out of sleep before, leaving her wide-eyed and thought-stricken into the early morning hours. No, the clock on her bedside table read a quarter to midnight. This felt like some internal alarm, something out of reach of her grasping mind.

Climbing from bed, she crossed the room to her door. The hallway was bruised with shadow and silent except for the quiet hush of an air vent. Allison glanced first one way, then the other. Nothing out of place or concerning. Only the dark and quiet of the manor at night.

Probably nerves. Anxiety gathering and reaching critical mass. It had grown over the last week into a strange fear interwoven with excitement. A giddiness at the thought of finally leaving this place once and for all to start something new.

The unreality of actually moving away washed over her again, and she was suddenly infinitely thankful for Oliver and Eleanor. To say they'd been the guardrails on her life so far was an understatement. Their love and kindness almost made up for her father's . . . behaviors. She'd told Oliver this the day before when they'd had a moment alone in the dining room. He'd smiled and looked at her in the same sad way he had so many times over the years, and it felt like he'd been at the precipice of saying something. But then the spell had broken as her father entered the room.

Allison shifted in the doorway, listening one last time to the silence before assuring herself it had been nerves that had woken her. One last day and then tomorrow . . . tomorrow they would finalize their plans before the equinox. Mom was adamant they be gone beforehand. It had something to do with what her father was planning. She had no idea what it was, but given the way things had been building over the last months, she didn't want to stay and find out. It felt like a storm was coming. Like the air was charged and about to—

A blast ripped through the quiet of the manor. Allison's heart seized, an electric shock of fear running through every nerve. Another vicious *crack* echoed down from somewhere above and adrenaline jetted into her veins. *Gunshots. Someone's shooting upstairs.*

A muffled yell rose and fell, coming from the direction of the stairway. There were no words, only a cry of raw pain that finally broke her free of her paralysis.

Allison stumbled away from her room, moving without thinking toward Isabelle's door, but when she opened it, her friend's bed was empty.

"Izzy?" she whispered, frantically searching for her in the dark. "Where are you?" She wasn't in the closet or hiding under the bed. She was gone.

What was happening?

She felt faint. Had someone broken into the house? What should she do? Hide? Try to get outside? Allison was starting for the closest window when the sound of hurried footsteps came down the hallway toward the room. Coldness flooded her.

She hadn't locked the door.

Allison rushed to the closet and slipped inside just as the bedroom door flew inward. She placed a hand on the handle but didn't dare pull the door shut, since whoever had just entered would see the movement. Hot tears gathered in the corners of her eyes as she tried to control her breathing, listening over her stampeding heartbeat.

More footsteps, much closer now. Right outside the door.

"Girls? Are you in here?"

Allison sagged and pushed the door open. Her mother stood in her robe just inside the room. Her face was stricken, hair askew. She rushed closer and pulled Allison to an embrace.

"What's going on?" Allison asked.

"We have to go. Come on." Her mother moved toward the door, then stopped short before stepping into the hallway herself. Her expression tightened, eyes widening, then she was locking the door and shoving Allison back toward the closet. "Inside, inside now," she hissed. Allison struggled for a second, trying to remain in the bedroom as her mother closed her inside the closet. "Be quiet" was the last thing she said before shutting the door.

Allison edged backward into the embrace of hanging clothes. What was happening? What had her mother seen? Why wasn't she hiding with her? Above the thudding of her heart came the sound of the bedroom door rattling in its frame. Then quiet.

"Vanessa?"

Her mother's name, even through the thickness of two doors, was enough to cause Allison's bladder to flex painfully. Because it was and wasn't her father who had spoken. It was his other voice, the one matching the emptiness that sometimes gathered behind his eyes.

"Leland, please," her mother wheezed. It sounded as if she were directly on the other side of the closet door, maybe with her back pressed up against it, a last line of defense. "Please, please, please stop."

A pregnant silence, then a bang and the splintering of wood. Allison flinched, almost screaming. Two more blows intermingled with her mother's cries, and she knew what was happening out there, could see her father kicking his way into the room. He was saying something over her mother's sobbing, something in that same vapid tone so much worse than rage.

Allison summoned all her courage to grasp the knob and twist it. She opened the door.

A gunshot rang out. Beyond loud and so close—it vibrated against her skin, all the way to her center. She nearly retreated but forced herself to step into the room.

The first thing she saw was her mother turning slowly away from her father, hands pressed tightly over her stomach, mouth a tight O of shock and pain. Liquid darkness spread from around her fingers, staining the pearl white of her robe black.

For a long second, Allison and her mother looked at one another, then Vanessa's knees folded and she fell to her side on the floor, hands finally coming loose to release a tide of blood.

Allison tried to move, to scream, to do something. The best she could manage was a quiet moan. Her mother made a feeble movement, trying to push herself toward the closet, then fell still. Slowly, Allison pried her eyes up from her mother's body to what stood in the doorway.

It was no longer her father. He had finally become something else.

He raised the gun he was holding, the muzzle's bore a black unblinking eye. "You're not her," Leland said quietly. Sadly.

There was movement behind him, a familiar shape there holding the length of the shotgun that had always hung above the great fireplace. He heard something and began to turn.

Allison sprang forward with a cry, and the room flashed white as the gun went off.

1

Someone was following her.

Mira glanced over her shoulder again, scanning the bus's crowded seats. No one was looking at her, at least not right then. But as soon as she faced forward the pressure of eyes resumed, like fingers probing the base of her neck.

She suppressed a shudder.

She'd felt it off and on over the last few weeks. Sometimes, like now, when she was riding the bus. Other times on the sidewalk, moving among the throngs of people. But she'd never been able to pinpoint someone actually following or watching her. When she'd told Shay about it, her friend said it was nerves. *You're anxious all the time. Of course you feel like someone's watching you. But sorry to say, you aren't that special.*

The bus slowed and Mira stood. It wasn't her stop but she got off anyway, pausing for a second on the streetcorner to see if anyone followed. The doors shut and the bus lumbered on down the Brooklyn street in a cloud of exhaust. City sounds washed over her and people streamed past. Everything completely normal. Shay was probably right.

Mira started to walk, hurrying because she had an extra block to cover now before her shift started. But even amongst the hustling crowd she felt completely alone.

From Grace Home to the care center where her brother lived was two buses and a significant walk.

That was how she measured distances in the city, not by miles or blocks but by transport. A cab, a bus, a train, a bike, walking. Traveling was an experience in itself. A way to reckon her place in the sprawling cityscape she'd lived in for the last five years her life.

And still she wasn't used to it.

She had friends who had been born here, who knew nothing else outside the lights and sounds of traffic, the voices of people they would never meet. They blended into the pace and flow as if it were second nature. She envied them, how comfortable they were, how they thrived. For her, the action and movement and noise had never normalized; she was still a novice sailor feeling the strange sway and tilt of a ship's deck beneath her feet.

Now she moved to the very edge of the sidewalk to avoid a happy babbling throng of teenagers and watched them pass, a pang of envy almost like hunger running through her. Then she turned onto a brick walkway, registering she'd arrived at her destination.

Village Gardens Assisted Living wasn't in the village and there were no gardens within view of the building where Aaron had spent the last two years. The grounds were well maintained but narrow and without many adornments, other than the random birdbath and wrought-iron benches set back from flaking ornamental fences.

It's only temporary, she reminded herself. Someday soon, he wouldn't have to stay here. They'd leave it behind, an obscure shape in the rear-view mirror of their lives, its definition and power growing fainter and fainter.

Mira signed in at the front desk, attaching her employee badge to her shirt. The hallways were clean with only a faint smell of disinfectant, and except for the chug of a floor polisher in a distant wing, the building was quiet.

Aaron was in his room. It had no windows. A windowed room was for kids whose relatives could pay for their accommodations, not for wards of the state. The plain walls were painted a calming shade of taupe, not that there was much taupe visible in his room. She would have given anyone a hundred dollars if they could find more than a two-inch strip of real estate between the sketches and paintings adorning every surface tape would stick to.

They were nearly all landscapes. A few done in charcoal but most vibrant watercolors, with a smattering of oil paintings thrown in for good measure. Aaron's work never failed to give her pause, no matter how many times she saw it. There was something *true* about the scenes he created. Some simple honesty in the bend of grass or the flutter of a bird's wings as it lit high in an oak.

Aaron sat at his desk, paging through a book of artwork she'd given to him for his fifteenth birthday several months before. The pages were becoming worn at the corners from use. He had always been slight but looked ever more so hunched in his chair, the only light in the room coming from a tilted lamp on a bedside table.

Mira lingered in the entry, raising two knuckles to the door and rapping out the five beat—*shave and a haircut*. Aaron didn't turn, only lifted his own fist to answer with the required knocked response—*two bits*. She smiled and stepped inside, their long-standing ritual complete.

"How are you?" she asked, giving him a hug before sitting on his bed.

"Good, good, good," he replied, still glued to the book.

"Are you still liking your book?"

"My book," he said, beginning to rock in his chair.

"That's right. It's yours."

Finally, he carefully placed a bookmark between the pages and folded it shut before facing her. It still stopped her to see how much he resembled their father, more and more as time went by. The same forehead below thin blond hair. The same hazel eyes, though Aaron's were beseeching as if he were continually asking a question. Asking why.

He reached out and touched her face. "Meery." What he called her since he'd learned to speak.

She put a hand over his. "Yep, I came to see you." He rocked harder and smiled at the floor. "What did you work on over the weekend? Did you paint anything new?"

Aaron sat thinking, then turned and shuffled through a stack of drawings piled four inches high on the corner of his desk. When he faced her again, he held out an eight-by-ten sheet of heavy art paper. On it, a winding lane cut before a tall stand of trees. Beside the driveway, a field rolled in gentle hills before fading into the yard of a two-story farmhouse.

"Home?" Aaron asked, and her heart flexed painfully.

"Pretty soon," she managed without a waver in her voice. "Not much longer." He nodded, accepting the response like all the hundreds of other times he'd asked. "Are you hungry?" He nodded again. "Let's get you some breakfast."

They ate cereal and toast in the cafeteria along with the rest of the kids housed at the facility. Mira was one of dozens of care workers moving between the children, some in wheelchairs, others with severe developmental disabilities, all needing some kind of assistance. When breakfast was over, she brought Aaron back to his room and helped him dress for the day.

"School?" he asked as she pulled a sweater over his head.

"No school today. Tomorrow."

"Outside?"

"You wanna go outside?"

"Now."

"Okay, let's go."

She helped him into his coat, returning to the times their mother had done the same thing before the two of them rambled out the door into the cool air of fall or drifting snow. Mira could still see her standing in the picture window watching them as they played, even then her shape behind the glass resembling a memory.

They sat on one of the benches after walking the narrow courtyard. A few other kids were outside with their care workers, their voices echoing off the nearby walls. Aaron pointed out a grackle on one of the lower branches of a tree and a finch bathing in the central bath. A siren started up like a moan, climbing to a shriek as it neared and a fire truck barreled past in the street, splashing reds and yellows against the buildings. When she looked at Aaron again, he had his hands over his ears.

"I'm sorry, Mira, I really am."

Mrs. Shepherd folded her hands over one another, and Mira had a difficult time looking away from them.

They were in the largest of the cramped offices off of Village Garden's lobby—Mira seated in a chair whose upholstery had seen better days, a narrow cluttered desk separating her from the facility's administrator. Mrs. Shepherd was a blocky woman and her hands matched the rest of her. They were hands well acquainted with difficult work. Decades of lifting people into and out of bed, on and off toilets, even cleaning floors when need be. Mira had seen her do all of it. Mrs. Shepherd unfolded them now and gestured vaguely at the paperwork before her, Mira's eyes following the movement.

"If it were up to me, I'd hire you on full-time; god knows we need the help here. But with the lack of grants and aid cuts coming next year, I don't have any choice. Your last day will be a week from this Friday."

"But I've been here two years; you said seniority—"

"It's not only you. I had to let Nick go, too."

"Isn't there something," Mira said, finally able to bring her gaze up, "anything else I can do? It doesn't have to be direct caring. I'll clean the bathrooms or wash windows, whatever you need. Just until I find something else."

"Those positions are already filled."

"But what about a counselor?" Mira scrambled, already knowing the answer. "You said you were two short. I could stand in for now and you could sign off on the paperwork. I could be like an intern or . . ."

Mrs. Shepherd was shaking her head sadly. "You need a degree. Or at the very least be certified by the state." She saw the look on Mira's face and went on. "And I think you should pursue it. You've got the heart for this line of work; I truly mean that. You're smart, patient, diligent, and most important of all, you're kind."

"But—" Mira was aghast to realize she was on the verge of tears. "I don't know what I'm going to do."

Mrs. Shepherd studied her. There was pity in her gaze—something Mira had become accustomed to over the past years. But she didn't need pity; she needed a paycheck. "I've written you the best reference I've ever given anyone, and I'll speak to any potential employers on your behalf. Beyond that, I'm afraid my hands are tied."

She stood and Mira followed suit. At the door, Mrs. Shepherd surprised her by gathering her into a hug. Mira stiffened, then sank into the embrace. "You keep your head up and everything'll be all right. You'll see, honey."

Mira held on for a few seconds after Mrs. Shepherd released her, gathering in the comfort and breathing in her faint perfume. It wasn't the same as her mother used to wear, but she pretended it was.

The rest of the day was spent helping Aaron and several other children with activities in the lounge, then lunch, then free time, which was Aaron's favorite since he always used it to paint. Between care, Mira tidied and cleaned, helped carry supplies in from a delivery truck, and read books to a group of kids in the cramped library.

As the light left the sky and bloomed beneath lampposts, Mira brought Aaron back to the cafeteria for dinner. She hugged him goodbye before dessert was served, saying she'd be back in two days. He watched her go, the constant question in his eyes following her out of the room and onto the street.

Outside, Mira drank in the open air, trying to shut out the sounds of the city before heading toward her bus stop. Her back ached from carrying boxes of food, and the fatigue from staying up late the night before, filling out paperwork, weighed on her like a lead vest.

Her eighteenth birthday was ten days ago. She'd been an adult for less than two weeks.

2

There was a woman waiting beneath a tree half a block from Grace Home.

Mira didn't know how she knew the woman was waiting, but she did. Maybe it was in the way she wasn't on her phone like most of the other pedestrians, or how she was inspecting each person who moved past along the sidewalk. Probably it was because she was standing still while the entire city seemed to be in motion around her. Except that wasn't exactly true since Mira wasn't moving either.

She was lingering beside the stairway of an apartment building, wondering why the sight of the woman had slowed, then stopped her in her tracks. There was nothing overly threatening about the woman. She wore a skirt, light blouse, and matching jacket along with no-nonsense flats. Tall and beginning to gray with austere features, she could've been forty or sixty. Someone's mother or even grandmother. But still Mira hesitated.

This was silly. She needed to get home. There was more paperwork Aaron's caseworker needed for his financial waiver along with the temporary housing application she'd fallen asleep over the night before. And a shower; God, she needed a shower . . .

She got herself moving. One foot after the other, trying not to look at the woman who was still scanning the crowd, *looking for her.* No, that was stupid. She would keep her head down and just walk on past like everyone else. In two minutes, she'd be inside Grace Home, safe and sound.

She was ten steps from the woman. Five.

She wasn't there for Mira, no matter what the paranoid part of her was saying. She glanced up at the woman when she was even with her, mostly to prove to herself she was being irrational.

"Mira Caine?"

The jolt of surprise was like an actual electric shock to her system made so much worse by somehow knowing the woman had been watching for her. It swept through her from head to foot and back again along with a thousand worries, and she stopped walking even as her brain cried out to keep going.

This woman would evict her from Grace Home. Tonight. She was there to say she couldn't be Aaron's guardian, that she wasn't good enough, wasn't strong enough. Her brother would be taken away from her, and there was nothing she could do about it.

"Yes?" was all she managed to say.

The woman smiled, offering her hand, and Mira felt an impulse to run away even as she reached out to shake with her.

"I'm Eleanor Madsen. You don't know me, but I think I would've known you anywhere."

"What?" Mira took a step back, suddenly thankful for the flow of people around them along with the reassuring lights of Grace Home a short distance away.

Eleanor shook her head, making an irritated sound in the back of her throat. "Forgive me; I get ahead of myself, especially as I get older. I recognize you from the television reports. So many times, people don't look the same in person as they do on the screen, but you're exactly the same."

Mira nodded, something falling into place. The news report. It had been over four months since the night she'd followed Sara Kinsey to the roof of Grace Home. Normally, the roof-access door was tightly locked, but that night it had been left open and Sara must have been watching for that exact chance. It was a good thing Mira had been watching her.

Sara was sixteen, waifish, and the quietest person at the foster home. She'd arrived a few weeks prior to her trip to the roof, and hadn't made any friends in the meantime. There'd been rumors about abuse by Sara's father, something that seemed to track whenever Mira caught a glimpse of the other girl's haunted gaze. And over the days leading up to the night on the roof, the look in her eyes had deepened as if she were receding somewhere further and further away inside herself. When Mira had followed her up the last flight of steps out into the open night air, she hadn't been surprised to find Sara standing on the building's edge, staring down at the street eighty feet below.

Mira had already felt a kinship with the other girl's solitude, and seeing how lost and alone she looked there against the drop shifted something internally and made her speak Sara's name.

Mira didn't really recall what she said afterward, only that she'd tried not to startle her. Slowly, she'd moved closer and kept talking until Sara began responding. Shortly after came the first of her tears, and by then, Mira was close enough to touch her but hadn't. She'd asked the right questions, gotten Sara to tell her about where she was from, about what had forced her up the flights of steps and onto the three-foot wall surrounding the building's border. Police had arrived but hung back, letting Mira's calmness gradually guide Sara to a sitting position, then off the wall completely and into her arms.

All of it had been captured on phones and cameras from onlookers below in the street and across the way.

By morning there was a deluge of emails waiting in Grace Home's inbox, almost all from news organizations. Andrea, the current manager, had been inundated with calls requesting Mira for interviews, podcasts, and a single slurred marriage proposal. Mira hadn't expected the attention and was put off by it. She'd made a simple statement to the most reputable newspaper, the same things most people said in situations like this—she'd just done what anyone else would have.

Now, looking at the well-dressed woman a few feet away, she said, "Thanks, but I've already spoken about that to the *Times*. I don't really have anything else to say."

"Oh, no, dear. You misunderstand me. I only came across your story a few days ago. I'm not here to interview you; I want to offer you a job."

They sat in a booth of Café Paris, a little eatery around the corner from Grace Home and Mira's very favorite place in the world for breakfast. They made crepes she dreamed about sometimes.

Eleanor said nothing until they'd ordered coffees and the waitress had left. Then she appraised Mira again, giving her another smile. The older woman carried a sense of surety and elegance in the comfortable but focused way she sat in the booth.

"I can't stay long," Mira said, opening the door to a quick escape if the lady turned out to be a weirdo. "I'm supposed to be back before seven."

"Don't worry; I'll be as brief as possible and out of your hair in no time, hopefully with both of us satisfied." Eleanor's eyes shifted up as if to check a catalogue in her mind. "Let's see; how do I start all this? I suppose I'm looking for a friend." When Mira glanced around the half-empty café, Eleanor suppressed a laugh. "That came out wrong. I'm looking for someone to be a friend and mentor for . . . well, what do I call myself in relation to Allison? *Housekeeper* would be the closest, since I clean and organize. But I also handle finances and see to certain details around the estate. I'm an RN, too, so a caregiver as well." She regarded Mira again. "But most of all, a mother, I suppose. Yes, I believe that fits best."

"Umm, okay."

"I don't suppose you're familiar with the name Wyndclyffe?"

"No." The strangeness of the conversation was getting to Mira. Would bolting toward the door be as uncomfortable as remaining in her seat?

"I'm sure there's information online," Eleanor continued. "Nowadays, it seems you can find almost anything on the internet, but I'll give you the basics. The Wyndclyffes weren't Rockefellers or Fords or Carnegies, but it's no secret their worth is equal to all of them, possibly surpassing a few other notable names here and there. Allison is the last of a long line, and I'm sorry to say she's had a difficult life despite her privilege."

The waitress reappeared, asking if they needed anything else, and they both declined. When she was gone, Eleanor sipped her coffee and said, "Forgive me for reading up a little about you prior to coming to the city. After I saw you talk that poor girl down off the ledge, I was curious if you'd be a good candidate."

"Candidate?"

"You and Allison have a lot in common, it seems." Eleanor paused. "I'm very sorry about the loss of your parents."

Mira tried swallowing but her mouth and throat were arid. "Thank you," she managed.

"Allison lost hers as well a few years ago. Very horrifically, I'm afraid. Her father, well, I won't go into details, but her parents died violently, and she was injured herself in the incident. If you care to know more, you'll have no problem finding the story on the internet." Eleanor's face had lost some of its former color beneath the café's lights. "Losing them the way she did changed her. She withdrew and became afraid of the outside world. Any friendships she had dissolved. She's been alone for a long time now."

Alone. That word, so cold and familiar. Mira cleared her throat. "I'm sorry, but I'm not sure what you want from me."

Eleanor blinked and seemed to come back from some inner distance. "Allison needs someone, a companion her age to spend time with. She's been in therapy and tried all sorts of medications, but nothing has really made a difference. When we saw the report about you saving that girl, I thought to myself, *Now, there's a person with empathy. Someone who cares.* The world is deeply callused to the needs of the less fortunate and the troubled. Finding a compassionate person is like stumbling on a four-leaf clover. Special, in other words."

You aren't that special. Shay's voice was there in her head, and even though her friend hadn't meant anything by it, the sentiment was something Mira had felt about herself for as long as she could recall. Nothing stood out about her. She wasn't beautiful, wasn't overly athletic, was smart enough but not gifted. In fact, she'd sometimes wondered if she was only the result of how other people saw her. Was she merely the daughter of the late William and Melody Caine, sister to Aaron? The sum of the parts of others? Extensions of their feelings, their love, their disappointment?

"I'm not sure I'm who you're looking for," Mira finally said.

"Exactly what a humble person would say," Eleanor said, tapping the table with a smile. "The article I read said you work at a care facility for disabled children; is that true?"

"Part-time. They keep almost all the employees at part time—"

"—So they don't have to pay a decent wage or benefits, yes, I'm sure," Eleanor finished with disdain. "Well, it's another mark in your favor; you're already suited to helping the less fortunate." When Mira started to protest, she held up a hand. "Please, let me explain my proposal and then I'll leave you in peace. That's all I ask." Mira deflated, settling back into her seat. Eleanor gathered herself and said, "Allison hasn't left the estate in years. She's afraid, you see. If you were to agree to the terms, you would come to stay at the manor."

"Where is it?" Mira asked, noting the spike of excitement she felt.

"On an island in the middle of the St. Lawrence River. The only job requirements would be to spend time with Allison, get to know her, try drawing her out of her shell. It would be on a trial basis, say a month. Your payment would be twenty-five thousand dollars—half up front and half at the end of the month. Room and board would be included, of course. And if you and Allison click, we would be happy to pay a hundred thousand for the forthcoming year."

The air in the café was gone.

Mira's lungs clutched at it like a child reaching for a toy on a high shelf but couldn't seem to draw any in. She started to pick up her coffee but her hand was shaking too much. "That's—that's a lot of money."

"It's nothing if we were able to get our Allison back."

"I . . . I don't know what to say. I—" Mira's heart rate hadn't calmed from hearing the offer, and she was seeing the sun-swept fields of her childhood, trees so green they almost hurt the eyes. And in the fall, the reds and oranges of the leaves defied imagination that anything could be that brilliant, that beautiful.

"Say you'll think about it." Eleanor finished her coffee and stood. She set cash down to cover the bill, then drew an off-white business card from her handbag and handed it to Mira. The stock was thick and heavy, almost as if the card was made from something metallic rather than paper. The shade of white was disturbing in a way she couldn't name. Embossed in spidery script in the center was the name *Wyndclyffe,* and below it a number.

"I find mulling things over a bit always provides perspective. Call whenever you've made up your mind, and we'll arrange the details." Eleanor watched Mira in a way that made her feel both small and very important at the same time. "I hope you'll come. I think you could help her."

Eleanor turned and headed for the door. "Mrs. Madsen?" Mira called after she'd gone a few steps. The older woman paused, looking back. "Why me, really? There must've been a lot of other options. People with more . . . I don't know . . . experience."

Eleanor's slight smile surfaced again. "Allison saw the report on you as well. She saw how you helped that girl. Maybe somewhere inside, she thinks you can save her too."

Then she was gone, and Mira was alone.

3

Mira's room was on the fourth floor.

Grace Home had once been a hotel and now housed kids with behavioral-health concerns, substance-abuse issues, and those in trauma situations. It was common in the city, old buildings retrofitted to become shelters—places the abandoned and broken could find help, if there was room.

Passing through the lobby, Mira spotted Andrea in her office behind the main desk, tapping away at her computer. Andrea glanced out at her, giving her a quick nod of acknowledgment as she passed. Andrea saw all and missed nothing. At least when it came to misconduct and curfews.

Mira went by the defunct elevator and mounted the stairs, huffing up the four flights before pushing out into the long corridor housing her room halfway down on the right. A few of the other kids' doors were open. Some music drifted out, mingled with laughter. Then she was unlocking her door—the privacy a perk of being of legal age.

After their parents' accident, there hadn't been any foster homes willing to accept someone with disabilities, so Village Gardens had been their only choice for Aaron. She'd wanted to be as close to him as possible, and the nearest foster family hadn't been in Brooklyn at all, so she'd opted for Grace Home. The facility was a safe, stable environment where she had the support she needed. At least, that was until her temporary placement ran out in a couple months . . .

Her room was square and spartan, a small attached bath its only luxury. She set her bag down and sank to the bed, the past week's exhaustion settling with her. She sat very still, letting everything inside her uncoil slowly so she wouldn't come apart with it all. The desk beside her bed was covered in stacks of paperwork. Endless forms to be filled out for what she was undertaking. Or trying to, if the world would let her.

Mira reached into her pocket and drew out the business card Eleanor had given her. It was heavier than it had any right to be. She reached over and snagged her laptop from beneath some papers and lay on her stomach on the bed. She brought up the browser, pausing before typing *Wyndclyffe, New York.*

Quite a few hits but not as many as she'd anticipated. She set the search to chronological order and began to read.

A brief Wikipedia entry detailed the family's origins—Sir Winston Wyndclyffe being the patriarch who first set foot in America in the late nineteenth century. Eleanor hadn't been joking—the Wyndclyffe money was old, from what Mira could gather. A break with English royalty had seemed to launch Winston's interest in the new world. He'd settled with his wife and two children in upstate New York, first on the mainland, then on Rift Island in the St. Lawrence River. The family gained attention by avoiding the local church, but what they lacked in the belief department, they made up for in donations. From what she could tell, the entire town of Yellow Bay opposite Rift Island grew because of the Wyndclyffes. A library, the renovations of a courthouse, as well as a promenade that would later become Main Street, were all paid for out of Winston's seemingly bottomless account.

Investments in lumber, rock quarries, and eventually railroads secured the family's status and future in the free world. Beyond that, the article dribbled to an end.

Mira chewed her lip and clicked the next link.

Murder. The headline from eighteen ninety-seven nearly screamed it. Rasmus Wyndclyffe, Winston's son, had apparently been stabbed to death in a barroom brawl in Yellow Bay. Justice had been swift. An Ernest Gouch was found guilty and hanged two days after the murder. A photograph accompanied the article portraying a gallows with a single form dangling from its center, the man's face thankfully shrouded by a bag. A group of people milled below the gallows, and a tall, well-dressed man, forever blurred in motion, was caught leaving the frame. The caption read, *Winston Wyndclyffe witnesses the execution of Ernest Gouch, his son Rasmus's murderer. None of the family Wyndclyffe cared to comment.*

Footsteps pounded by the door. Mira glanced up until they receded into quiet, then read on.

A few more notations, mostly concerning an ever-growing list of philanthropy in the north half of the state with a sprinkling of announcements about galas and soirees held on the Wyndclyffe grounds throughout the early and mid-twentieth century.

The last article of note gave her pause, and as she read, an unpleasant tingling began in the base of her stomach that had nothing to do with missing dinner.

September, 2021: Leland Wyndclyffe, heir to the Wyndclyffe estate and fortune, kills his wife Vanessa and wounds two others including his only daughter, Allison, in a domestic rampage.

Mira scanned the page, eyes alighting on words like *reclusive* and *eccentric* before traveling on to others such as *mental instability* and *unmedicated.* Statements given by staff members of the Wyndclyffe estate painted a vivid picture leaving room for generous imagination.

Late on a Saturday evening, Leland Wyndclyffe loaded one of his hunting rifles and shot a member of his staff before gunning down his wife Vanessa as she hid with their daughter Allison, who was also wounded. Another staff member intervened and shot Leland before he could take the life of his daughter. Allison and the wounded staff member survived after being airlifted from the Wyndclyffe estate.

The article went on to say Leland had been remote and lethargic as of late, though that was well within his typical character. At the very end were the words, *The tragedy leaves behind only one living member of the family, Allison Wyndclyffe, 16 years old, who could not be reached for comment.*

A single picture adorned the report. It was a shot taken from a distance and magnified of a stone façade, one wall of an enormous house, if Mira had to guess, with an ornate window in its center. The drapes were pulled aside and a girl stood there, only a vague outline amongst deeper shadows.

Mira's door burst open, and she jumped so hard, her laptop spun sideways and rebounded off the wall.

Shay stood in the doorway like a triumphant conqueror before flinging the door closed behind her. She crossed the room in two steps and leapt onto the bed, half-landing on Mira. "What's up, bitch?"

"Uh, God, get off!" Mira yelled, shoving her best friend as hard as she could. Shay rolled to the end of the bed, laughing. "You scared the hell out of me."

"Gotta keep you on your toes."

"You don't, though."

"Should have locked your door."

"I guess."

"Where were you? You missed dinner."

"I—"

"Ooo, what's this?" Shay picked up the Wyndclyffe card and turned it over, eyes sparkling along with the fake diamond studs lining the curves of her ears.

"A job offer."

"You better accept if this is their business card. What's the job?"

"Mentoring a girl?"

"Mentoring?"

"Yeah . . . like being a friend?" Shay stared at her, one of her sculpted eyebrows cocked much higher than the other. "Like do stuff together and try to help her get back to normal. Here, read this." Mira spun the laptop around to face Shay and watched as she pored over the most recent article. When she was finished, Shay sat back and let out a long breath.

"So, you're supposed to, what, go to this person's house and hang out with her or something?"

"Something like that." Mira hesitated. "They actually want me to live there for a month on a trial basis."

"Nope. Nuh-uh, they're going to traffic your ass."

"The lady I talked to seemed legit."

"That's what they do; they use people who seem trustworthy to lure you in, then bam! You're drugged and on your way to some billionaire's sex island. No way; shut that shit down."

"But why would they want me?"

"You're young and pretty and vulnerable. If they did their homework, they know you don't have any family."

Mira looked away and stood from the bed. Shay caught her hand. "Hey, sorry. You know what I mean."

"Yeah." Mira moved to the desk and sat. She sorted a stack of papers and then stared at the faded tile floor. "I heard back from the temporary housing place upstate."

"And?"

"And they're full, just like the last two. They put me on a waiting list."

"How long's the list?"

"They said a year." Mira looked at Shay. "A year. I can't leave Aaron in that place for another year. He wants to go home." Her vision blurred. "*I* want to go home."

"Hey, hey." Shay came to her, pulled her into an embrace, which only made the tears flow harder. She stifled a sob against her friend's shoulder. "You have that plan, right? The little steps you always tell me about? Which one are you on?"

The "steps" were how she saw the future. A stairway leading upward, or backward if she were honest with herself. When their family left Connecticut for their father's promotion in the city, she'd been thirteen and Aaron was ten. She hadn't known then how much she would miss the quiet of the country, hadn't known how much it would affect Aaron. For the first year, the hustle and bustle of the city had been exciting in an all-consuming way, then it had lost its luster. By the time the drunk driver crossed his lane of traffic on the freeway and barreled at seventy miles an hour into their parents' vehicle, she'd already been thinking about the home they'd left behind. It wasn't much later she started envisioning the stairs, each tread taking her and Aaron closer to their goal, taking them back to a better time and place. She'd even gone so far as asking the local realtor to let her know if their old home ever came on the market again. He hadn't called.

"All the paperwork's done to become Aaron's guardian," Mira said, reluctantly leaving Shay's embrace. "But I don't want to file it until I have a place for us to stay and a steady job. We need to get out of the city. I thought we'd get used to it, but . . ."

"Sometimes places belong to people, and sometimes people belong to places," Shay said. "There's nothing wrong with either." Mira sniffled and swiped at her eyes. Shay appraised her. "Look, we talked about me coming with you guys as soon as I'm eighteen. That's six months. Then we'd have two incomes and I could help with Aaron."

"I can't ask you to do that."

"I'm fine with it. We could be like those guys in that book you made me read."

Mira felt a smile surface. "*Of Mice and Men.*"

"Yeah, yeah. We could get a place and we'd be in charge. No one else."

"It didn't work out too well for them."

"That's because they're men."

They both laughed. Mira shuffled more papers around the desk. "It's really sweet of you, but I think this job might be a sign. It might be the break we've been waiting for. The money's really good, like beyond good."

"Trafficking pays well."

"I'm serious."

"So am I." Shay paced across the room and back. "How long have we been friends?"

"Two years? As soon you got here."

"And right away, I knew you were different from anyone else I'd ever met. You care about people. Like really care. That's why you were able to stop that girl from taking a walk off the roof. You saw she was hurting and gave a shit. I know it's part your parents being gone and Aaron's situation, but I think you're just built that way. And now you hear this girl's sob story and you want to go help her, too. You ever think you might get yourself into trouble going out of your way for everyone else?"

"It's an opportunity."

"Is that all it is?"

Hot blood pulsed in Mira's face. "So, it's wrong to want to help?"

"If it costs more than you have, yes."

Mira shook her head and turned toward her desk. "I have a lot to do before bed." There was a long pause, then Shay let out a deep sigh and knelt at her side.

"Sorry. I worry about you. You're going all the time. You never do anything for yourself."

"This is for me." Mira took one of Shay's hands in her own. "How about you be my safety net? You don't hear from me on a regular basis, you call the cops. You'll know exactly where I went and who I'm with."

"Can't depend on Andrea to keep track of you. She'll fill your room the moment you step out the door."

"For sure."

"For sure."

Shay studied her for another beat. "Okay, if you're committed. But I'm on record against it."

"Noted."

"What are you going to tell Aaron?"

The job offer was so new, she hadn't had time to think about not seeing her brother for a full month. The thought sent a sickening ripple of sorrow through her.

"I don't know."

When she was alone again, Mira snacked on a protein bar but only managed to eat half. She went to the room's small window and opened the sash.

The city flooded in.

Normally, she only tolerated the noise, but tonight it felt necessary. It was a sign she was still connected to something, not adrift like she'd felt so often in the last two years. Outside, the city's sprawl glittered, and she thought of the building's rooftop—how she liked the look of everything better from up there. She recalled the times she and Aaron used to climb out of their bedroom window at night to look at the stars. They would lie on the day-warm shingles and gaze upward for hours. In the rural Connecticut sky, the Milky Way wasn't just visible; it was tangible. All those stars had weight, and she loved feeling their density settle over her. From their roost they'd been able to see all twenty acres of the property. There was something deeply calming about being high up and having a vantage of everything surrounding you. It was easy to spot anything wrong, see troubles long before they came near and tried stealing everything you loved.

For a second, she could hear a phone ringing, ringing through the past. Could feel it in her hand as she picked it up and answered. Could hear the words that changed everything, feel them seeping into her mind, staining her heart dark with grief.

The memory had soured her stomach further, and she grimaced. Out of reflex, she imagined a different outcome of that night. Let herself sink into another reality where her mom and dad were still alive and Aaron was at home, exactly where he should be.

Mira shut the window and readied for bed. The building was quiet now; lights out had come and gone. When she climbed beneath the covers, she saw Shay had left the business card on top of the comforter. She picked it up and studied it again. This was a chance to finally move out of the city. An invitation, an opportunity. Something good.

Then why, she asked herself much later as sleep finally began to drag her under, did the business card make her uneasy?

Bone, her dream voice whispered as she faded. *The card is the color of bone.*

4

The wind raked furrows in the dark water of the river as Mira waited for her coffee.

She stood off to one side of the shop's long counter facing the wide windows, the sidewalk and street front, the rock-slabbed shoreline, the water.

And out there, a half-mile distant, slumped the dark shape of Rift Island.

It rose from the water gradually with rough edges defining to smoother hills. Trees grew in clumps dotting open fields before becoming a solid forest in the center of the island, concealing any structures behind thick foliage. Several boats bobbed between the island and shore, occasional whitecaps flaring like bared teeth.

The barista said Mira's name and she collected her coffee, sipping greedily. It was good, very good—bold but creamy and hot enough to be almost painful. She definitely needed the caffeine; the drive from the city had started before dawn in a rented car and continued into more rural country revealed with the pallid gray of morning. The trip itself had gone well even with her nervousness upon leaving Grace Home and driving for the first time alone outside the city. All in all, she'd been behind the wheel for more than six hours before finally pulling into the town of Yellow Bay.

The town itself was quaint, touristy without being kitschy. Hashtag streets of residential neighborhoods gave way to a modest business district fronting the river. Main Street followed the border of rocky shoreline, shadowed by a walking trail dotted with few pedestrians. Given the overcast skies and wind, it was surprising to see anyone out. The temperature hovered at forty degrees, and there was a dry bite to the air unfamiliar to the city's atmosphere. It felt a lot like fall in Connecticut when the wind would turn and march down from the north. In a way, it was refreshing even with the chill it drove into her bones. The coffee definitely helped.

"Ugly, ain't it?"

The voice came from beside her and she startled. She'd been lost, gazing at the island, mind freewheeling. The woman who had spoken sat a few seats away, a black coffee steaming on the table before her. She was dressed in jeans and a heavy knitted sweater stained at the hem. Her mottled gray hair was chopped just below her ears, adding to the roundness of her features.

"I don't know. Can't really tell from here," Mira said, recovering from her surprise. It wasn't often a stranger talked to her out of the blue in the city. And if they did, it usually wasn't a good thing.

"Well, let me put any guesswork to rest. It's ugly." The woman gave her a wink and smiled, holding out a hand. "Agnes Pinter, but people call me Nessie. Supposedly since I'm out on the water so much, though I'd wager some think I'm a monster."

"Mira Caine; nice to meet you," Mira said, shaking the offered hand.

"What do you think of our thriving metropolis?"

Mira smiled. "It's nice. Quaint."

"Quaint it is. Only about fifteen hundred people. Bit more during the summer months, but they're all gone now. Back to the city, which is where you're from, I'm guessing." Mira nodded. "What brings you to our little burg?"

Mira hesitated. "I'm thinking of moving here." It wasn't a far throw from the truth. Once she'd officially decided to accept the job offer, she'd opened up the gates of her imagination and explored the potential new world beyond. Yellow Bay wasn't their hometown in Connecticut, but it did remind her of it. If this trial month worked out, she wondered how Aaron would react if they moved here. She could see them resettling to be closer to the island so she could commute each day—Eleanor hadn't specified anything different on the phone when Mira talked to her early that week to confirm she'd be accepting the offer. In the evenings, she could come home to a house outside of town. Maybe one with some rolling fields set back from the road. Someplace

Aaron could settle into comfortably. Somewhere quiet. And with the year's salary, she could afford the best in-home services for him while she worked.

"There's no college here, though. You look about college age."

College. She hadn't thought about her own future in quite a while. Maybe if the job worked out there would be time to again. "I was thinking after college."

Nessie studied her for a beat. "Well, there are worse places to put down roots. In fact, I've got a cousin who's a realtor if you're serious. Name's Martin Randle. His shingle's hung out over on Second Street. Can't miss it."

"Thank you."

A few grizzled old-timers shuffled through the door, most heading to a booth in the back while the tallest of the group went to place their orders, noticing them as he neared the counter. "Captain! Thought you had a charter this morning," he called, and Nessie shook her head.

"Pulled out last minute."

"There's a joke there—"

"That you'll damn well keep to yourself in public, John Taylor," Nessie said, a hard glint in her eye. The old man threw back his head and laughed before ordering coffees for his group.

"Captain?" Mira asked, partially intrigued and partially to kill time before the boat arrived from the island.

Nessie waved a hand. "Piloted an iron ore freighter for a dozen years or so. Duluth to Rochester, mostly. Old assholes think it's funny to call me that, but they won't get within reach when they say it. Speaks volumes." Mira laughed, beginning to like Nessie a lot. Nessie shifted in her seat and nodded out at the island in the distance. "Got an interest in our local haunted house? Seen you looking at it for quite some time after you came in."

"Actually a little, now that you mention it," Mira said. Learning about the place she was going to spend the next month, possibly more, couldn't hurt. Even if it was just ghost stories and superstition. She took her coffee and motioned at an empty chair next to Nessie.

"By all means."

"Every town has one, I guess. A haunted house," Mira said.

"Well, that's ours out there, for sure. I'll be seventy-three next month, and I can't recall a time in my life where some rumor or another wasn't traveling around town about that place." Mira recalled something Eleanor said on their last phone call. *The neighboring town is, how do I put this politely . . . nosy as all hell. Over the years, we've kept Allison's situation under the radar. It wouldn't do for her to see herself splashed across a page of one of the local periodicals or on the TV. In the city, the name Wyndclyffe may have fallen by the wayside, but in the north, people still know it well.* So far, her opinion of the gossip seemed accurate. "Though it's mostly all bullshit, pardon my French," Nessie went on, bringing Mira's attention back.

"Mostly?"

"Well, they say there's always a kernel of truth in every legend, right? And there's legends surrounding that island going back a hundred and fifty years. My daddy told me some that would curl your pretty hair up tight. Lights floating on the water, odd voices chanting, strange-colored fires burning, things like that."

Mira glanced at the island again. As far as haunted islands went, visually, it fit the part.

"Old Winston Wyndclyffe," Nessie went on, "he was patriarch of the lot, was said to be a devil worshipper. That's why he got the heave-ho from his homeland. Wasn't praying to the right god, so they ousted him. Word was he'd brought his customs with him. Someone my grandfather knew said their dog was taken and sacrificed, and someone else who worked clearing trees on the property when the house was being built swore they saw Winston drinking blood from a mason jar." Nessie shrugged. "Though you didn't see the townsfolk turning away the money he donated every year."

The article she'd read online had touched on the family's shunning of religion. Odd for the time period, but devil worship? More likely it was rumors literally demonizing the rich. "Interesting," Mira said, sipping her coffee. "Ever seen anything strange?"

Nessie shifted in her seat again, this time slightly away. "No." She fidgeted with her cup. "Well, once. Years ago, but I'd rather not talk about it. Not polite discussion with someone as young as yourself." Mira read her body language and didn't reply, her guess proving correct a few seconds later. Silence was sometimes the ultimate question. "You don't scare easily, do you?"

"No. I don't think so."

"All right. I suppose it's water so far under the bridge, it's out of sight. I mean Leland's been dead for almost two years now." Nessie scooted closer to her, voice lowering conspiratorially. "It was back in twenty-nineteen or -twenty; can't recall which now. Maybe that's my brain trying to get rid of the memory, who knows, but it was late afternoon and I was coming around the north side of the island. I'd gone out fishing, I supply a couple of the meat markets here with catches when I can, and was finished for the day. It was starting to rain, part of why I was heading in, and the wind was up, a few rollers coming from the lake." Nessie's eyes grew distant and she paused. "He was there at the edge of the trees, Leland Wyndclyffe. He was naked and staring out at me as I passed. It caught me so off guard, I didn't know what to do. No one else around, just me and him, and him with not a stitch on. He stood there staring, and he was saying something, too. I could see his mouth moving but couldn't hear. It seemed like he was repeating the same thing over and over, like a chant. He stayed that way until I was out of sight."

Nessie sat back and glanced around. No one else in the shop appeared to be listening, and Mira was grateful because the shudder that went through her was noticeable. "I tried to tell myself it hadn't happened, but I knew it had," Nessie continued. "Weirdest damn thing I've ever seen in my life, and let me tell you, darlin', I've seen a lot."

Mira registered a shape detaching from the island's mass that slowly materialized into a small boat.

"I'd say the more money, the crazier people seem to be. I've had a few out on my charters who were doozies. But let me tell you, no one holds a candle to those Wyndclyffes. Cursed family if there ever was one."

Mira pried a smile loose and offered her hand as she stood. "Well, I need to get going, but it was very nice to meet you. I'll check in with your cousin if I decide to go house-hunting."

Nessie squeezed her hand once and nodded. "Martin'll do you right. Remember to tell him I sent you." Her expression darkened slightly as she released her grip, a cloud scudding across blue sky. Mira wanted to head for the door but was pinned in place by the older woman's gaze. "You look like them a little. Got the appearance." Nessie's demeanor changed, all earlier warmth receding. "You a relative? A cousin?"

"What do you mean?" Mira asked, a blade of unease sliding across her skin.

Nessie didn't look away, just nodded at the island. When she spoke, her voice was low again. "One of them."

Mira glanced through the glass. The boat was mooring at the longest dock extending into the water. "Sorry, I have to go."

As she exited the shop, she realized she wasn't only hurrying but stifling the urge to run. Petals of acid bloomed in her stomach. Nessie had suggested, what . . . that she resembled the Wyndclyffes? Had the woman pretended to be friendly only to alienate an outsider? Maybe now Nessie was seated with the other old-timers in the back booth, head thrown back with laughter at messing with a young tourist. Maybe it was a game and they kept score.

She stopped at the rental to retrieve her luggage, then made her way down the winding ramp to the docks, her hard case's wheels clacking the whole way.

Meeting the man with the boat was a blur. Jeff, the groundskeeper, was large with long gray hair intertangling in an unkempt beard stained by tobacco. His greeting mirrored his appearance, a gruff hello, before he directed her into the bow of the boat and loaded her luggage with ease. They cast off and Jeff fired up the engine, first idling out into deeper water, then slowly getting up to plane as they cut away from the mainland.

Mira looked back only once. Once was enough to see the coffee shop's front window. Enough to see Nessie framed there, watching her with dull eyes like old coins.

5

To the east the river gradually narrowed, other islands smudges in the distance, black chalk on a gray canvas.

The water in the west widened until it opened to the stunning expanse of Lake Ontario. Mira had been out on it once years before with her family. They'd gone sailing with a business associate of her father, and she'd fallen in love with how the wind had been their only engine on the water. The only mar on the memory was when she and Aaron had gone swimming. The cold was like a vise on her body the moment she jumped in. *July!* Her brain had cried as if it could change the fact of the biting temperature. She'd never felt cold like that, before or since. And now, surrounded by the same expanse in the grip of fall, she could only imagine how frigid the water would be.

Ahead, the island loomed, as if it were growing and she was shrinking.

Rift Island was approximately two square miles, forested with patches of open field, and given the blurry satellite photo she'd studied extensively, beset with a house of epic proportions in the shape of a capital T. There was only one picture she'd been able to find on the internet of Wyndclyffe Manor. It was black-and-white, taken sometime before it was fully completed. Even under construction, the building was imposing—massive walls of stone and mortar rising into the sky in uneven lines.

As waves rose and broke across the boat's hull, she returned to the reason she was here in the first place. A month of friendship for twenty-five thousand dollars—half the amount already in her bank account. She'd refreshed it online over and over after signing the contract, and after twenty-four hours, the money had appeared, adding to the existing pathetic three digits like a miracle. And there was the promise of so much more if she were able to succeed in helping Allison. Lifechanging money in every sense of the words. Beyond that was the deeper urge Shay had pointed out. Allison had suffered a loss like her own but so much worse. To have your father kill your mother and try to kill you was . . . unthinkable. If she could help her, she would.

As far as she was concerned, everyone deserved help.

"Wanna catch that piling for me?"

The boat slowed the same moment Jeff spoke. They were idling up to a long concrete pier lined with steel pilings disappearing into murky water. A ladder moored in the concrete sat between two of the supports. Mira glanced at Jeff, who nodded at the incoming piling they drifted toward on their own rolling wake. "There's a rope there with a clasp. Hook it to the eye in the beam."

Mira steadied herself after finding the tie rope and secured it to the nearest pillar. Jeff did the same at the aft and gathered her luggage as she stepped from the boat's swaying deck to the ladder. When she was atop the pier, Jeff handed up the luggage, the bulk of his shoulders shifting beneath his coat.

"I'd take you up myself, but the waves'll beat the boat to pieces if I don't stow it now," he said. He pointed to a set of stairs leading up from the pier, which wound away into the trees. "Up the stairs and follow the path to the house. You can leave the bags; I'll bring them in a bit."

"Okay, thanks!" she called, but he didn't acknowledge her, only unhooked the boat and reversed away from the pier with the practice of someone who had done the maneuver countless times. She watched for a moment as he guided the vessel down the shoreline to a damp-darkened boathouse thrust out over the water.

Mira glanced back at the mainland—Yellow Bay's streets and buildings shrunken to a child's playset. Everything she knew was there across the water. She'd debated for days whether to tell Aaron she was going away for a while. His grasp of time wasn't concrete, only the days of the week she came to see him holding any real weight. In the end, she'd visited him the day before she left, saying she had to go on a little trip and she'd have a wonderful surprise for him when she came back. Twenty-five thousand would get them into a house or apartment outside the city, and even if she weren't able to make progress with Allison, the money would allow her time to find a steady job. It was the breathing room they needed—in the end, worth the time they'd spend apart, though she had cried most of the way home after leaving his small room at Village Gardens. This would be the longest they'd ever been away from one another.

But she'd also felt an undeniable surge of freedom climbing in the car that morning and leaving the city and everything, *even Aaron*, behind. Shameful as it felt, the burst of liberty when the open road unfurled and everything tied to the city and that life faded away was intoxicating. It was probably just the unburdening of responsibilities, but that didn't keep the guilt from creeping in like it always did whenever she attempted to do something for herself.

A nervy part of her suddenly cried out to go back, to forgo the urge to help the girl who lived there, to forget the money.

Instead, she turned and headed along the pier to where it met the stairs and started up them.

The path at the top of the rise wound into a copse of trees and curved out of sight. It was six feet wide and concrete, just as the stairs had been, and free of any of the detritus of the woods. Someone, probably Jeff, kept it unnaturally clean. The woods themselves were sparse, shin-high grass growing beneath the canopy, bramble scattered amongst trunks of older growth. Every so often, a bench appeared along the path's edge, an inscription, always the same, carved into the backrest in sweeping cursive.

MORI ET RENOVARE

Mira murmured the words to herself and picked up the pace.

Gradually, sky appeared in greater and greater patches until the trees fell away completely and she stepped onto a sweeping plain. It rolled gently away to the west, grass undulating with the wind. She'd climbed high enough for the waterway below the island to spread out and meld with the gray reaches of the great lake in the distance. She paused, breathing in the sharp air. It felt cleansing in a way a deep inhale never did in the city. The only smells were the soft decay of freshly fallen leaves and the flat emptiness of open water.

Cresting the top of the path's rise, she stopped again, this time not to indulge the view but to acclimate to it.

Wyndclyffe Manor stood before her in all its stone-cut glory. It rose at least four stories to crenelated rooftops peaked here and there by stern watchtowers and chimneys. Its breadth went at least a football field in either direction from a center where a wide porte cochère shaded a grand entryway. Leaded windows dotted the entire front, many behind terraces on the upper floors. A flower garden complete with low manicured hedges filled up the middle of the drive's turnaround. She could hear the trickle of and splash of fountains but only just over the beating of her heart.

Mira took in the structure a second time. It really was as sprawling as it appeared and not some optical illusion. To the right and farther back a stone garage appeared, four overhead doors gleaming whitely. Tucked beside the left wing was the suggestion of a pond's edge, reeds swaying in the breeze and punctuated with the sharp quack of a duck.

This must be what commoners feel like seeing royalty's castle, she thought, nearing the covered entrance. A sense of awe threaded with envy for something they could never have.

Dark oak double doors ten feet high split at their middle seam as she reached the top step, and Eleanor Madsen appeared in the gap. She smiled, subtle lines etching her face. She wore no makeup and her age was more apparent in the daylight.

"Mira, so glad you made it okay."

Mira took Eleanor's outstretched hand and shook it, slightly out of breath both from the walk and the manor's spectacle. "Thank you. This is . . . Wow" was all she managed before a burst of unexpected laughter escaped.

"It's quite something the first time, isn't it? Don't worry; it's like any other house after a while. Just a lot of rooms and windows. Come in, come in." Eleanor stepped aside.

The same interior voice from on the pier called out—an insecurity she'd struggled with all her life. The voice of reason, of responsibility, one that avoided risk or anything new and frightening.

"Okay?" Eleanor asked.

Mira nodded, slinging the thoughts away. "Yes, I'm fine." She hesitated a second more, then stepped inside.

6

A flood of vertigo poured over her as if she stood at the open door of an airplane, readying to skydive.

It was the sheer openness. The ceiling wasn't there. Or at least it was so high, it didn't seem to be. Fifty feet overhead, milky skylights slanted in great sheets, bathing everything below in a muted glow. A double grand staircase rose out of dark hardwood floors, and stone pillars shouldered crossing supports that could've been ribs of an ancient ship. Shining lacquer or the flatness of split rock made up every visible surface.

Mira turned in a half-circle, taking it all in. Hallways stretched off in either direction and at least a dozen heavy doors branched from the main entry. A massive fireplace yawned, tall enough for a grown person to stand up in, and above it hung the mounted head of an enormous water buffalo—black polished eyes and great horns curving toward the ceiling. Wrought-iron sconces shone and the smell of antiquity was nearly overwhelming. Age had never had a scent before, but here, it did. It was like a mixture of faded smoke and the leather covers of books.

"It's incredible," she heard herself say.

Eleanor laughed. "You'd think you'd still be awed by it, but after twenty years, it's just a big house."

"That's how long you've been here?"

"Next month. I was hired by Phillip and Angelica, Leland's parents. He was only twenty then. Time does go by, doesn't it?" Eleanor started off around the right staircase. "I'll play tour guide before you go get settled. Forgive me if I drone; it's been ages since anyone visited."

Mira followed her deeper into the house. Ornateness drenched everything from the paneled walls to the carved molding abutting ceilings inscribed with delicate scrollwork. It was a barrage to the eyes. How could anyone ever get used to this, to the beauty of it all? The only disturbing thing was the taxidermy.

It was everywhere.

Head, shoulder, and full-body mounts of animals hung every ten feet along the walls or perched on ornamental stands. They ranged from the exoticness of African kudu with its spiraled horns to a more domestic ruffed grouse, tail feathers spanned like a deck of cards.

Mira tried looking past the preserved death, but it was as if the walls were staring at her. Her stomach gave an unpleasant lurch, and she was thankful for the distraction when Eleanor started talking.

"The east wing goes back to the rear gardens; I'm sure Oliver will give you a tour of them later if you'd like. There's a grand ballroom this way and a full lounge. The kitchen is off to the right here, and the formal dining room is through those double doors." Mira caught a glimpse of a wooden table that could easily seat fifty guests along with the sense of high ceilings through the dining room's doorway, then they were moving on to another opening, which Eleanor stepped through.

"And this is where we typically eat. Little less ostentatious, don't you think?" The room they stood in was perhaps twenty by twenty and modern. In the center stood a utilitarian table with a distressed finish surrounded by equally used chairs. Several granite countertops lined the walls below dark wood cabinets. A modest flatscreen TV hung from one wall. No preserved pelts or shine of horn anywhere in sight. Good. "The staff dining room. You can find most anything you need in the refrigerator to make a quick meal or snack if you're hungry. Feel free to help yourself whenever."

Eleanor led the way out of the dining room and turned toward a veranda overlooking the back property. To the left, the pond she'd spotted earlier wrapped the rest of the way around the north wing, a few ducks paddling lazily on its surface. On the right, the four-stall garage's end was barely visible. Ahead, the garden sprawled in several acres of trimmed grass and flowerbeds, intersected by hedges and the occasional tree. Benches and chairs were arranged in groups in a half dozen places, and it was easy to imagine the parties and gatherings that had been held there over the years—the women in dresses and men in suits wandering among the greenery, drinks in hand. She could almost smell mingling scents of perfume and alcohol.

"It makes me a little sad," Eleanor said, breaking the silence. "Looking at so much grand space going to waste. There used to be wonderful events here; Angelica kept a ledger of every party with a list of guests and invitations in the library upstairs. You wouldn't believe some of the famous names in there. I'd go and read through them sometimes and think about what it would have been like to be here in the roaring twenties." She laughed quietly again. "But I suppose any well-to-do home was something to behold back then."

"It's really impressive. It must be a lot of work to keep up."

"Jeffry does a wonderful job with the grounds. Oliver and I do our best on the interior, but to be honest, it's been somewhat overwhelming since Allison's decline. We're more worried about her than some dust on the chandeliers, and it does show." She grimaced. "Please forgive any mess you happen upon. If something is in the way or you can't stand looking at it, just let us know. And feel free to explore. While you're here, this is your home as well."

As they returned to the main entry, Eleanor noticed her looking at the head of a male lion caught in a jaw-splitting roar and must have read the distaste in her expression. "Dreadful, isn't it? The one thing I've never gotten used to, all these poor animals. Killing wasn't good enough; they had to preserve death, too."

"Who . . ." Mira asked, motioning at a rash of doves in mid-flight.

"Phillip, almost all of them. Leland hunted some, but his father was the gamesman of the family." Eleanor's face creased and she continued on without saying any more.

At the base of the stairs, a man appeared out of the far hallway and came toward them. He was tall with iron-gray hair cut close at the sides and longer on top. His craggy features were creased kindly in smile lines around his mouth and eyes. As he neared and held out one large hand, Mira guessed he was several years Eleanor's senior.

"You must be Miss Caine," he said in a cultured European timbre, squeezing her hand firmly. He seemed to search her face for a moment before coming back to himself. "I'm Oliver Branson, estate manager. So very glad you agreed to come. We're thrilled to have you."

"Thank you." Mira struggled for a moment. Between the travel and the grand surroundings, she felt off-balance. "I really hope I can help."

"Us too, us too," Oliver said. He gave her another long look before focusing on Eleanor. "You've given her the grand tour?"

"Just the main floor, really, and only shown her a few of the rooms."

Oliver waved his hand. "You'll learn your way around soon enough. Most of the main floor is guest suites. I can lead you upstairs and give a more general layout if you'd like?"

"That would be great."

"I'll be in my office if you need me," Eleanor said, beginning to turn away.

"Did you check on Allison?" Oliver asked.

"Yes, just before Mira arrived. She's in the back garden."

"Good, good. Okay, if you'll follow me," Oliver said, heading for the stairs. Eleanor gave her a quick smile, then started down the nearest hall. As Mira fell in a few steps behind Oliver and climbed the lushly carpeted treads, she tried to recall seeing anyone in the back garden from the veranda but couldn't. All the tables and chairs had been empty.

The second- and third-floor layouts mirrored one another with a few exceptions, the main being the library on the third, which took up almost the entirety of the north wing.

The room was completely lined with shelves stretching halfway to the twenty-foot ceilings, tomes filling up every inch of space. Massive pillars grew from the floor, with flowering buttress supports fading into shadow. There was even an honest-to-God rolling ladder system on either side of the room Mira could barely restrain herself from climbing onto.

"This is the largest private library north of New York City," Oliver said from the doorway. "At least, it was the last time I looked it up. I wanted to show it to you because this is a very special place to Allison. She spent days and days here growing up." He stopped as if stumbling upon an unpleasant sight. She almost pressed upon the point, asked questions she'd formed upon reading the article about the most recent Wyndclyffes' fates, but held off. "All of the Wyndclyffes were voracious readers, especially in the earlier years. Before the internet," Oliver continued, saying the last word like a curse. He frowned, then held up one finger as if he'd recalled something. "Speaking of that, did Eleanor mention that the phone service is dreadful on the island?"

"She didn't."

"It is beyond spotty. If you need to make a call, I'd suggest using our landline, though that isn't always reliable either. We do have Wi-Fi, but with the thick walls and floor, it's—"

"Spotty?" Mira finished for him, continuing around the room.

"Yes, *spotty* is being kind." She wasn't surprised at the tech issues and lack of contact with the outside world. In a way, it was liberating. The city was a never-ending source of distractions, all the senses constantly barraged. Here there was a solitude. What would Aaron think of this place? As she traversed the wide room, her eyes drank in the spines and titles. "What else does Allison enjoy besides reading?"

"She loves the outdoors, the gardens, the forest. There's a path leading down to the river, and she spends time there, though she's been keeping indoors as of late. She does watch a bit of television and receives some magazines—Jeffry picks them up twice a week from the mainland."

"I love to read too, so we have that in common."

Oliver looked relieved. "Well, again, you're welcome to the library and anything herein." He paused, gazing around the room, his profile presented partially in shadow lending more definition to the lines in his face.

"How long have you worked here, Oliver?" Mira asked.

"Twenty-eight years. I was only twenty-four when I was hired on. Fresh out of Oxford and fresh off the boat. My great-grandparents knew the Wyndclyffes before they left England. That was my 'in,' so to speak. I've been here ever since, given a few excursions."

"That's a long time to spend on an island."

"It's home," he said simply. "Shall I show you your room?"

They left the library, and Mira gave it a final longing look before returning to the corridor. Oliver led her toward the second floor along a hallway of more taxidermy she tried to ignore while focusing on sculpted busts featuring Homer, Euclid, and several others she didn't recognize. Their alabaster gazes followed her movements. Past the sculptures, a painting featuring an English foxhunt adorned almost an entire wall from floor to ceiling, the riders and mounts life-size. As they passed the mural, Mira had to look twice to confirm what she was seeing. The hunters astride their horses were somehow . . . off. There was an incongruence to their features, as if the artist had suffered from cataracts. Mouths blurred into noses and eyes, and she wasn't sure, but she thought she counted one too many fingers on a hand holding a rifle. Horses' breath steamed from flared and dripping nostrils. Dogs yowled silently, jaws frothing, a reddish gleam set deeply in their eyes. But the worst was the fox. At first, she didn't notice it at all, then couldn't look at anything else. The fox stared out from the shade of alien ferns at the far corner of the painting. Its face was as wrong as its human hunters—elongated, the features too pointed—but its expression was what caught Mira's attention and held it. Pure calculating malice dripped from its blackened eyes. It grinned out of the oil it had been rendered in, each whisker a sharpened needle, every tooth a promise.

"Miss Caine?"

Mira flinched, realizing she'd stopped in front of the painting. Oliver watched her questioningly. "Sorry," she said, catching up and resisting the urge to look at the mural again.

"A bit hypnotizing, isn't it?" Oliver said, gesturing at the wall as they moved down to the second floor.

"A little."

"I've always detested it. Gives me the creeps. Though I'm biased; I hated 'the hunts,' as my father called them. Here we are."

They stopped at the second door from the stairway, and Oliver opened it with a flourish, bowing slightly with a smile. "Your humble accommodations, madam."

She stepped past him, trying to leave the unsettling sensation from the painting in the hall. The bedroom was a wide space featuring a sitting area complete with loveseat and matching chair, a squat Victorian dresser, and a four-poster bed sans canopy. A bank of windows lined the far wall. Above the dresser, a mountain goat's head stared down. Her reflection was a faint smear in its dark glossy eyes.

"I hope it's adequate," Oliver said.

"It's wonderful, thank you," Mira said, looking away from the goat. She noticed her luggage had been deposited at the foot of the bed. Something else occurred to her then. "I didn't see the staircase to the fourth floor; is it in another part of the house?"

Oliver cocked his head. "Fourth floor?"

"Yeah, isn't there one? I could've sworn . . ." she trailed off. The height of the building didn't match with the tour. Its exterior dimensions must've been an illusion; three stories could easily become four, given the spectacle at first glance. Oliver watched her, seeming to wait for something. The silence drew out. Mira glanced away, unsure of what to say.

"If you're hungry, I'll have Gael bring up a light lunch," he said finally.

"Thank you. That would be great."

"When would you like to meet Allison?"

"Well, whenever, I guess. After lunch?"

"Of course. I'll see to it she's ready. If you need anything further, you can just dial the one on the phone and it will ring our offices downstairs." Oliver stepped into the hall and began to shut the door, but paused. "Miss Caine, if I may?"

"It's just Mira."

"Mira. All right. Allison isn't just like family to us; she is family. I have to say this, and I mean no offense. I'm slightly dubious of Eleanor's confidence in this plan. So I ask, do you really believe you can help her?"

"I . . . I'm . . ." She floundered slightly, all of the doubts crashing down at once. *What am I doing here?* "I'm a good listener and I think that's sometimes what people need most. I'll really do my best."

The lines at the corners of Oliver's eyes crinkled. "That's all we ask."

7

It was the best sandwich she'd ever eaten.

Roasted steak sliced thin on a toasted ciabatta bun with lettuce, sun-dried tomatoes, and a sauce that would've made any Manhattan chef weep into his whites. Mira set aside the empty plate, looked around, then picked it up and licked it clean. Her hunger had sneaked up on her and become a caged animal the moment Gael Danforth knocked at her door with the silver tray.

The manor's chef was young and strikingly handsome, slender with hair so blond it was almost white. If she had to guess, she'd put him five years her senior. He'd presented the meal, paused only to introduce himself with a handshake, and asked if she had any food allergies he should be aware of.

"Nutmeg. I've gotten really sick a few times," she'd replied.

"One bee sting will kill me. Allergies are the worst, right?" He'd given her a dazzling smile, and she'd noticed the suggestion of a dimple on one cheek beneath a fine layer of scruff.

For a second, she'd been unable to come up with a response. "For sure," she finally managed.

"Anything you're particularly fond of?"

She thought for a moment. "Silk pie?"

"Now we're talking."

With that, he'd left her with a slight bow to enjoy her lunch.

Stomach pleasantly full, she set about siphoning the contents of her two suitcases into the ornate dresser drawers. When she was finished, she explored the attached bath and let out a gasp. It was literally larger than her entire room at Grace Home.

The windows along the bedroom's wall gave a panoramic view of the pond, rippled with wind, the ducks absent now. Beyond the pond and yard, the forest took over. A crushed-shell path led from the rear gardens out of sight beneath dark overhanging branches, assumedly the one Oliver had mentioned that ended at the river. *He stood there staring, and he was saying something too. I could see his mouth moving but couldn't hear.*

It was like Nessie had spoken directly into her ear. Mira's meal shifted unpleasantly and she turned away from the view. Nerves, that was all. Leaving Aaron along with the weird encounter in town would be enough to make anyone uneasy. And there was the residual worry Shay had instilled in her, but that was slowly ebbing. The offer *had* sounded too good to be true, but the estate was legitimate and there didn't seem to be anything weird about the staff so far. Jeff had been gruff, but maybe that was just him. She tapped out a quick text to Shay letting her know she wasn't in danger of being trafficked and hit Send.

As she passed the dresser on her way out of the room, she looked at the mirror hanging above it. The frame was interwoven silver vines, expertly joined so that none of the welds were visible. Wide silver leaves sprouted at all four corners. At the top, spelled in the same delicate weaving, was the phrase she'd seen carved into the backs of the benches along the path.

On her phone, she brought up the web browser and typed in the Latin. The search wheel spun. And spun. And spun. One bar on the Wi-Fi connection. She waited another ten seconds, then shut down the search and left the room.

There was no one in the hall or on the stairs. The entry echoed with her footfalls and she debated which direction to go. *Should have just hit the damned one button on the room's phone.* But she hadn't, so now it was hide-and-seek.

She found Eleanor in her office, a room halfway down the main corridor in the south wing. The space was mostly bare with only a wide desk, laser jet printer, latest Apple desktop computer, and a leather rolling chair the women herself sat in. There were no decorations on the walls save for one, a black-and-white picture of the manor in summer—lush grass and blooming flowers near the front walk.

"All fed and settled?" Eleanor asked, pulling off a pair of bifocals and standing.

"Yes, the food was amazing."

"Gael is an excellent chef. We're lucky to have him. He's from Yellow Bay, and when we heard he was graduating from culinary school, we snatched him up immediately. Wonderful guy, though he's too handsome for his own good, if you know what I mean."

Mira smiled. "I'll be on guard."

"Good." Eleanor straightened. "Now I suppose you'd like to meet Allison. I'll show you to her room; she's waiting."

They moved into the northern wing past a piece of modern art resembling a virus, and another painting that didn't instill quite the same amount of disquiet as the fox hunt but nearly.

It was a framed six-foot square canvas depicting a woman's face, though completely dislocated by an interspersed jigsaw puzzle of blank squares, the features scattered. The woman's mouth was where her forehead should be, an ear at chin height, an eye peering out the top right corner.

Mira looked away and nearly bumped into Eleanor, who had stopped in front of a door.

"She normally naps in the late afternoon before supper, so this may be a good time for you to get to know one another. I guess we'll leave that up to the two of you." Eleanor wrung her hands and looked past Mira. "I don't have to tell you we're all nervous. There's been so much promise and subsequent failure in her treatment . . . it's been demoralizing. I hope . . ."

Mira placed a hand on her arm. "I'm sure we'll get along great. We'll take one day at a time."

Eleanor brightened and Mira was moved to see the shimmer of tears in her eyes. "I'll be in my office if you need anything." She started away but turned back after a few steps. "Supper will be served in the staff dining room at six thirty. We'd love if you could join us." She continued down the hall, the click of her shoes trailing in her wake.

Mira watched her go, then gathered herself, touching the cold doorknob. She breathed deeply and opened the door.

8

The room was large and ill lit.

For a second, Mira had the sense she was standing in an auditorium stretching on and on into oblivion, but it was simply the patterned darkness broken by soft blades of light cutting between tall curtains on the far wall. A fireplace almost as large as the one in the entry sat to the right, while a desk and barrage of mismatched furniture were positioned to the left. Beyond the field of chairs and loveseats arranged in semicircles was a king-sized bed. At its foot was a coffin.

Mira blinked. No, not a coffin—a cedar chest alarmingly similar in shape and size. On the opposite side of the bed was an open door she assumed led into a bath.

There was no one else in the room.

Mira glanced around again, then took a step forward. "Hello?" She'd barely uttered the word when something shifted in the closest chair.

A girl sat staring at her where there hadn't been one before.

Mira took an involuntary step back, unable to help herself.

The girl had faded blond hair hanging loose on slim shoulders. Bird shoulders, her father would have called them. She was narrow-waisted and -hipped, with skin so pale it was almost translucent. But her eyes were wide and luminous, even in the low light. They drank Mira in, unblinking. And there was a hesitant beauty about Allison, a timidity that made Mira want to apologize even though she hadn't done anything wrong. When Allison sat forward, Mira saw why she hadn't noticed her in the first place—she wore a blouse and matching ankle-length skirt almost exactly the same shade as the chair she sat in.

She wasn't there before, Mira thought wildly before coming back to herself.

"Hi, I'm Mira. You must be Allison." Mira didn't move closer, didn't reach out. She waited.

Allison studied her for another few seconds. "You look just like you did on TV. That's good."

When she said nothing further, Mira gestured at a seat opposite Allison. "Is it okay if I sit down?" A slight nod. Mira settled into the chair and glanced around, looking for an icebreaker. "I like your room. It's so open."

Allison looked at her surroundings as if seeing them for the first time. "It's the biggest bedroom in the house. My mother and father's."

"Oh . . . it's really nice." An awkward silence stretched out. Two minutes with this girl and she was already out of things to say? "Oliver and Eleanor told me you like being outside," Mira said, grasping at anything. Another nod. "I grew up in Connecticut, about a half hour from the ocean. We could smell it sometimes when the wind was right. The island reminds me of it a little."

Allison's wide gaze landed on her and traveled away. "I've never been there. Connecticut, I mean. I haven't gone anywhere in a long time." She crossed her arms, cupping her elbows as if she were cold.

"When was the last time you left the island?"

"I don't know." She began to rock slightly, forward and back.

Mira cringed internally, changing tack. "So, Oliver said you like to read?"

"Sometimes."

"What's your favorite book?"

She was a long time answering. "You'll laugh."

"I won't. I promise."

"*Alice In Wonderland.*"

"I like that one too. It's kind of trippy." Allison blinked and Mira toyed with the hem of her shirt. "Why's it your favorite?"

"Not because of the weirdness; I hate that about it. My mom used to read it to me when I was little. I loved the sound of her voice."

Mira smiled. "My mom used to read to my brother and me. Mostly Dr. Seuss and Berenstain Bears." When Allison didn't respond Mira shifted in her chair and said, "I don't know if Eleanor told you, but I lost my parents too." Allison had been looking at something over her shoulder, but now her gaze came back and held. "They were in a car accident a few years ago. And, um . . ." Mira fought a sudden surge of emotion. "I know it's not the same, but we have that in common."

Allison studied her for another moment, then stood and made her way to the windows, pushing a button, which moved a set of power curtains aside. The view was expansive, the pond almost directly outside the window. When she made no move to return, Mira rose and went to stand beside her, keeping a comfortable distance between them. She was intensely reminded of being on a rooftop ledge months before next to another girl.

"I know why you're here," Allison finally said.

"Is that okay?"

A shrug. "I think it's a waste of time."

"Oh." It was all Mira could come up with. What was she supposed to say to this deeply damaged girl? Why had Eleanor put so much faith in her? She didn't know what she was doing, had no idea where to go from here.

Somewhere outside the room a chime tolled, drifting faintly through the walls. One. Two. Three. Four. Five. Silence. Allison tilted her head, listening, then went to the door, opened it a crack and peered out. She touched the doorknob once, twice, three times.

"Everything all right?" Mira asked.

"Do you want to see the grounds?"

Mira hesitated. "Uh, sure."

Allison led the way out of the room and down the hall to the front entry. For a second, she paused there, staring toward the back of the house. The main corridor was dim now, shadows gathering along the floors and beneath the furniture. Allison squinted into the gloom, motionless. Waiting.

"What is it?" Mira said.

Allison straightened and glanced over her shoulder, a tentative smile blooming. "Nothing. Let's go."

They filed outside, and as Mira was pulling the massive door shut behind them, a clock began chiming again somewhere deep in the house.

SEPTEMBER 2021

"What do you mean, you're leaving?"

Allison kept her back to her best friend, afraid to look at her expression, but she could see it anyway in her mind—the hurt creases in Isabelle's brow and how her frown always made her look so much younger than her fifteen years, more vulnerable.

Allison turned away from the river. Isabelle sat on the turtle rock higher up the bank. They'd named it both for its shape and mottled coloring the first time they'd come to this place, staking another claim to the shaded stretch of silt and piled rock, making it theirs, something they shared. Like a secret.

The sun had slid free of the clouds and nudged back the morning chill. Allison turned her face up to it for a moment before going and sitting beside her friend. "Mom and I, we're going . . ." She'd almost slipped. Her mother had been adamant about keeping what she'd confided to herself. Her father couldn't find out. If he did . . . But this was Isabelle. She told her everything. And what would she think if one day she was just gone? "We have to go," she said quietly.

Isabelle's frown deepened. "Where?"

"I don't know; she wouldn't tell me. Just away."

"For how long?" Allison shrugged, not meeting her gaze. "But you're coming back, right?"

"I don't know." This was what she'd truly been afraid of from the moment her mother took her on a walk down by the river and revealed her plans. Izzy had always been more like a sister than a friend, and Allison had been aware of the younger girl's instability on some level from the start—her fear of other people and places and change in general, which had only worsened over the years. It was maybe one of the things that drew them together, since Allison had played the protector while urging Isabelle to be more adventurous.

And now she was saying goodbye.

"But what will I do? Does my mom know?"

"No, and you can't tell her. This has to be a secret until we leave. My dad can't find out." Isabelle stiffened at the mention of her father and glanced around as if he might come striding out of the woods right then. "I can't be here anymore. It's too much. The last time, I didn't sleep for days. By the end, I had no idea where I was. *Who* I was. I think that's what he wanted." Allison reached out and took one of her hands. "I'll let you know where we are as soon as we get there. And you can come visit." She said the last with a false hopefulness they both heard.

Isabelle pulled her hand free and stood, taking Allison's former place by the water. "If he changes, would you stay?" she said after a time.

"What do you mean?"

"If your dad was different . . . nicer. Would you and your mom stay?"

Allison considered this. "I don't know. He's always been . . ." She swallowed, struggling for a moment to drown out the memory of her father yelling in the next room, yelling right in her face. "I think it's something my mom needs us to do. Maybe someday it'll be different." When Isabelle said nothing and didn't turn around, Allison went to her side, unsurprised to see tears staining her friend's face. When she tried wiping them away, Isabelle stepped out of reach.

"You're leaving me," Isabelle said, her voice hushed.

"It won't be forever."

"You don't know that."

"Izzy, please."

Isabelle shook her head, her features tightening in anger. Then she was running away, back up the path toward the manor.

"Izzy!" But she was gone.

Allison slumped and stared out over the river, throat tight, her own eyes stinging. A fish jumped and a loon called, long and lonesome somewhere toward Lake Ontario. Truth told, she hadn't ever cared for open water all that much. Especially the lake. The darkness beneath the waves reminded her of her father—how on the surface he was smiling while underneath there was something deeper. Colder.

Gradually, she straightened. It would be good to leave this place. Good to leave the memories behind, even if it meant leaving Isabelle, too. She'd make it up to her someday, somehow.

Fixing the promise to a permanent place inside her, Allison turned and started up the path into the trees as the loon called out once more and then fell quiet.

9

Mira had never seen a triangular window before, much less one set in the outside corner of a building.

It was in a flattened alcove high up on a northeast corner of the manor. She wouldn't have seen it at all if she'd been closer to the wall, but a hedge almost fifteen feet tall blocked the way, forcing them to detour around its perimeter. Mira stood looking up at the window, hands shoved in the pockets of her light sweater, wishing she'd taken the time to retrieve a jacket from her room. The breeze carried a damp chill.

"Kind of weird, isn't it?" Allison said from beside her.

"Uh, yeah. It's different."

"My great-great-great-grandfather built this whole place. Well, not him. He was rich, so he paid workers to do it. But he had them make stuff like that." She raised her chin toward the odd window.

"What room is it in?" Mira asked.

"Not sure. I've never seen it from the inside," Allison said, then started away.

The library.

It had to be, though she couldn't recall seeing it earlier. It was definitely on the third floor and she thought she had her bearings straight enough to be sure where the room was located. The oddness of its shape struck her in equal parts charming and eerie, like a sweet birthday card from someone you didn't know.

She wasn't sure if she believed Allison or not. How could you live in a house your entire life, even a place as large as this, and not know what room a window belonged to? Maybe Allison was testing her, teasing a little bit to see how she'd react.

Mira watched the glass for another moment, waiting for movement or a light, something, she couldn't say what, then scanned the blank face of the wall above the third floor. There was a lot of it. Enough for a fourth level or a very high roof enclosure.

"You coming?" Allison called from farther along the hedge.

Mira gave the window a last look and hurried on.

They walked slowly, hugging the hedge's curve. The yard widened more and more as they rounded the side of the manor. Here and there were decorative lawn sculptures—a rearing horse, a regal stag—along with birdbaths empty except for small amounts of rainwater and slimes of algae.

"So, you're staying for a month," Allison said quietly.

"To start with. I can stay longer if I need to."

"Don't you go to school?"

"I graduated last spring. I was the youngest in my grade. My mom wanted to keep me home an extra year before kindergarten, but my dad insisted I go as soon as I could."

"Why?"

"He thought being the littlest would make me tougher."

Allison was quiet for a time. "Did it?" she finally asked.

"Maybe some." Mira glanced at her. "You do homeschool?"

"Yeah."

"Do you like it?"

A shrug. "It's okay. I do my work whenever I want. Eleanor takes care of everything else. I'll be done sometime this winter."

"Did you ever go to school anywhere else?"

"No. My father didn't trust schools. He didn't trust a lot of things." Allison glanced away and Mira was struck again by how delicate she looked, like spun glass in the gray light. What would it be like to only know one place your entire life? Without any contact other than your family with the outside world? What would that do to a person?

On the opposite side of the hedge, the pond revealed itself. In the city, this would be considered a lake. A retaining wall lined the pond's boundaries, tall enough to sit on. Past it, a smattering of trees marked where the deeper forest began.

"Wow," Mira breathed. "It's amazing."

"It's prettier in the summer," Allison said. She stood a few paces back and to the right, hunched in the cool air. "Everything's dry and dying now. Winter's coming."

"I always loved fall," Mira said, getting lost in the view. "It's my favorite season. At our old place, we'd take long walks when the leaves turned and started falling. My brother Aaron and I would try to catch them before they hit the ground."

"Aaron," Allison said, as if she were tasting the name. "Is he younger or older?"

"Younger."

"Where is he?"

Again the guilt came roaring back. Mira took a step toward the retaining wall. "He lives at a facility for people with disabilities. But I'm moving him out soon."

"Moving where?"

"I don't know yet." Mira looked up. "A place like this with lots of space. Like where we used to live. He's always wanted to go back."

"You don't like the city?"

"No. Not really."

"I went there once when I was young. Everything was so big and loud. It was terrible. I'd want to leave too."

"It was never really home." A gust of wind coasted across the yard, rippling the pond's surface in silver ridges.

"And that's what you're looking for? Home?" Allison said, her voice soft and distant.

It was what she'd been looking for ever since the night the phone rang and her life had come completely apart. But the meaning of the word was drifting further and further away. Because now she understood home wasn't a place or a building. It was the people who filled it.

Mira swallowed thickly. "I think maybe we should go in. I'm starting to get col—"

She turned to find the space behind her empty.

There was only the wall of hedges and vacant yard to either side. "Allison?" The other girl was nowhere to be seen. But she'd been there moments ago, had just asked her a question. Mira called her name again, her voice very small in the vastness of the grounds.

"Help ya with somethin'?"

Mira spun and found Jeff the groundskeeper standing a few yards away. He held a long-handled pole with a net at one end and wore the same clothes as when she'd met him earlier, plus a set of tall rubber boots ending just below the knees. She hadn't heard his approach at all.

"Did you see where Allison went?"

He studied her for a time. "Nope."

"She was just here."

The groundskeeper didn't reply. He swept the net out over the water, collecting some floating leaves, and pulled it back in. His movements were practiced and unhurried.

Mira glanced around again, still shaken. She moved to the pond's retaining wall and looked down, studying the dark, placid surface and her wavering reflection until it was broken by the silver flash of scales. Mira startled, a laugh escaping her. "There's fish in there?"

"Yuh. Lake trout and sunnies mostly."

"It must be pretty deep."

"Least twenty feet, since the fish survive the winter after freeze-up." He telescoped the pole outward again, swiping up a floating clump, and Mira tried placing his accent. A Yankee for sure, but she thought he must've grown up farther north. Central Maine was a good bet, by the sound of his *a*'s. Her grandfather had been from a little town east of Bangor, and she could still hear him telling her about the fishing boats he'd worked on as a young man in the same drawling brogue.

"How long have you worked here?" Mira asked, trying to make polite conversation.

Jeff shot her a look out the corner of his eye and went back to skimming the pond. "Long enough." He paused. "Sorry. Not used to guests. 'Bout fifteen years, give or take." When he moved the pole again, she noticed old blue-green ink extending from beneath his shirtsleeve onto the back of his hand in the shape of roughly drawn flames. Shay had a tattoo like it on her shoulder, a heart on fire licking up toward her neck—a birthday present from Shay's mother before she'd been arrested for heroin possession. But Shay's ink was all smooth dark lines, and she would've bet Jeff's tattoo had been done in prison.

"You're here to see if you can help her, then," he said, continuing his work.

"I am."

"Be staying long?"

"For a while."

"From the city?"

"Yeah."

"Not born there, though."

It seemed she wasn't the only one good at placing accents. "Connecticut."

He nodded. "Stayed a summer in Tall Pines Village. Worked at the resort there. Pretty place."

"I've been through there." She glanced around. "The grounds are beautiful; it must be a lot of work."

"Keeps me busy. Less so come winter. I'm mainland from December through February."

The inflection of his last words as well as his body language told her he was done talking. "Well, thanks for bringing my luggage up," she said, stepping away from the wall and walking past him. She angled toward the shell path she'd spotted earlier from her room but stopped short when Jeff spoke again.

"Wanna be mindful if you go in the woods. 'Specially at night." She watched him, eyebrows raised. "Wouldn't wander at night."

"Haunted?" she asked, getting the same vibe as she had after Nessie's initiation. Jeff stared off into the trees, gaze veiled and thoughtful. She glanced in the same direction. Shadows grew like mold between the trunks, and a stillness she hadn't been aware of before lay across the grounds. Thick and expectant.

"Nah. Cougar," Jeff finally said. It came out *Coogah*. She waited to see if he'd crack a smile, but he only gestured at the wall of trees bordering the yard. "Least that's the legend. Supposed to have been one or two here since the place was built. Wouldn't put much faith in it, but I've found a few skunks and porcupines torn up over the seasons." He fixed her with a look. "Somethin' out there."

She couldn't help but scan the tree line again, desperately craving to be inside the safety of the manor. "Thanks," she said slowly, not knowing if she meant it. Mira turned and changed course away from the shell path, following the pond's edge toward the garden. She willed herself not to look back in case Jeff was watching her, but when she climbed the rear steps, he was still combing the pond with the net.

Back and forth. Back and forth.

10

At a little before six-thirty, Mira changed into a comfortable pair of jeans and a long sleeved T-shirt, and made her way to the staff dining room.

After her conversation with Jeff, she'd gone looking for Allison but found her bedroom door closed and locked. Not wanting to disturb her if she was napping, Mira had lain down herself, surprised by falling asleep almost immediately—the early morning and long drive apparently catching up with her.

Oliver and Eleanor were already seated at the table when she entered the room. They welcomed her as Gael appeared, rolling a small cart before him loaded with dishes. The atmosphere was one of a small family with quips and asides interspersed amongst questions about daily routines, which created a familiar ache of longing in her chest.

The fare was better than any restaurant she'd frequented in the city, featuring pickled capers and fried clams as appetizers. The main course was trout, "Caught right from the pond!" Oliver exclaimed, basted in a white wine shallot sauce, accompanied by roasted asparagus and fresh carrots.

As the food was placed on the table Mira kept glancing toward the door until Eleanor seemed to notice. "Is everything okay, Mira?"

"Isn't Allison eating with us?"

"Her anxiety medication affects her appetite," Oliver said. "She dines on a different schedule than we do."

As they ate, Oliver and Eleanor chatted about the weather and the coming winter. They asked her about Grace Home and her friends. Everything except her first meeting with Allison. The question was there as the elephant in the corner everyone politely skirted past. Gael joined them between courses, sipping at a glass of red wine but never touching any of the food. She liked the casual way he leaned against the counter with a white towel draped over one shoulder and how whenever he wasn't talking, his gaze seemed to find her own and hold it.

When dinner was finished (she had managed to down a large piece of silk pie Gael set before her with a wink), they moved next door to a modest lounge where a stone fireplace crackled with flames. Beside the fireplace, a large bay window overlooked the garden. Twilit fog hung across the grounds like laundry left out and forgotten. Oliver poured himself a finger of brandy and sat in an overstuffed chair.

"Would you like anything else?" Eleanor said. "A cup of coffee or tea?"

"I couldn't," Mira said, placing a hand against her stomach. Oliver and Eleanor chuckled.

"If Gael ever decides to leave, I'll follow him wherever he goes," Eleanor said, settling into a seat beside the fire.

"So, he works full-time here?"

"He does. His mother passed away not long ago and left him his childhood home in Yellow Bay, but he rarely goes there. He's got a room on the ground floor, and feeding us keeps him pretty busy most days."

"He's an excellent chef."

"We're certainly spoiled," Oliver agreed. He tasted his drink, then winced as he reached out to set it down on a nearby table as if the movement pained him. "A satisfying meal should never be taken for granted. Life is a strange sequence of events and one has to savor the good alongside the bad." His face darkened, and he seemed to go somewhere else for a moment before brightening again. "And there is always hope. The one true renewable resource humankind has at its disposal."

"Forgive him; he waxes poetic at times," Eleanor said without rancor.

The fire snapped cozily and the elephant moved away from the corner toward the middle of the room. Mira thought for a moment, then said, "I'm sure you're both wondering how things went today."

Oliver smiled. "We are, but wouldn't dream of intruding."

"We didn't talk a lot, but I know she cares very much about both of you." Oliver and Eleanor shared a look, so much passing between them. "I think it's just going to take time."

"The one thing we don't have," Eleanor said quietly.

Mira glanced from her to Oliver. "What do you mean?"

They considered one another before Oliver motioned to Eleanor. "Go ahead and tell her; she needs to know."

Eleanor took a moment to gather herself. "Leland, Allison's father, was always . . . troubled. From a young age he struggled with depression. His father, Phillip, called it melancholy, another way of skirting any responsibility."

"He wasn't treated for it?" Mira asked.

"No. Phillip was like the rest of the Wyndclyffe patriarchs, secular and secretive. Distrustful of the outside world. He saw mental illness as weakness—a flaw that could be overcome with enough initiative, and ignored if it wasn't." Eleanor shook her head. "He instilled this nonsense in Leland and also passed down his paranoia of doctors. Instead of getting proper help, Leland walled himself and his family off from the outside world. He was strict with Allison and would yell sometimes. Never in front of us, but we could hear him and Vanessa fighting, even with the thick walls."

"If we ever would have thought he was capable . . ." Oliver said, trailing off and shaking his head.

"He was acting strange leading up to . . . that night. Removed, quiet, spending lots of time alone." Eleanor glanced at Oliver but he seemed miles away. "The gunshots woke me. Leland had taken one of his rifles into Oliver's room and shot him twice. It was a miracle he didn't hit anything vital."

Mira watched Oliver, imagining the terror of waking to gun blasts in the dead of night, feeling the pain, the panic . . .

"Then he went looking for Vanessa and Allison," Eleanor continued. "Vanessa tried hiding them in a closet, but he found them and—" She grimaced. "By the time I got there, Vanessa was gone and Allison was pleading with him. I'd loaded the shotgun that used to hang over the mantel and managed to sneak up behind him."

Mira let the implications settle in. The news report she'd read took on weight. She was sitting across from those who'd lived it. She could feel the violent memory hanging like smoke in the room.

Mira was quiet for a moment before sitting forward. "I'm so sorry."

Eleanor gave her a tired smile. "It was beyond horrible. Allison was wounded by a ricochet and lost a lot of blood." She glanced at Oliver, but he was still distant. "What I'm about to tell you is confidential and covered in the nondisclosure agreement you signed before arriving, but beyond that, Allison's comfort is our utmost concern. Did she say anything about her diagnosis?"

"No. Not really."

"I've mentioned the anxiety and panic attacks, but it's more serious than that. She also suffers from something called depersonalization. In her case, Allison sometimes feels detached from herself. Almost like she's someone else watching her life. The physicians think it's a self-defense mechanism from the trauma she endured, a way to separate herself from it." Eleanor paused, her brow drawing together. "She's also had bouts of catatonia. All of them directly after anyone presses her about that night. She recedes until she's no longer here. At times, it's taken her weeks to begin responding again." She licked her lips. "We want to apologize for keeping this from you, but we were afraid you might refuse our offer if you knew."

There it was. The other shoe dropping. Something had been missing but she hadn't been able to figure out what it was. "How many times has this happened?"

"Seven," Eleanor said. "Seven times she's disappeared within herself, and each time we were afraid she wouldn't return." She shared another look with Oliver. "And this brings us to the real reason why you're here. Now that you've seen this place and have a grasp of the Wyndclyffe wealth, you must also understand the weight of such a fortune. After her parents' deaths, everything was to be bestowed to Allison upon her eighteenth birthday. Everything. Leland's lawyer, a detestable man by the name of Browning, executed the will to the letter. It was only later he returned to us, highlighting a clause within a clause." Eleanor made a small quotation sign with her fingers. "'At any such time should the recipient die or be deemed unsound of mind, all assets will be forfeit to the secondary successor.' A single sentence that's brought nothing but heartache."

"So, that means—"

"The successor in the will is a fund-management group Leland created, and to who Mr. Browning serves as primary counsel," Eleanor continued. "Mr. Browning's last visit was during one of Allison's regressions. He's found a judge who has granted a motion to have Allison's mental state assessed a few months from now, prior to her birthday." She paused and looked at the nearest table as if searching for a drink where there was none. "If she's deemed unsound of mind, she'll be removed from the estate and placed in a care facility. We'll all be torn apart."

"And we can't let that happen," Oliver finished, appearing to come back from wherever he'd gone.

A quiet fell over the room, broken only by the fire's occasional snapping. Mira breathed out, long and slow. "I'm sorry, but I don't know if I can help."

"She saw you save her," Eleanor said quietly. "We all did. You talked that girl down off the edge of a building."

Mira shook her head. "That was . . ."

"Heroic," Oliver said. "And that's what Allison needs. Someone brave, someone she can trust. A friend." He finished his drink in one long swallow. Mira sighed, a dozen impulses pulling in different directions.

"Don't make a decision now," Eleanor said. "Sleep on it and give us your answer in the morning. The offer stands. Even if you trigger another bout of catatonia while trying to help her, you'll still be paid for the month." She reached out and took one of Mira's hands in her own. Her skin was warm and papery smooth. "We only ask that you try."

11

A full moon rose from the trees in the east like a disgorged egg.

Mira stood, watching it ascend from the front steps, its initial color a sulphurous yellow bleaching to white the higher it climbed. Though the wind had died, the night continued to cool and the air nipped at her exposed skin. She pulled her jacket tighter and began to pace the wide landing.

She moved slowly and methodically. A thinking speed, her father would have called it. He'd gone on his share of walks when considering something—a problem at work, a decision about Aaron's treatment, a fight with their mother. Almost always, he'd come back enlightened, and she'd inherited the practice from him. Very few things couldn't be solved by a long walk.

But with darkness an oppressive blanket now beyond the glow of the outdoor lights along with Jeff's warning about a cougar stalking the island, she settled for moving back and forth on the safety of the steps.

She should've known there was something more to Eleanor's offer. Shay had been right to a degree. Oliver and Eleanor weren't trying to traffic her, but they hadn't been honest either. Not only did Allison's mental health rest solidly on her shoulders, but so did the means to a fortune she couldn't even guess at. The idea of leaving swept over her again but just as quickly subsided with the thought of Allison in someplace like Village Gardens. Somewhere strange and frightening, away from the people who loved her. Somewhere that wasn't home.

Mira was making her way back to the far end of the steps when she realized she was no longer alone. A shadow hovered beside the main entrance, then it shifted and the light revealed Allison's features. "Hey."

"Hey. How long have you been there?"

"A minute or two."

"I didn't even see you."

"I'm good at that." Allison moved to the top stair's edge and sat. She'd changed from her skirt and wore a pair of dark leggings and a down jacket. Mira sat beside her. They both studied the moon. "It's something I look forward to every month," Allison said after a moment, nodding to the sky. "People are supposed to change with a full moon. It affects us like it does the tides, since we're mostly saltwater."

Mira laughed. "I guess that makes sense. Do you feel different?"

"No. I always hope I will, but I don't."

They were quiet for a time, then Mira said, "You disappeared on me this afternoon."

Even in the low light, the wrinkles on Allison's brow were prominent. "What do you mean?"

"We were talking out by the pond, and then you were just . . . gone."

It was Allison's turn to laugh. "I said I was tired and I was going in. You must not have heard me."

"No, you . . ." Mira replayed their conversation. Had Allison said something prior to vanishing? She couldn't recall. At the time, she'd been thinking of home and had been mesmerized by the pond, how it had rippled with the wind.

"I think you might've been daydreaming," Allison said.

"Maybe."

An owl hooted somewhere far away, and it was such a lonely, haunting sound, Mira both hoped it would and wouldn't come again.

"So, they told you," Allison said, bringing her back.

"Told me?" She was lost for a second, then realized what the other girl was referring to. "You mean your diagnosis?" Allison nodded, still not facing her. "How did you know?"

"Sounds are funny in this place. They carry."

"Oh."

"I'm guessing you'll be leaving, then."

"What?"

"I mean, why would you want to hang out with a crazy person, right? Except for the money of course."

"I don't think you're crazy."

Allison scoffed. "Sure you do. Everyone does."

"I don't." There must've been something in her voice, because Allison glanced her way. "And neither do Eleanor and Oliver."

Allison picked at one of her fingernails. "They're desperate."

"Maybe. But they want to help you. So do I."

"No one can help me." Her voice was suddenly full of venom. "The drugs make me tired and make food taste weird. That's what the doctors were interested in, seeing what the chemicals would do to me. The therapists asked stupid questions and then never really listened. They just wrote stuff down on their little papers."

Her anger both was and wasn't surprising. A lot of the kids at Grace Home carried around the same resentment. They were there because they were no longer safe in their homes, or they didn't have homes at all. And the anger went deeper than that, all the way back to their parents or lack thereof. And without them to blame, they blamed themselves. She waited to see if Allison was done, and when she started to rise from her seat, Mira said, "You feel like an experiment instead of a person."

A long pause, then Allison whispered, "Yes."

"Well, I'm not here to try and change you. I'm here to listen."

"You don't want to hear what's wrong with me."

Mira studied her for a beat, then looked up at the floating moon. "My brother loses control of himself sometimes. Really loud noises or too many people around him at once makes him panic. He runs away if he can and lashes out if he can't. It doesn't matter who he's hurting. One time, we were at the beach and some boys set off a bunch of firecrackers. Aaron broke my dad's glasses and hit me so hard, my eye swelled shut for two days. It's not his fault." She let the words hang in the air and waited.

"All the doctors say it's here," Allison finally said, touching one temple lightly. "Why I'm sad, why I panic. Sometimes, I believe them. But most times . . ." She glanced over one shoulder as if making sure they were alone. Mira couldn't help herself and did the same, a part of her looking for someone else standing in the shadowed portico. ". . . things are wrong. They show up in bad places. Days don't line up right. Hours get lost. And I'm not even me sometimes—" She drew in a deep, shuddering breath.

Mira reached out and gently took her hand. Held it. They sat that way, gazing up at the sky together.

"I only want to help if you want me to," Mira said.

Allison looked down at their hands still lightly clasped. "Meet me in the garden tomorrow. Even if it's raining. The garden doesn't change."

Then she rose and was gone, leaving Mira alone in the silver-dappled air.

The shower was strong and almost scalding. Mira leaned in to the spray, letting it course over her face and hair as if it could wash away the day.

One day. It's only been one day. It felt more like a week had passed since she'd left the city. As she recounted everything that had transpired since her arrival, the last notions of leaving spiraled away like water down the drain at her feet. She and Aaron needed the opportunity too much to give up so quickly, and witnessing Allison's naked vulnerability cemented her resolve.

Mira shut the water off and grabbed a thick towel from a stack beside the shower. She looked in the mirror as she dried her hair, noting the shadows beneath her eyes. *You look like them a little. Got the appearance.* Nessie's words floated in her mind. She hadn't seen any pictures of Leland or Vanessa yet, but she and Allison looked nothing alike. Allison was blonde, while she had dark hair. She was taller and heavier than Allison, and Allison's features were more aquiline, while hers were rounded.

Mira huffed a quiet laugh. Nessie had definitely been messing with her. Just another joke among the mainlanders at the expense of the secluded island folk and anyone involved with them. It really didn't matter where you went, big city or rural town; cruelty was as casual as chewing gum for some people.

When she checked her phone again, still expecting notifications that weren't there, she saw it was only a little past nine o'clock. It felt much later and she was bone-tired despite the afternoon nap. As she was setting her phone on the bedside table, she paused, opening the messages app and finding her and Shay's conversation. She'd asked her to stop in to visit Aaron when she could and water the single spider plant in her room. Now she typed, *Hey, got settled in here fine. Hope you had a good day,* and hit Send. The message progress bar crept across the screen, then stopped. She watched it for thirty seconds before flicking back a screen. Maybe it would send at some point in the night and she'd get a pissed response in the wee hours of the morning. The thought made her smile.

She started to exit the messages screen but found herself scrolling down instead. There weren't many other texts, since Shay was really her only friend. Just a few acquaintances she'd met over the years, along with some members of Aaron's care team. At the bottom, the last two names were still there, though she feared (and hoped) someday they wouldn't be. If they vanished, it would be a sign to let go. To move on in the best way she could.

She touched her mother's text thread first.

The retreat was fantastic! You'll have to come next time.

Lol
Yoga's not my thing mom

Doesn't have to be. You can just pretend to meditate and check out cute guys.
No one will know the difference.

Mom!

Haha! Thanks again for helping out with your brother over the weekend.

No problem! Anytime

Then her father's.

Hey sweetie, we're getting pizza. What kind do you want?

Whatever's fine

Be here around six?

Yep!

Hey, are you in class?
Got a quick question.
Give me a call when you're free.

These conversations forever suspended in time—so casual and carefree. No way to know they were the last ones. Now they were precious amber moments she couldn't get herself to let go of. She returned to her mother's text string, hesitated, then began to type.

Hey mom, you won't believe where I am. This place is incredible.
Ten of our houses would fit in here.
There's this girl who needs my help but I don't know what I'm doing.
I don't know if I'll be able to take care of Aaron.
I'm scared.

She was very still for a moment, then deleted the text and closed the app and sat looking at the darkened window, throat painfully tight.

"I really miss you guys," she finally whispered, swiping at her eyes. She set the phone on the bedside table and turned out the light before climbing into bed. She lay on her back, letting the large open space settle around her, getting used to the faint sounds of the manor. It was mostly quiet, and after her night vision adjusted, she found herself looking up into the face of the mountain goat.

Back out of bed. She pulled the desk chair over close to the wall and stood on tiptoes, finally managing to unhook the head mount from where it hung. The fur had an undeniably dead feel to it, like bristles of a broom, and she resisted the urge to heave it away from herself.

She carried it to the small pocket door beside the entry and drew it aside, revealing a shallow closet. Mira set the goat's head on a waist-high shelf, then turned it so the eyes faced the back wall. With that done, she shut the door and went back to bed, detouring quickly to wash her hands.

The second time, the bed seemed made for her and she sank into it, releasing a sigh. Sleep bore her away so quickly, she was under almost as soon as her eyes closed, Allison's words her last conscious thought.

Meet me in the garden. Even if it's raining. The garden doesn't change.

12

Aaron sat on the end of Mira's bed, watching her as she woke.

He smiled sadly and a triangular piece of his skull broke free and fell to the blanket, inky darkness bleeding from the hole.

Mira tasted blood and sat up. For a second, Aaron was still there, then he smeared away to nothing, his smile the last thing to evaporate. She looked around the dim space, and when the recollection of where she was finally locked into place, she sagged back to the pillows, exhaling long and slow.

A dream. Nightmare. Vivid.

The relief was soothing liquid flowing through her. Aaron was fine. He was safe at Village Gardens. Everything was okay. She considered trying to fall back to sleep but knew it wasn't going to happen. She rose instead and dressed for the day.

Her last message to Shay hadn't sent. In fact, it wasn't even on the screen anymore. Must've deleted when it timed out or something like that, though she'd never seen it happen before. Of course, she'd never been on an island in the middle of a river without adequate cell coverage either. Maybe it was for the best. It had been late. She'd catch up with Shay that afternoon.

In the dining room, Oliver leaned against the far doorway, eating an apple. He nodded to her as she came in.

"Good morning," she murmured.

Eleanor turned from where she stood at a coffee sideboard. "Morning, Mira. How'd you sleep?"

"Really hard, actually," she said, settling into a chair. "The bed was super comfortable."

Eleanor smiled. "Good to hear. Coffee?"

"Yes, please."

"Cream?"

"Just a little."

Eleanor fixed a cup and brought it to the table, setting it before her on a plate. She turned the handle clockwise so it faced Mira's right side. Considerate. "Thanks." The coffee wasn't the best she'd ever had—that award still went to Anthony's Bistro on the corner of 7th and 4th—but it was a close second. She sipped deeply as Oliver finished his apple and tossed the core in a wastebasket near the wall. Still chewing, he tipped them a wave and disappeared into the hall.

Eleanor hovered near the refrigerator, gazing out the window to the garden. Mira eyed the fresh fruit on a platter in the middle of the table but held off. "So, I've thought it through, and I'll try and help Allison. I'm still not sure I can, but I'll do my best," she said after taking another galvanizing sip of caffeine.

Eleanor beamed. "Good. I'm so glad. Will you be needing anything else before you begin the day?"

"No. I don't think so."

"Okay. Well, then, lots to do." She gave Mira another quick smile and left her alone. Mira sat at the table, sipping her coffee until the claustrophobic silence of the room got to her and she picked up a banana along with her cup and headed out the door.

She stepped from the back stairway and went straight across the garden, following the crushed-shell path as it wound its way toward the wood line. The day had dawned unseasonably warm, and a trickle of sweat ran between her shoulder blades and down the small of her back. She finished the banana by the time the path met the woods and took the dregs of her coffee onward.

The path was as well maintained as the rest of the grounds—as hard as she looked, she couldn't spot a single fleck of shell outside the well-defined edges. The woods themselves closed quickly and quietly around her, trunks growing within feet of one another until it felt as if she walked down some primeval hallway.

At the bottom of a gentle decline, the trees receded and the shore transitioned to river. A rock resembling a weathered turtle shell sat to the left, and she dragged her fingertips over its pebbled surface. She stood on a large oblong stone near the bank and watched a distant boat chug along the Canadian shoreline.

The sun was planished gold on the water and she breathed in its warmth and the murky scent of the river, filling herself with the moment of calm as she finished her coffee. A well-worn memory returned to her then of a trip her parents had taken them on to the ocean before moving to the city. She and Aaron had walked the beach most of the afternoon, searching for shells to bring back to their mother while gulls wheeled and called overhead in endless circles. Her dad had stood by her side, ankle-deep in the water, and told her to close her eyes as the waves came in and out. Told her to feel how the sand moved beneath her feet with each one. *It's the sea's heartbeat,* he'd said, and from that point forward, she never thought of it any other way.

Now she smiled, nostalgia filling her as she turned away from the water with a last longing glance.

Halfway up the path, Mira slowed, then stopped. To the left a gap in the trees opened enough to see the semblance of a trail. It led deeper into the interior of the forest. She hesitated, then stepped off the crushed shells into lush knee-high grass.

It was definitely a trail, no mistaking it once she was thirty or forty paces away from the main path. The underbrush had been cleared away, though some had begun creeping back in here and there. But the ground was well worn beneath the grass, as if hundreds of feet had compacted it over lifetimes. The wind swelled, lashing branches together overhead, and she looked around. Would she hear the cougar before it pounced? She guessed not. Just the impact and shearing pain of claws and teeth.

Mira picked up speed until she was almost at a jog. The trail wound in a crescent shape, curling ever toward the center of the island. A blue jay screamed somewhere off to the right, and she nearly cried out with it. Her heart had sped up, prodded by fright as well as exhilaration. She couldn't name the boundary between fear and excitement but felt one foot planted firmly on either side. Then the trees were gone and she was stumbling to a stop, taking in her surroundings.

She stood in a perfect circle.

The ground was flat and even, expanding at least thirty feet in diameter before running up against the forest. No other paths diverged from the circle she could see, and a single blackened stump in the very center was the only visible adornment. Mira moved forward, exhilaration dwindling. Her foot struck something, and she realized she'd been wrong: there were other features hidden in the long grass, stones of matching general shape and size. All of them were perhaps two feet long and wide, and they formed a second ring within the circular clearing. There were twelve in all. *Seats,* she thought suddenly, not knowing why, and stepped around the nearest rock.

The stump had been a tree of unnatural size at one point, at least three feet across. Weather had taken its toll, and its general shape slumped to one side, spilling bark and rot to the ground. But the evidence of fire was apparent, faded soot and char staining its outer edges in cracked and flaking points.

And something else littered its blackened depression. Small scorched twigs and broken oblong shapes piled atop one another, bleached whiteness shining through the ash.

No. Not twigs. *Bones.*

Mira leaned closer, telling herself they weren't what they looked like. She reached out to touch one of the shattered pieces and thought of sticking her hand between the bars of a lion cage. She drew back, wiping her palm on her pantleg.

Strange lights and fires, Nessie had said. And sacrifice. Though she could still hear the distant buzz of an outboard motor and rush of a jet somewhere to the south, it was as if she'd stumbled into another time. Fire had danced in this circle, licked shadows away from stone, and warmed those who stood watching. And what had they done here? What had they witnessed in this cove of trees?

Her spit was thick and acidic in the back of her throat. Mira sidled to the trail, chiding herself for letting her imagination go wild while at the same time knowing this was a bad place.

Once more on the trail, she reluctantly turned her back on the circle. This time, she did run.

13

Mira stopped to catch her breath when she was safely back in the garden.

She stood facing back the way she'd come, hands on her hips, lungs burning slightly. The path was vacant all the way to the woods, where it fell out of sight. Had she really expected to see something there? Something that had appeared the moment she turned her back on the strange clearing and pursued her up into the sunlit garden?

Just burned sticks; that's all they were. You saw an old campfire, nothing more.

She forced a laugh and looked around, making sure no one had seen her fleeing her own imagination. The grounds were empty, as were the manor's battalion of rear windows. A good thing. She was embarrassed now with the sun shining down and threatening to burn her exposed skin if she stayed still long enough. As she turned away from the woods, movement across the garden caught her attention.

One of the doors on the long garage was swinging slowly closed. Then gradually open. Closed. Open.

The wind was gentle and coming from the right direction. It had blown the door open. Someone would come along and close it. She hesitated, chewing the inside of her lip, and started toward the garage.

When she reached the door, a smell met her, seeping from inside, something chemically sweet. Not quite rot, but unpleasant just the same. She reached out and started to pull the door shut but found herself pushing it inward instead.

A short hall opened into the building, created by two parallel shelves reaching almost all the way to the ceiling. Various gardening tools hung from hooks, and bags of fertilizer were stacked neatly. Beyond the shelves, a light glowed in the greater part of the garage.

"Hello?" She listened. No reply. Nothing. Eleanor had told her to explore . . . She debated for another moment, then went inside.

This part of the garage was partitioned off from the rest of the building in a workshop/storage area. The room was wide and mostly open with shelves and cabinets of different heights lining the walls. The center of the space was taken up by two long worktables, and in the middle of the closest, the head of a monster stared at her.

Mira's stomach did a sickening swoop but she caught herself before she could cry out. What glared from its place on the table was vaguely deer-shaped with dark, jutting antlers. The rest of the head was chalky white with two empty holes where its eyes should've been. The neck extended down almost to where shoulders began, then ended flatly with a swiveled device anchoring it upright to the table.

Mira looked around, breathing shallowly. The smell was more pungent here. It crawled up through her sinuses and covered the back of her throat. Swallowing made it worse. She could taste it. She moved toward the table, drawn by morbid curiosity.

It was some kind of model or mannequin, made from a type of hard foam. She touched the neck lightly and thought of a plaster-of-Paris sculpture she'd made in seventh-grade art. Running her fingers upward, she grazed the horns, then slowed, leaning closer, before jerking her hand back. The horns were real. She'd been expecting them to be fake too, plastic or aluminum. But they were striated bone.

A loud click and growl came from behind her and she spun.

The long low freezer near the wall cleared its throat, rattled once, then purred evenly.

Mira sagged and turned back to find Jeff standing beside her, a knife shining in one hand.

She wasn't able to hold back the scream this time and flinched away from him.

"Whoa! Hey, calm down. Didn't mean to startle ya," he said, holding his hands out. He followed her gaze down to the knife and set it on the table.

Mira took another involuntary step back before gathering herself. "You scared the hell out of me."

"Thought ya heard me when I came in."

"I didn't." He grunted what might've been an apology, then stared at her. "The door," she said, motioning from the way she came. "It was open and I yelled, but no one . . . You . . . I wasn't snooping."

Jeff's lips twitched beneath his beard and he turned to the table. "It's fine. You got the run of the place, I'm told."

Mira glanced around, her face growing hot, and started for the door. But part of her curiosity was still piqued as Jeff began unfolding something brownish gray from a canvas bag. After a moment, she realized it was an animal pelt, and then everything in the workshop began to make sense.

"You do taxidermy?" she asked.

"Ayuh."

"Did you do the animals inside?"

Jeff slowed in his work. "Not all. Some were done before I got hired on. But yeah, quite a few. Father was a taxidermist. Picked it up from him."

She watched with macabre wonder as a deer's face was revealed in the folds of skin and fur. It was flattened, and the openness behind the eyeholes and mouth caused a sense of revulsion within her she'd never experienced before. With a few deft movements, Jeff laid out the pelt and then began spreading some type of adhesive onto the mannequin.

Mira swallowed thickly. The glue was what smelled. Or maybe it was the cured hide. She didn't know and didn't care. She needed to be out in clean air with the sun on her face.

"Sure you think it's barbaric, but it's an art just like anything else. Shitty taxidermy is a mockery of death."

"What's good taxidermy?" Her face heated again. She'd spoken without meaning to. Jeff either didn't seem to notice or care. He finished applying the glue and began fitting the deer's skin onto the model in short precise movements.

"Is the *Mona Lisa* a celebration of death just because whoever the hell posed for da Vinci is dead?" He shot her a look out of the corner of his eye.

"I guess not."

His fingers worked and worked, fitting the deer's skin up and around the molding like a straitjacket. Its face hung limply and Jeff pressed it tighter and tighter to the faux skull.

Mira was hypnotized. The rudimentary shape beneath the skin was becoming something else. It was taking on life with each minor adjustment. Then Jeff was rummaging in one of the table's drawers and pulling out a bag with large black marbles inside.

Not marbles. Eyes. Two-inch points of metal jutted from them like the studs of earrings, and these Jeff shoved into the empty sockets, driving the points into the soft molding. When they were set, he used the knife he'd been holding earlier to tuck in the excess skin around the eyes until the holes lined up perfectly.

The deer stared at her, mouth agape.

"Okay, I'm . . . gonna go. Thanks, uh . . ." She trailed off, starting in the direction of the door. The fascination had vanished, leaving behind a hollow sickness in her center. *Hollow like its eyes and mouth had been.* Her stomach clenched and she pressed the back of her hand to her lips, stifling a belch.

As she passed a low set of shelves on her way out, something caught her eye. Another mannequin, this one in the shape of a human torso with arms ending at elbow length, sat in dusty shadow. There was no head. A few dozen small X patterns were scattered across its chest.

She stared down at it, fighting off grotesque thoughts growing like mildew in the corners of her mind. She startled when Jeff spoke from close behind her.

"You shoot bow?"

"What?"

"Archery," he said, motioning to the nearest wall where a compound bow hung, its quiver full of arrows. "That deer I'm mounting now, I got last fall over in Pennsylvania. Hittin' a smaller target like this is good practice." He went to the torso and knelt, pulling it out into the light. She understood now; the *X*s were where the broadheads had sunk into the target. Jeff looked up at her. His grin was hidden in his beard but on full display in his eyes. "Keeps it interesting too."

She was nodding. Nodding and walking backward, breathing the foul air which felt as if it was plastering itself to her lungs like the glue on the deer.

Then she was stumbling outside and hurrying toward the manor, not allowing herself to run. As she was nearing the house's back steps, the garage door closed solidly behind her.

14

Allison waited for her at the farthest table in the garden.

The rest of the morning had passed with Mira slowly coming down from the high of her fear and disgust, part of the manic energy burnt on a rowing machine in the second-floor gym after she'd showered away the stink of the taxidermy shop. Another shower, then she'd dressed and contemplated stopping into the dining room for a late lunch, but her appetite was a withered thing cowering in the corner of her stomach. Instead, she filled her aluminum water bottle and went to find Allison. Her room had been vacant and the halls empty and quiet. When Mira looked out the veranda windows, she'd spotted Allison immediately, partially because of how brightly she was dressed.

Allison wore dark leggings and a vividly red sweater. Her hair was held back by a yellow headband, and in the full light of day, she looked truly beautiful in a rigid way.

"Hey," Mira said, settling into a seat opposite her.

"Hello."

"How's it going?"

"Okay."

"How'd you sleep?" Allison made a so-so gesture with one hand. "Have you always had trouble sleeping, or is it the medication?"

"I used to sleep good. Really good. And dream." A brief smile surfaced, submerged. "Now there's nightmares."

"Want to talk about them?"

"Don't want to scare you."

"I'm pretty hard to scare." When Allison didn't respond, Mira shifted in her chair and glanced around the garden. "It's gorgeous here."

"One of my favorite places.

The wind sawed in the trees and a chipmunk appeared beneath a nearby table, beady black eyes studying them, then it was gone beneath a hedge. "So, what do you normally do?" Mira asked. "What's your day look like?"

Allison squinted into the apexing sun. "School stuff in the morning, usually. Lunch. Then I read or take a walk." She shrugged. "Boring, right?"

"No, sounds nice, actually."

Allison surveyed her. "How about you?"

"Well, it depends, but usually, I work at my brother's facility, then it's back to where I live. Hang out with friends—well . . . friend—then dinner and then read or watch a movie." Silence fell between them again, the expectant kind that always seemed to accompany getting to know someone new. Mira shifted in her seat and said, "So, do you want to show me more of the house?"

"Didn't Oliver give you the grand tour?"

"It was good, not grand." Allison smirked. "I'd love to see more of the third floor, especially the library."

Allison froze. "I don't go there anymore."

"Oh. Why?"

"It's a bad place. The walls . . . they *crawl.*"

Crawl. Like Mira's skin was doing. "Okay, well, somewhere else, then?"

Allison fidgeted with her sweater's cuff. Slowly, her expression sharpened and she looked up, the breeze toying with a strand of her hair that had come loose. "Do you want to see something really weird?"

Mira followed Allison down the deserted third-floor main hallway, their footsteps padding silently on the thick carpeting. The level was deathly quiet and still. In fact, the entire manor felt abandoned. They could've been the only two people on the island.

They turned right at the hallway's T juncture and continued on, passing numerous doors on both sides. "Ollie usually keeps it locked, but sometimes he forgets after cleaning," Allison said over one shoulder.

She stopped at a door on the left and looked at Mira, crossing the fingers of her free hand. Mira smiled and did the same. Allison tried the knob. It turned. "You won't even believe it," she said, and opened the door.

Mira didn't know what she was expecting, but it wasn't this.

The room was at least as large as Allison's bedroom, possibly bigger, and wreathed in shadow except where light rimmed a set of heavy curtains blocking off the exterior windows. The ceilings were high and the space was cluttered with muted shapes beneath drop cloths that sprang in to definition as Allison snapped a series of light switches on.

They were tables, dozens of them lined up beside one another, spanning the far wall and wrapping around each end of the room—all of them covered by protective sheets. Huge oil paintings hung every few feet on the walls, and a full suit of gleaming armor stood in one corner, clutching a battle axe twice as tall as Mira.

"Holy shit," she breathed. Allison giggled and moved deeper into the room, skirting a few objects under their tarps. "What is all this?"

"A museum. Kind of," Allison said. "Close and lock the door." Mira did as Allison drew back the floor-length curtains, flooding the room with daylight. Dust motes spun thickly in the air as the last shadows fled. "My great-great-great-grandfather was fascinated with really bizarre stuff." Allison moved from table to table, pulling the drop cloths away to reveal what was beneath. Mira blinked, walking along the rows, eyes sliding from object to object.

The items seemed to be generally grouped per table. On the first were stacks of leatherbound books, the ancient skin cracked and creased along the spines. The next held a collection of coins set in velvet-lined glass boxes, their markings archaic and faded. The table after that gave Mira pause, her eyes traveling over the items gleaming in the light.

Weapons. All manner of them, ranging from daggers and spears to bulky pistols and rifles with huge iron barrels and hammers. Allison stood on the opposite side of the table, gauging Mira's reaction. "What do you think?"

"I . . . I don't know. It's wild."

"Winston, my great-great—you know, he was really into the occult. Almost everything in here has something to do with that or death. A lot of it's just really creepy, like this," she said, picking up a wicked-looking dagger made from dark steel with a blackened handle and a small ruby set in the hilt. "This was supposed to have belonged to one of the grand inquisitors in the Spanish Inquisition. He must've been a hands-on kind of guy—this rust on the tip isn't rust. It's blood." She held the dagger out for Mira's inspection. Mira took in the corrosion but shook her head when Allison offered for her to hold it.

"Unreal."

"That's nothing," Allison said, moving down the table to pick up a smooth piece of wood that appeared to be carved from a tree limb. Its end was pitted and blackened, and Mira couldn't help but think of the burnt stump in the clearing. "This is one of the torches they used to burn the witches in Salem. And here's a noose from a hanging during the Civil War."

Mira swallowed thickly. The room seemed suddenly too dry and cloistering. She could taste dust and thought it held the bitter flavor of violence. As if the objects had leaked their past deeds into the air like some kind of cruel radiation.

"Even these coins are blood money," Allison was saying. She'd set the noose down and gone to the table with the currency. "Payments or bribes for assassinations and abductions. He was obsessed."

"Why?" Mira asked. She stared at a jar containing what she'd first thought were white stones. But they were teeth. Very small teeth.

Allison moved to one of the largest paintings on the wall and Mira followed. The subject was a man in his later years with iron-gray hair swept back from a tall forehead. He wore a dark suit and rested one hand on an ebony cane. But his eyes were what caught Mira's attention and held it. They were piercingly blue, like pieces of glacial ice honed to points. They stared out of the oil with clear contempt, as if he had seen all of what the world had to offer and found it lacking. "I'm not sure, but I think it had something to do with his son being murdered," Allison said, her voice catching on the last word. She cleared her throat. "My father's grandfather said it changed him. Tainted the rest of his life. He was never the same."

They stood looking at Winston's likeness for a time before Allison finally nudged her and pointed to the opposite corner of the room. "You have to see this."

When Allison yanked the dust cover up and off, it took Mira a second to recognize what was underneath. Then she smiled and stepped forward, touching the antique gramophone's horn. "No way. Does it work?"

Allison grinned, pulled a record from beneath the player's stand, and placed it on the turntable. She wound the hand crank on its side with a sound of a huge zipper being drawn up, and the record spun. Gently, she lowered the arm and needle onto the record's edge.

Faint scratching came from the horn, then a woman's voice poured out—high and mellifluous, singing in another language. Mira listened, gaze rapt on the turntable, this recording from another era filling the room and her ears with sudden life and long-departed beauty. When she glanced up, Allison's eyes were closed and her features had relaxed.

They stayed that way for a time until the RPMs began to slow and the woman's voice devolved into a molasses growl before finally halting completely. They shared a look, then burst out laughing.

A quiet thud came from somewhere nearby.

They both froze, staring at one another. Listening. Waiting. Oliver's voice echoed down the hall. "Hello? Is anyone up here?"

"Quick!" Allison hissed, covering the gramophone again. She hurried to the tables, tossing Mira a sheet. Mira flung her cover quickly across the table holding the books and helped Allison straighten the last sheet. "The lights," Allison said, and began drawing the curtains closed. Mira raced between the rows of shrouded shapes and snapped the lights off just as the sound of footsteps stopped outside the door. The knob rattled. Mira stood staring dumbly as Oliver grunted and a key ring jangled.

"Mira," Allison whispered. She was leaning out from the gap in the closed curtains, a blade of light illuminating her. She waved her hand frantically. "*Come on!*"

Mira stumbled away from the door, giddy with fright and excitement, wondering what the hell she was doing, why they needed to hide, but unable to stop herself. She leapt over a short cabinet and slid in beside Allison. They spent an agonizing second making sure the drapes were firmly shut before the sound of the lock turning across the room froze them still.

The door opened and the lights came on.

Mira tried not to breathe and felt the nakedness of her exposed feet a few inches below the curtain's edge. She turned her head sideways, pulse thundering in her ears. Allison was there beside her, bathed in the light shining in through the tall windows. They shared a look and Allison bit her lower lip, stifling a laugh. Mira felt the same insane urge to giggle and choked it down as Oliver stepped farther into the room.

"Hello?" he said again. Mira's muscles quaked. Her heart shuddered. Any second the curtains would be yanked aside, exposing them, and she'd be sent away. The best chance she had at making a new life for her and Aaron gone because of a stupid game.

The seconds stretched out like taffy, pulling her nerves tighter and tighter.

Oliver grunted and the lights snapped off. The door shut and the lock clicked. His footsteps receded and were gone.

Mira breathed out, sagging with relief. "Oh my God, he almost caught us," Allison said, laughing. They drew the curtains aside and stepped into the newly darkened room.

"Why did we have to hide?" Mira asked.

"Eleanor and Oliver don't like me being in here." She shrugged. "Besides, it's fun."

Mira didn't know if she agreed, but didn't say anything as she followed Allison out of the room with a pause at the doorway to make sure Oliver really was gone. When Mira pulled the door shut behind them, she couldn't help but notice they'd left the curtains partially open, and some of the light shining in landed on Winston Wyndclyffe's portrait.

As Allison took her hand and led her back down the hall at a half-jog, still on the lookout for Oliver, Mira told herself Winston's eyes hadn't seemed to glint in the afternoon light.

15

Mira sat on the edge of her bed, tapping a pen against her front teeth—a terrible habit she fell into no matter how many times she corrected herself.

She'd been adding to a list of things still needing to be done prior to moving Aaron out of Village Gardens. It was a long one. Securing a place for the two of them to live was only the beginning. There was the exit paperwork to complete for her to leave Grace Home as well as for Aaron. And once their home was secured, she would need to find a PCA for him during the day while she worked.

That particular thought gave her pause. What did she actually want to do for work?

Prior to her parents' accident, she'd been interested in everything from veterinary care to writing. College had seemed a distant destination in the future she'd eventually arrive at. Then everything had changed and she hadn't had any time or will to think about what was to come. There'd only been the now with its smothering grief, the future a dark pitfall of uncertainty. But with the income from helping Allison, college could be back on the table again. She might even have time to dream. Maybe a little.

She thought back to Mrs. Shepherd's encouragement as well as the remainder of the afternoon spent with Allison in her room. How the other girl had come alive when Mira began playing music off of her phone and they'd discovered their shared worship of Billie Eilish. It was wonderful to see her smiling and hear excitement in her voice. She'd pondered a career in the mental health field, and if this was what it was like to help someone with that type of anguish, she could see herself doing it for the rest of her life.

Needing to move, Mira set the list aside and stretched. When that didn't satisfy her, she left the room, wandering to the stairs and up to the third floor. The door to the library was open, and as she neared it, a faint voice came from inside. She slowed, stopping short in the doorway.

"Winter's coming. It'll snow soon. You always loved the first snow. Remember what you told me when you were little? You said, 'The snow cleans everything for the next year.'"

It was Oliver. He was somewhere across the library, his voice barely audible. Mira leaned to the side, trying to spot him and whoever he was speaking with. All she could see were the eastern bookshelves and one support column.

"I think you were right. Everything will be clean this spring. Everything will be better."

Mira edged into the room, scanning the dark stacks. He wasn't on the right-hand side of the great space or sitting in any of the overstuffed chairs. There was no sign of him in front of the windows either.

She took another step and squinted into the shadows. She could see almost all of the room, and he should've been right in front of her. There was a low rumbling and clicking, then silence. She took a step to the right, trying to see the farthest corner, where some of the window's heavy drapes were piled. A support column invaded her view. She moved to the left and Oliver materialized out of the dark.

Mira stifled a gasp. One second, there had been nothing but empty space, then Oliver had been there as if stepping through a portal. He turned to the window, stared out for a beat, then started in her direction.

She reversed quickly, almost bumping her hip on the doorframe, waited a second, then came back inside, acting as nonchalant as possible. Now it was Oliver's turn to startle. He halted, hand coming up to his chest as if to hold his heart in place. His head craned forward and peered through the low light at her, not moving, not saying anything.

Mira cleared her throat. "I'm sorry; I didn't mean to scare you."

Oliver took a step toward her. "Oh, that's all right. I was just . . ." He half-looked over his shoulder as if trying to recall something. When he faced her again, she swore there was a hint of worry behind his eyes. "What can I do for you?"

"Oh, nothing. I just thought I heard someone in here . . ." She trailed off and Oliver surveyed her.

"Well, yes," he said, smiling thinly. "It was me."

"Right. Sorry. I—"

"It's almost time for dinner. Walk with me?"

"Uh, sure."

Oliver led her down the corridor in the direction of the staircase. "So, your stay is satisfactory so far?" he asked.

"Definitely. Everything's been great." That wasn't exactly true, but she wasn't going to mention the encounter with Jeff in his taxidermy studio or the nightmare about Aaron that kept creeping into her thoughts all day.

"Wonderful. We want you to be as comfortable as can be," Oliver said as they stepped onto the second-floor landing. "Also—" he began, but his words were cut off by a loud chiming. Mira flinched, glancing at the source.

The grandfather clock she'd noticed a few times stood in an alcove off to the left. It was enormous, at least eight feet tall and made of some dark wood glossed to an onyx shine. It was wider than any other similar timepiece she'd ever seen, at three feet, maybe more. A large door concealed its interior workings and its face was inscribed with tall Roman numerals.

"Damned thing," Oliver said between chimes. "Still startles me from time to time." The clock finished its report on the hour and Mira stepped closer to it. "The story is old Winston Wyndclyffe brought it straight from England on the boat," he went on. "Had it custom-made around the time Queen Victoria was taking the throne. Must've cost a fortune, and I wouldn't even want to guess its worth now. We've actually discussed auctioning off a few of the oldest relics to donate to charities, but Allison won't have it. I think it must be some subconscious effort to keep things the same as before."

It ticked and whirred quietly. To her it sounded like secrets being whispered. The time itself appeared correct.

"I'm surprised she's resisted selling it—she's hated it since she was a little girl. Said it gave her nightmares," Oliver said.

"It's really . . . unique," Mira said, studying it and liking it less and less.

"That it is. And believe it or not, it's never been wound, to my knowledge." She looked at him, and he held up his hands and smiled. "I know, I know. What clock runs continuous perfect time for the better part of two hundred years? The man who I took over for told me it was the old-world design, something to do with a special counterbalance the maker created. It boggles me, to be honest. If someone could do this for a clock, why can't they create the same in an automobile?"

Mira walked around it and finally stood back. "It chimes on the hour?"

"Every hour."

Weird. She hadn't heard it since the day before when Allison counted out the correct time by tapping on the doorknob. But the chimes had been two too many. And they'd been clear, even downstairs. "Are there any other clocks in the house?"

"None that make any noise."

Mira stared at the clock, waiting for what, she didn't know.

"Shall we?" Oliver said as he started for the stairs. Mira nodded and followed, resisting the urge to look back at the clock as she went.

16

Mira picked at her food.

Even with the fresh salad and sumptuous roast chicken Gael had prepared, she couldn't get herself to eat more than a few bites. *Still acclimating*, she thought, and pushed a bit of mashed potatoes around her plate. She'd been off ever since this morning, and given the oddity of the room Allison had shown her on the third floor along with the adrenaline rush and subsequent crash, her nerves were still a little taut.

"Au revoir, an evening come down to dusk. Though remorse for the hours, rejoice upon tomorrow, now closer to a morning's trust," Oliver said, turning his glass around in slow circles. When Mira raised her eyebrows he smiled and shook his head. "One of my favorite poets, Patrick Degras. He was hopeful in much of his work, which I like very much. Do you enjoy poetry, Mira?"

"Some, but I haven't read a lot."

"Any favorites?"

She thought for a moment. "I love Robert Frost and Emily Dickinson."

Oliver nodded. "Wonderful stuff. I still say Emily Dickinson is the greatest writer of the nineteenth century, bar none. In fact—"

"Ollie, you're boring her," Eleanor said. She'd been mostly quiet during dinner, only commenting on how wonderful everything smelled when Gael set the food before them. "Besides, Dickinson is phenomenal but not the greatest by any means."

"And who would you contend holds the spot?" Oliver asked.

"I think you've forgotten a man named Edgar Allan Poe."

Oliver issued a mock sound of outrage. "Poe? Oh come on. He was a genius for sure, but Dickinson towered."

"Maybe you'll have to settle this the old-fashioned way," Mira said, smiling a little.

"How's that?" Eleanor asked.

"In a read-off with an impartial judge. Pick what you each think is the best from your particular writer, read it aloud, and have the judge choose a winner."

Oliver threw his head back and laughed. "Forgive me, but I won't enter into competition with someone whose reading preferences typically feature a tanned shirtless buffalo on the cover!"

Eleanor squinted and threw a crust of bread at him which he ducked. Mira laughed. "Enough, enough!" Oliver raised his hands in surrender. "All kidding aside, I'm right about Dickinson." Eleanor picked up a second piece of bread and he cringed. They all laughed again.

When everyone quieted Eleanor said, "How was Allison today? She seemed in a better mood."

"Good. We're getting to know each other."

"Wonderful to hear. And your accommodations? Everything's okay?"

"It's been great. I'm not used to this much space. My room would fit in one of the bathrooms."

"I lived in New York for a time when I was very young. I can sympathize."

"You said you were from Connecticut originally," Oliver said. "What brought you to New York, if I may ask?"

"My father's job. He was a sales rep for a medical equipment company."

"Ah, and do you have any siblings?"

"One. A younger brother."

"And are you both true-blue New Yorkers now?"

"No, not really. The city is . . . very big, very loud. We're actually hoping to move someday."

Eleanor poured herself a little more wine. "I felt the same way when I lived there. Couldn't wait to leave. I wished I loved it, you know? There was so much life and vibrancy, and for some reason I felt . . . outside of it all."

Mira caught herself leaning forward. Hearing her thoughts coming out of Eleanor's mouth was hypnotizing. "I always thought I was so strange, not fitting in."

"And your brother feels the same?" Oliver asked.

She hesitated. "He's intellectually disabled. He's never really moved on from where we lived before."

"Oh, I'm sorry." Oliver shook his head. "None of our business, really. I apologize if we overstepped."

"No, not at all." But she could feel a fist tightening in her center again. She sipped her water. "How about you two? Close family? Any children?"

They shared a look and Oliver drank from his glass. "I was married a long time ago," Eleanor said. "I have a daughter around your age."

"Oh, does she—" Mira started to say, but Oliver interrupted her.

"You're a remarkable young woman; I'm sure your parents would be very proud of you."

She was at a loss for a moment. Would they? Or was she making the wrong choice being here, so far away from Aaron? She couldn't tell anymore. Nothing felt right with them gone.

She didn't know if it was the day or the blunder into painful territory all around, but there were sudden tears in her eyes. A phone was ringing somewhere in her head again, always waiting for her to pick up and hear the terrible news. She tried swallowing, but her vision swam, and she stood from the table. "I'm sorry; excuse me."

The dining room blurred further, but she made it to the hall before the tears actually broke free. She swiped them away, not slowing as she took the stairs two at a time.

She shut the door to her room harder than she meant to and went to the window. Night draped itself across the island. In the distance, lights of some vessel bobbed above the fathoms of Lake Ontario. A bit of weather had rolled in during dinner and the glass was speckled with rain.

After all this time, to cry in front of a pair of kind strangers. She'd mourned her parents, held Aaron as he cried his heart out when she explained Mom and Dad wouldn't be coming home. All the worst was over, done with. But was it? Grief never truly went away, it only dulled with time. And once in a while, when everything was just so, it would light up like a supernova and burn your center out.

She gazed down at the yard below.

Something was moving down there.

A subtle shifting near the tall hedges farther along the building. She cupped her hands around her face to shield the reflection and waited, watching until her eyes began to water. Had she seen something, or had it been her imagination? Something . . . crawling?

A knock on the door made her jump so hard, her forehead clipped the windowpane with a dull thud. She let out a nervous laugh, rubbing the spot and went to the door.

Eleanor waited outside, hands wringing, concern naked on her face. "I just wanted to check if you were okay."

"I'm fine, thank you. I'm sorry—"

"Nonsense, don't apologize. Ollie feels terrible for bringing your parents up."

"It's okay. It's funny how it can sneak up on you, isn't it? Most people think mourning eventually ends. But it doesn't; it just changes."

Eleanor looked down. "I suppose so." She cleared her throat and reached out to squeeze Mira's arm. "Please accept our apology, and let us know if you need anything." She started down the hall, then turned back. "I hope you'll still want to join us for dinner going forward?"

"Of course."

"Good. I'd hate to ruin things before they got started." She smiled and gave her a little wave. "Good night."

"Good night." Mira watched her until she was out of sight, then shut the door, hesitated, locked it. Back at the window, the darkness had thickened, obscuring the grounds. It had been her nerves earlier. Or Jeff. Or an animal. Maybe one and the same. She smiled a little at that.

Before she readied for bed, she dialed Village Gardens on the room's phone. There was a buzzing undercurrent beneath the ringing on the line, like a fly droning against a window in another room.

"Village Gardens, Lily speaking."

"Hey, Lily, it's Mira Caine."

"Hi, what can I do for you?"

"I was just checking on Aaron. Making sure he's doing okay." The line's humming strengthened.

"Sorry, didn't get that."

"I said I was making sure Aaron was doing all right."

"He's fine. He had a good day. He's sleeping now. You didn't want me to wake him, did you?"

"No, no, that's—" She swallowed back some of the remaining emotion from dinner. "Just tell him I called in the morning and that I'll be back soon."

"You got it. Enjoy your trip!"

She hung up and sat on the edge of the bed. Everything she loved in the world seemed very far away.

When she was finished in the bathroom, she shut off the light, plunging the room to black. *So dark here.* New York never slept, that was true, and it also never really got dark either. Fluorescent, sodium arc, neon, some kind of light was always shining. But here, darkness fully defined itself.

Lying there, she replayed the day, thinking of Aaron in his own bed in a room without windows in a city he wanted to be away from.

"It'll be okay," she whispered into the dark. It was as close to a prayer as she could manage.

17

Sleep wouldn't come.

No matter which position she got comfortable in, no matter how long she kept her eyes shut, nothing.

At one in the morning, Mira gave up and climbed out of bed, donning a pair of sweats and a T-shirt. She'd brought a paperback and found it still tucked away in a pocket of her suitcase. She carried it to one of the chairs and started to settle in but stopped, looking at the book before setting it down and unlocking her door.

The corridor was cool and silent, lit by every third wall sconce. She headed for the stairs, throwing a quick glance at the grandfather clock on the way. It had tolled correctly all the hours she lay awake (she'd counted each chime). Maybe she'd simply tuned it out before.

The third floor was the same cocoon of quiet but even darker. She drew her cellphone out and turned its light on, swiping it back and forth. At least she didn't have to worry about waking anyone; everyone else's rooms were on the ground level. Approaching the library's door, Mira paused and turned the handle.

The door creaked inward and she stepped through the gap, sweeping the light in an arc once inside. For a moment, she thought there was someone else there with her. Not that she saw them. The cell phone only lit up ten or fifteen feet of space, then merged with shadows hanging from the tall ceilings. It was more of a feeling, a sense another had breathed the same air only seconds before. That they'd been waiting for her.

The walls . . . crawl.

"Stop it," she said, not bothering to whisper. She was being stupid and letting the gravity of the manor and this room creep her out. There was nothing here but a bunch of dead writers' voices all lined up along the walls.

A flick of a switch and several chandeliers lit up. Mira made her way around the room, absently dragging a couple fingertips along leathered spines, which gave her a shiver of pleasure up her own. There was a medical section, while another wall seemed to hold only classics, everyone from Chaucer to Brontë to Dickens to Wolfe. She found an ancient-looking collection of Poe and couldn't resist taking it down. Another wall held charts of seafaring lanes, maps of the St. Lawrence islands, and county surveys for the entire state of New York dating all the way back to the late seventeen hundreds. A smaller section contained contemporary works, and she paused there, finally selecting two mysteries and a thriller that had only come out the prior year. She smiled to herself, seeing the extensive romance section, all of the spines wrinkled and cracked.

Mira found a settee and matching footrest by one of the windows, rain still speckling the glass, and settled in.

She came awake to a sound sometime later, unaware she'd fallen asleep. Her neck ached from the awkward angle it was bent at, and her mouth was sandy. The book she'd been reading lay splayed open on the floor. Its fall must've been what woke her.

Mira sat up, checking the time—almost three thirty—and yawned. The comforting atmosphere of the library and the author's fluid prose had lulled her. She knew she'd be able to sleep now. As she climbed out of her seat, something across the room caught her eye.

A thin blade of light shone from the bottom of the wall.

Her head tilted and she tapped the book against one leg. She was awake. She moved closer, pausing at the edge of the light. It fanned across the carpet in a faint gold spray at her feet. The nearest chandelier hung behind her, no chance of a reflection bouncing off the paneled wall. Kneeling, she brought her face to the floor.

There was a half-inch gap along a three-foot section of the wall. Flooring, different than on which she knelt, was visible on the other side. She sat up on her haunches. *There is no way I just found a secret door in an old library*. But she reached out to touch it just the same.

At first, there was nothing, no give, no movement, and she wondered if something had come loose in her mind. Maybe if she looked over her shoulder right now she'd see herself still asleep in the chair.

The idea was chilling enough to keep her eyes forward, hands searching the seamless wall. Just as she was about to lean back to floor level for another look, the panel moved. Not sideways but inward. An inch, no more. She pushed harder and the wall gave.

A sliding door revealed itself as it sank in and to the left, gliding away in a familiar low rumble and clicking. Inside was a short, narrow passage. Mira gaped, still not really believing what she was seeing.

The passage was a pace in length. It opened into a square space half the size of her bedroom that appeared to be an office—a desk and chair being the prominent fixtures along with a tall bookcase taking up one wall. Two floor lamps flanked the desk, one glowing on a low setting.

Mira turned around, taking in everything. There were no adornments on the walls, no paintings or photos, and the walls themselves were rudimentary without decorative flourishes common throughout the rest of the manor. A bay alcove jutted outward in the farthest corner, a triangular window set within it.

She looked at it for a moment before realizing she was looking at the inside of the triangular window she'd spotted outside from the grounds.

A hidden window in a hidden room.

But was it supposed to be hidden? For all she knew, the office door might typically be left open for anyone wanting to come in and jot some notes down or study a book in even deeper solitude. Except Allison had said she'd never seen the triangular window from the inside, so there went that theory . . .

Something occurred to her then. This must've been where Oliver was when she'd heard him earlier. Heard him talking to someone. The skin on the back of her neck tightened and Mira rotated, half-expecting someone to be there when she turned around. Still alone. At least she knew why she hadn't been able to see him. She went to the triangular window and peered out. Darkness. Only the swaying tops of the tall hedges were visible. She returned to the bookcase.

If the books in the library were old, she mused, these were primeval. She pulled out a faded leather casement bound by rawhide and flipped it open. An illustration of a vivisected man met her. She stifled a sudden lurch in the back of her throat. The drawing was archaic but finely detailed. *Overly* detailed. Exposed muscle and tendon glistened, skin stretched translucent, intestines roped limply. The next page was a woman opened from groin to throat. The next a boy.

Mira snapped the book shut and replaced it on the shelf, stomach roiling. An unpleasant tingling ran down her arms to her fingertips. What the hell was this? She scanned other volumes but couldn't bring herself to touch any of them. Most held no titles on the spines, and the ones that did sported unpronounceable names, many in Latin. The entire place gave off a bad vibe, like an ugly secret, almost as if this were an extension of the display room down the hall. Maybe this was overflow, the worst of the worst of Winston's demented collection. And there was something else too, another undercurrent she was becoming gradually aware of. A scent. Something at first she denied but which another deep inhale confirmed.

The smell from the taxidermy studio.

It was faint but there. A chemical undertone laced with rot. She glanced around, searching for some mounted animal she'd missed initially, but there was nothing.

Time to go. As she started across the room, her eyes fell on the desk which she'd given only a cursory glance. It was large but simple, its surface clean and clear of everything save a glass pen holder and a small book. Compact and thin, the book was more along the lines of a journal. A title had been etched in the cover and most likely embossed with some type of precious metal, but it had flaked away over time, leaving only the indentations of letters. She traced their molded shapes.

"*Metamorphi*," she read. Opening the cover, and bracing herself for another illustrated horror, she saw the Wyndclyffe motto emblazoned within a triangle. *Mori et renovare.* There was no author name and no publishing information. The next page was typeset in paragraphs of more Latin with wispy pencil marks along the margins. As she bent closer to read the handwriting, a sound jerked her upright.

When she turned to the entry, she fully expected to see Oliver or Eleanor standing there, outrage and disapproval plain upon their face. But the doorway was empty. She started toward the library and almost paused to turn off the lamp, then thought better of it and hurried out of the office, somewhat ashamed at the sense of intrusion. What had gotten into her the last couple days? She was never this nosy. Maybe it was simple curiosity fueled by the grandiosity of the manor. Still, she needed to contain herself if she wanted to be able to stay.

With a slight pull, the hidden door reappeared, sliding seamlessly back into place, the wall once more whole. *The walls crawl.* Was this what Allison had meant? Maybe the hidden room held some kind of negative memory or meaning. Maybe there would be a way to ask her about it without triggering something painful from the past. As she started back toward her pile of books on the settee, she found she was still holding the journal.

She heard another quiet thud from a direction she couldn't pin down. The hallway? The next room? She didn't wait to find out. Gathering the books she'd pulled from the shelves earlier, Mira hurried across the library, pausing only for a second to flip off the chandeliers. The faint glow from beneath the hidden door seemed to bid her farewell as she stepped into the corridor and started toward the stairs, but a level of unease lingered as she put more distance between her and the library.

I shouldn't have gone in that room. There hadn't been much dust on the desktop or bookshelves. Someone kept it neat and clean. But the book feels important, it wouldn't have the Wyndclyffe motto on it if it wasn't. Maybe it'll give me a better insight into Allison's family history. I'll take a peek at it, and if there's nothing useful inside, it'll be easy to put back without anyone knowing. Hopefully . . .

Near the top of the stairs where the first and only sconce glowed on this level, she passed a picture hanging at eye level, giving it half a glance. As her foot found the first stair, she halted. *It's nothing, keep going.* She hadn't seen what her mind said she had. *It's late and you're tired and nerved up and just go to bed,* she thought even while retracing her steps to the picture.

But she had seen it right.

The picture was in black and white and depicted a car decimated by a high-speed crash. Its front end was a congealed mess of bent metal and shredded plastic. A single headlight hung askew like an ejected eye. The windshield was a spiderwebbed mass, obscuring everything behind it. The car sat at an angle on the edge of a highway due to two of the wheels missing on the left side. Beyond the wreck, the rear end of a truck was barely visible. Maybe it was the other vehicle involved in the crash, maybe an ambulance bumper, she couldn't tell. Couldn't take her eyes off the car. Off the surroundings. Off the license plate where only one letter was visible at the border of the frame. An *L*.

No.

She spun away from the picture.

No.

Down the stairs, clutching the books to her chest, which tightened past the point of discomfort into pain.

Couldn't be.

On to the second-floor landing and down the hall to her room.

Inside, sagging against the door, forehead pressed to the cool wood.

She hadn't seen it, and if she had, it wasn't what she thought. Wasn't possible. Her stomach squeezed upward, and for a long, agonizing moment, she was sure she would be sick. Deep breaths, in and out. With each one some control returned. When she felt steady enough, Mira made her way to the bed and sat, mind whirring with rational explanations.

She'd been overly emotional lately. Last night at dinner, she had cried thinking of her parents. It had been on her mind, and seeing some strange picture in the middle of the night while low on sleep was nothing to freak about.

Yes, it felt good to think these things. Steady. Sure. Real.

Mira stood and stacked the books on the bedside table. She ran a glass of water from the tap in the bathroom and listened to the wind outside. Probably what she heard in the office and library. An old house still settling on itself.

In bed, she drew the covers up to her chin and reached out to flick the bedside lamp off but left it on instead. It was a small concession, one she could live with.

Only a strange and random photo. Nothing recognizable. Not really. She'd seen one picture of her parents' crash shortly after their deaths, and only briefly. Had never gone to the site itself. But in the darkest hours, when she was missing them terribly or when she went to phone one of them out of reflex, she thought of the place where they died.

It wasn't the same photo, just one that looked like it. She rolled over, trying to embrace sleep that had been so close only a short while ago. It was a long time coming.

18

A knocking pulled her up through fathoms of sleep to bright daylight.

Mira stared around with the shell-shocked feeling of the violently woken as the knocking came again.

"Hold on," she called, climbing free of bed and glancing at her phone. Almost noon. "Damn it," she hissed, throwing on some clothes.

Gael waited in the hall with a covered tray when she opened the door. "Morning. Eleanor asked me to bring up some brunch since you didn't come down for breakfast."

"Oh, thanks. I . . . overslept."

"No problem." She stepped aside and combed through her hair with her fingers as Gael moved into the room, setting the tray on the table in the sitting area. "There are scrambled eggs and crepes. I hope you don't hate both."

"That's wonderful; thank you." He made a charming half-bow. For a giddy second, she thought he might take her hand and kiss the back of it, that she might let him, but he only smiled and started for the door. "Gael, do you have a second?"

"Sure."

He waited expectantly, hands held behind his back. "Never mind," she said finally. "It's nothing."

"Nothing is never nothing, as my mom used to say."

She paused, considering. "Could I show you something?"

They made their way up the stairs side by side. Gael wore a white uniform that set off his eyes, and his cologne was something subtle and light she kept trying to catch as she breathed. She found herself sneaking glances at him as they climbed. He was one of the more attractive men she'd encountered in person, and there was something alluring about him. Maybe it was the way he waited expectantly whenever she spoke. Like he actually cared about what she was saying. She thought of the last date she'd gone on and was a little horrified to find herself struggling to remember it.

"Enjoying your stay so far?" Gael asked as they turned on the landing and went up again.

"Yes, the island's amazing. How long have you worked here?"

"Let's see; almost two years. I got into the Culinary Institute of America right after high school, and Eleanor hired me as soon as I graduated."

Mira did a quick mental calculation. If the culinary course was two years, that meant Gael was only twenty-two, not really that much older than she was. She cleared her throat. "Eleanor mentioned you have a house in Yellow Bay?"

His jaw tightened almost imperceptibly. "It was my mom's. I don't go there much."

"No other family?" She said it trying not to look at his ring finger, and failed. Thankfully, he didn't notice.

"None to speak of."

They reached the third floor, and the reason for coming here settled over her again. There was the photo on the wall. She moved toward it, heart beginning to pick up speed. *Was this the best thing to do? What would Gael think of asking about it? Would he even know anything?* She nudged the reservations aside and moved as quickly as she could, stopping before the photo. Mira tried looking at it but could only raise her eyes so far before dropping them again. She motioned at it instead and said, "This picture—do you know where it was taken?"

Gael squinted, stepping closer. "That's Main Street in Yellow Bay."

"What?" She finally gathered the courage to face what she'd seen last night in the full light of day.

It wasn't the same.

The picture was sepia-toned and depicted a wide street with storefronts on either side, antiquated signs above the doors. There were two vehicles in the frame passing one another: a Studebaker and a Chevy pickup that had been manufactured sometime before mid-century. Their windows were dark, with no suggestion of people behind them.

"I don't . . . I thought it was . . ." She stepped closer, having to actually touch the picture to make sure it was real.

"You okay?"

She was adrift, mind wheeling, trying to gain traction like a person skidding toward a cliff. "I'm—I thought . . . it was something else," she finished lamely.

"The picture?"

"Yes, I'm sorry for dragging you up here." She regained a thin sense of composure and smiled. "Thanks for humoring me. I think I got confused."

"No problem. There are much worse things to do besides walking and talking with a pretty woman in the morning."

She blinked, feeling her heart speed up once again. "Um . . ."

"Can I walk you back to your room?"

"Sure."

They went back down the stairs, and she resisted the urge to look over her shoulder at the photo, to make sure it was still there, still the same.

"I got turned around a few times the first month I lived here," Gael said. "It's easier to do than you think."

"It's a big place."

"If you want a more in-depth tour, I'd be happy to show you around," he said as they reached her door. When she hesitated, he rushed on. "And if not, that's totally fine."

"No, no that would be . . . really nice, actually."

He smiled again, and this time, he did take her hand. But instead of bringing it to his lips, he just held it gently for a moment, then let go. "I hope you enjoy the brunch."

Mira smiled, watching him go, then stepped into her room. With the door shut, she sagged. She'd been mistaken, that was all. It was actually a huge relief. With sleep clearing away some of the cobwebs along with the brilliant light coming through the windows, the idea of the photo seemed not just strange but absurd. *Would Gael say anything to the other staff about it?* No, she didn't think so. That same giddiness was back, an electric, rubbery feeling at the memory of how his hand felt holding her own.

What about the letter? What about that capital L *on the license plate?* she thought, sitting down in one of the chairs and pulling off the tray's lid. Had she mistaken that detail too? Made it up out of the blue?

It had been dark and very late. She'd been tired and a little freaked by the secret room in the library. The mind plays tricks, especially at night. The assurances were flimsy, so she reinforced them by breathing in the exhalation from the tray's contents. It was heavenly and she leaned forward, letting the sweet steam roll across her face.

But the location. None of the background loo—

Enough. She dug in to the scrambled eggs. They were light and delicious, and the toast was still warm. *It was a mistake in the dark*, she thought, tearing into a fruit-filled crepe. She wasn't going to let stress and an overactive imagination ruin everything.

She finished the food, every last bite, then dressed for the day. As she was wrangling her hair into a bun, her gaze landed on the journal she'd lifted from the office. It felt strangely rough in her hands when she picked it up, something she hadn't noticed in the early-morning hours. Opening to the first page with the handwriting, she brought it close to inspect the faded spidery script.

He is gone. My beautiful son is no longer. I am without heart and my soul withers. If this is what constitutes life, I reject it.

Mira frowned and read on.

Winter, but the work has already begun on the circle. I feel hope for the first time in months.

She turned the page.

Excitement—the waiting has ended. The time is near for rebirth.

She turned the next page and saw another large triangle emblazoned with a word in Latin at each point.

Inanis. Imple. Fieri.

Below it was a line written by a different hand in much-fresher ink.

He missed the forest for the trees. The key to everything. The bloodline.

Mira sank to the bed. If she was reading this correctly, the first scribblings were attributed to Winston Wyndclyffe concerning his slain son Rasmus, the latter possibly Leland. But what the hell was this thing? Its scant pages were filled with Latin except for the notations here and there. Near the very end, there was a hand-sketched diagram of a circle with a point in its center and several other large dots surrounding it.

Just like the clearing in the woods.

She snapped it shut, studying the worn cover again. So, it was a journal passed down through the family. Some sort of guide. But a guide for what?

She opened the much-larger tome of Poe and placed the ledger inside.

A glance at her phone jolted her up off the bed and toward the door. It was much later than she'd thought. Allison would be waiting for her.

19

Grass crunched under their feet.

They walked with the manor looming behind them, shadows thrown forward by a cool afternoon sun. Mira had found Allison in the garden again at the same table in the same chair. This time, the other girl had brightened the moment she saw her, smiling widely as Mira apologized for sleeping in.

"It's fine. I just enjoyed the sun while I was waiting."

"It's gorgeous out," Mira said, shielding her eyes.

"I thought I could show you more of the island. If you want . . ."

"That would be great."

For a time, they walked side by side without saying much, Allison occasionally breaking the quiet to point out a one feature or another. There was more ease between them, the silence no longer awkward. Reaching the edge of the forest, they turned east, walking along the natural boundary with the rolling field sweeping away on the right. "So, what's it like where you live?" Allison finally said, peeling a long blade of grass into strips.

"It's okay. It's basically a big building of little rooms. There's a lot of other kids there and it's always noisy."

"So, boys live there too?"

"Yeah, quite a few. But they have their floors and the girls are on others." Mira glanced at her. "Anybody special in your life?"

A hint of color appeared on Allison's cheeks. "No."

"No one? I don't believe that."

"I mean, I was texting with a guy from Yellow Bay a while ago. His dad is a plumber and he came with him when a pipe broke a couple years ago and we talked. But . . ."

"Cute?"

"Yeah."

"What's his name?"

"Evan."

"So, are you still texting?"

Allison's smile faded a little. "Not lately. He went away for college and just kind of quit responding. So . . ." She shrugged. "I'm sure he met some other girl who wasn't afraid of . . . everything."

Mira chewed at the inside of her lip. "Do you like it here?" she asked as casually as she could, keeping her eyes forward on the horizon while watching Allison's reaction in her peripheral vision.

Allison looked away, her hand dragging the tops of some dead grass as they walked through it. "It's the only place I feel good. Normal. Everything else is . . ." Her voice trailed off.

"How do you feel when you think about leaving?"

"Anxious. Afraid. The island's safe." Allison seemed to catch herself and fell quiet.

"What scares you about leaving?"

They arrived at a downslope in the field, small thickets of brush to either side they passed through like a gate. A scree of stunted trees appeared, then fell away to reveal the eastern end of the island. They stood on a higher outcropping overlooking a slew of rock descending to the water's edge.

"My father used to say that everything wrong with the world was right here." Allison tapped the side of her head. "If people were different, if they learned to evolve, then the world would be a better place."

"Is that mostly what scares you about leaving? Other people?"

"Yes. I don't know what they're thinking. What they'd think of me."

"Well, I think you're cool."

Allison glanced sharply at her as if to see if she were joking. "I know something's wrong with me. Maybe I'm meant to be this way." She paused. "Maybe I deserve it."

Mira took her hand. "No one deserves to suffer. *Everyone* deserves help." Allison swallowed loudly and looked away. When Mira started to release her hand, she held on tighter. They headed back the way they'd come, branching left instead of right, keeping the water in view as they walked. "So, there was this really cute boutique I saw in Yellow Bay on my way here. And an old bookstore, too. What do you think about going with me to do some shopping?"

Allison halted, her hand loosening and falling from Mira's. "Leave the island?"

"Yeah, but maybe just for the afternoon? I'm guessing Jeff could bring us across."

Allison shook her head. "I don't think so."

"I'd be with you the whole time." Allison started away, moving faster than their previous pace. Mira winced and caught up with her. "I'm sorry. We don't have to—"

"No, it's fine. I'm just really tired. I'm going to go lie down. I'll see you later." Allison kept her head straight forward, and after a moment, Mira quit trying to keep up with her. She watched Allison go until she was lost around the sprawling side of the manor in the distance. Mira swore quietly and began walking again. *Too hard. You pushed too hard.*

As she angled toward the front portico, a sudden dinging from her pocket startled her, and it took a second to recognize the sound of a received email. When she checked the device, she saw a flood of emails had come through, backlogged from when she'd left Yellow Bay. Nothing of real consequence, and no texts. None from Shay, though. *Weird.* A high point in the field must've helped catch a signal. She tapped out a quick message to Shay and watched it zip away.

As she reached the front steps, she noticed Jeff trimming the corner of the tall hedges at the far end of the manor, and her mind returned to what she'd seen from the window the night before. *Thought you saw.* It was dark; could've been anything. Jeff paused in his work, his head turning toward her. Mira looked away and hurried up the steps inside.

When she placed her hand on the doorknob to her room a few minutes later, it wouldn't turn. Her palm slipped on the wrought-iron knob and she frowned, trying to recall if she'd shut the door upon leaving. Yes, she could remember swinging it closed behind her, the solid *thunk* of it following her down the hall.

Mira grabbed the knob with both hands and turned. Nothing. It wouldn't budge. She blew a strand of hair away from her face that had escaped her bun and retraced her steps downstairs.

When she stepped into the office doorway and knocked on the jamb, Eleanor was squinting down at a sheaf of papers in one hand through a set of glasses. "Mira, what can I do for you?"

"I think I locked myself out of my room."

Eleanor chuckled, setting the papers aside and drew out a ring of keys. "Don't worry; happens quite a lot, actually." She strode past and Mira followed her to the stairs. "Drafts close doors and the locks are finicky, to say the least. I've done the same to myself a half dozen times over the years, and don't say anything, but Oliver still does it at least once a month," Eleanor said over her shoulder, chuckling again.

On the second floor, Mira stopped before her door and began to apologize for the inconvenience but realized Eleanor had kept walking. Mira cleared her throat and she glanced over one shoulder. "It's this one," she said, embarrassed to be correcting her.

A strange look passed over Eleanor's features. "We have you in this suite," she said, pointing to the next door down the hall.

Mira looked from the door in front of her to the one Eleanor motioned to. For a second, she questioned herself, then shook her head. "No, I'm sorry, it's this one. Second from the stairs."

Eleanor moved to the next room and produced a key but, before inserting it in the lock, tried the door. It opened. She glanced inside, then stepped back. "I think you may have gotten confused," she said. "Easy to do around here."

Mira looked at her room's door one more time before sidling up to the next suite.

It was her room.

The sitting area was just as she'd left it, her brunch tray and dishes still on the table. The bedspread was thrown aside from where she'd climbed free only hours ago, and her sleeping clothes lay in a small heap on the floor.

Mira took it all in while her mind rejected what she was seeing. She'd been staying in the second room from the stairway for two days. Not the third. Not the first. The second. She stepped inside and took inventory. The books from the library were still on the bedside table as was the half-glass of water she'd set there before finally falling asleep early that morning. Outside, the view was almost identical, except she was definitely closer to the tall hedges. Not a lot, but some. She turned back to Eleanor, half-smiling. "It's a joke, right?"

"Sorry?"

Mira glanced around again. This was her room, the same shade of walls, the same bed, all of her belongings in the same place, yet it wasn't. "Could you . . . could you show me the second room?"

"Well, I suppose. It's storage, but we can give it a look."

They returned to her room's door and Eleanor's keys rattled in the lock. Mira watched from beside her, an uncanny tingle of fear in her center. It was like when she'd had a strange mole removed from her shoulder a year ago, then waiting days until the results showed up.

Rotten anticipation.

The door unlocked and Eleanor opened it, reaching inside the darkness for a switch. In that moment, Mira's stomach sank lower, with the stale smell coming from the gap in the doorway. It was the scent of a long-closed space. Light bloomed within and Eleanor nudged the door wide.

It was a storage room, filled nearly to the ceiling with all manner of things.

Shapes beneath drop cloths, old furniture, desks, stacked chairs, lamps, paintings, everything grouped tightly with only a narrow space down the center to move through.

Mira registered everything as a wave of vertigo washed over her, leaving behind small black dots in the corners of her vision as it receded. She braced a hand as casually as she could against the doorframe.

No.

She stepped inside and ran her hand along a chair's back. It was solid. Real.

Eleanor was saying something, her voice slowly tuning back in like a radio station from distant airwaves. "—mostly, but we haven't used this one for overflow in a few years." Mira faced her. "Are you all right? You're very pale."

The black dots tried to blossom into flowers of darkness, but she tightened her grip on the chair and forced a smile. "I didn't sleep well last night; must've gotten completely confused."

"Take my word for it. It's actually one of the reasons Jeffry says he won't stay in the manor. He's afraid he'll get lost in here." She laughed and Mira joined in halfheartedly.

Back in the hall, Eleanor pulled the door shut and relocked it. "Is there anything else I can do for you?"

"No, sorry I bothered you with this. I think I'm just tired."

"No bother at all. See you at supper."

When she was gone, Mira retreated to her bedroom, stopping at the threshold as if something waited for her within. As she scanned the area again, she slowly turned to the small closet near the entry, hesitated, then pulled the door open.

The goat's head was inside, facing the wall, just as she'd left it. Mira stared at it for a time and shut the door. She brought her hands up to rub her eyes but paused, feeling soft grit between her fingers.

Dust. There had been dust on the objects in the next room.

No one had set foot in there for months.

20

The room's phone crackled and buzzed in her ear.

For almost half an hour, she'd sat motionless on the edge of the mattress and stared around the new-familiar room. Spent long minutes dissecting everything to see if she could catch something out, some discrepancy in her surroundings, all while a nagging voice spoke louder and louder from inside her.

It's finally happening—you're losing control. You thought you were so strong, but something broke inside when you lost them, and you've been trying to ignore it ever since. Now you can't deny it anymore. You won't be able to take care of Aaron. You can't even take care of yourself.

She shook her head like a dog with water in its ears. When she'd managed to gag the voice, she picked up the phone and dialed Village Gardens.

Checking on Aaron was the best thing she could think of at the moment. It would ground her to hear his voice and make sure he was doing okay. As the phone at Village Gardens tolled for what felt like the fiftieth time, she considered telling him they might be leaving the city for good. But that might be jumping the gun altogether.

"Village Gardens Care Center, Lily speaking," a voice suddenly said in her ear.

"Lily, hi. It's Mira Caine." The phone line fluttered with static.

"I'm sorry, who?"

"Bad connection, it's Mira Caine, Aaron's sister."

"Oh, hi. What can I do for you?"

"Just checking in again. How's he doing?"

More static invaded the earpiece and she drew it away from her head, wincing. "—okay, although he's been a little down lat—" Lily's voice faded in and out.

"Lily, sorry, I can't hear you."

"—ut he's drawing a lot, which is go—" Static roared. "—outside as much. He's been asking for—" Another long blast of noise, then the phone went silent.

Mira held the handset for a second, looking at it, then redialed. This time, the static was a steady roar. She listened through it for a ringing on the other end, but there was nothing. Finally she hung up, fearing what Lily had been trying to say at the end was Aaron had been asking for her. Maybe it had been a mistake not to tell him how long she was going away for. She'd thought it would spare him worrying, but now she wasn't so sure. Hopefully, Lily would tell him she'd called. She'd make it a point to ask Oliver later about the phone lines and the Wi-Fi again. If all else failed, maybe she could have Jeff pilot her across the river to a point where she'd get better reception.

In the bathroom, she splashed cold water on her face and studied her reflection. "It's okay. It was a glitch; that's all. It happens sometimes." But even as she said it, the denials inside her came roaring back, and she found herself striding out into the hall and moving toward the next room. She stood with her back against the opposite wall and turned her head from right to left, examining each memory of her accommodations even as she studied the two doors.

She had been staying in the second room.

She couldn't have been.

It was a paradox.

So, what was the answer? Somehow, all of her things, not to mention the contents of the second room, had been switched around while she was out with Allison? They'd only been gone an hour or so. Impossible.

Mira bit the inside of her cheek, hard, but the pain did its job. She came back to the moment, head slightly clearer. What did sane adults do when they encountered something that didn't fit into their rational worldview? They shrugged it off as strangeness. A mistake. An oddity. And then they moved on. They didn't obsess. They let it go.

Mira opened her eyes.

The door across the hall mocked her.

"Let it go," she said to the empty air.

* * *

Dinner was served on the back veranda, the sun making a brief appearance before it fell below the western horizon. Gael lit an outdoor gas heater, which threw warmth across their table along with hot tea and coffee.

Mira ate with gusto she didn't feel, but the excellence of the food made it bearable. Eleanor made no reference to her earlier mix-up, and she was thankful for it. The more time that passed, the more she could convince herself she'd made a simple error. The manor was enormous, the number of quarters staggering. She shuffled the incident to a back room of her mind, turned out the lights, and shut the door.

After dessert had been served and they were all sipping coffee, she set her cup aside and said, "Could I ask you about Leland?"

Eleanor and Oliver shared a look and sat forward. "Go ahead," Oliver said.

"You said he had . . . mental health problems."

"Probably manic depression," Eleanor said, nodding.

"Did his father suffer from something too?"

"No," Eleanor said. "Phillip was coldly practical to the point of cruelty. One of the reasons he couldn't seem to be bothered about his son's condition. Or his wife's . . ."

Mira absorbed this. "Leland's mother . . ."

"She never had a diagnosis either, because Phillip wouldn't allow her to receive one," Oliver said. "He was so distrustful of the outside world—thought most of his business associates were out to get him. He saw Angelica's depression as something that could be potentially exploited. Cold-hearted bastard—pardon my French."

Eleanor grimaced. "Without any type of treatment or medication . . ." She glanced at Oliver. "It was too much for her."

"So she—"

Eleanor nodded quickly. "It was a terrible affair and affected Leland deeply. They were very close—he once said she was the only other human being who truly understood him. And what's even worse, he was the one who . . ." She trailed off, giving Mira a meaningful look.

Found her. Mira digested this new information as a flock of blackbirds careened overhead in a storm of wings and disappeared into the evening. "Why do you ask? Did Allison say something?" Eleanor said.

"No, I mean, not really. She said her father didn't like people very much."

"Understatement of the century," Oliver murmured.

"I guess I was just curious about her family history, how many people before her had things they were struggling with."

"Hereditary, yes," Eleanor said. "Sadly, she was predisposed to suffer from something."

Winston's words came back to Mira then, the odd references in the journal still in her room. Mental illness had traveled down through the generations like an inevitable river, all the way to the girl she was now slowly coming to know.

"Leland had very strange . . . habits," Oliver said, gazing away over the grounds. "He would go outside late at night and not come back in until the early-morning hours. Sometimes, he would eat a particular food for weeks and force the diet on the family as well. Equinoxes in particular were extremely tense. His behaviors would become more pronounced. He would spend longer hours teaching Allison her lessons—sometimes, they would go outside and be gone for days on end. Vanessa would be more on edge, jumping at everything."

"And she had her own emotional issues, particularly with living here," Eleanor added. "Vanessa despised the island, wanted to move, but Leland wouldn't hear of it."

"Why didn't she divorce him?" Mira asked.

"It was no secret she'd signed a prenuptial agreement. She was afraid of losing custody of Allison. Even with us testifying to his instability, Leland would've had the upper hand in a divorce," Oliver said, drawing out a thin cigar and lighting it.

"Oliver, please," Eleanor said. "Put that disgusting thing out; you'll make Mira sick."

"It's okay," Mira said. "I don't mind."

"We're out of doors," Oliver said. "It's my one vice; leave me to it."

Eleanor rolled her eyes. "I've told him those things will be his end, but does he listen?"

"Everyone must die from something. If not from these, then from your nagging. Both a slow, painful death."

"I could make it quick, then."

Mira smiled as the two entered a stare-off, which ended with Oliver dropping Eleanor a slow wink followed by her laughter.

"I know it's very early," Oliver said after they'd both quieted. "But do you feel Allison is responding well to you?"

Mira thought of how Allison had bolted at the end of their walk. "I think it's going to take a while, but I hope so," she said carefully.

Oliver puffed his cigar, the fragrant smoke spooling around his head. He raised his cup of coffee. "To hope."

"To hope," Eleanor said, picking up her cup as well.

Mira joined them. "To hope," she said, clinking their porcelain together in a brittle sound that carried across the quiet veranda.

PART 2

IMPLE

21

Mira rubbed the last of sleep from her eyes and headed downstairs.

After dinner the prior evening, she'd been overcome by exhaustion despite the coffee and had fallen asleep shortly after dark, her plans of returning to the library to translate the notebook derailed by bone-weariness. There had been dreams, nightmares actually, though she couldn't say what they'd been about. All that had followed her up out of sleep was the sensation of being chased, something directly behind her reaching out to grasp and pull her back. As she made her way to the first floor, she wondered if she were getting sick, but other than a mild headache, she didn't notice any symptoms. *Don't stay up all night sneaking into secret rooms in libraries and you'll be fine.*

When she stepped into the dining room, Oliver was leaning against the far doorway, eating an apple. He nodded to her as she came in.

"Good morning," she said, settling into a seat at the table and gathering her own apple from the bowl of fruit in its center.

Eleanor turned from where she stood at the coffee sideboard. "Morning, Mira. How'd you sleep?"

"Great; I was really tired."

Eleanor smiled. "Good to hear. Coffee?"

"Yes, please."

"Cream?"

"Just a little."

Eleanor fixed a cup and brought it to the table, setting it before her. She rotated the handle so it faced Mira's right side.

"Thank you," Mira said, relishing the heat and bitterness. Maybe the brew did rival the fare at Anthony's Bistro. She sipped deeply and

Oliver finished his apple, tossing the core in a wastebasket near the wall. He gave them a wave and disappeared into the hall.

Eleanor stood looking out the small window to the garden. Mira's stomach growled, asking for more than fruit, and she placed a hand against it. "I appreciate you both being so open about Allison's family history," she said. "It really helps to understand a little more about her."

Eleanor glanced at her and nodded. "Good. I'm glad. Will you be needing anything else before you begin the day?"

"No. I don't think so."

"Okay. Well, then, lots to do." She gave Mira a smile and left the room.

Yes, Mira thought, getting up to fix herself some toast and a hard-boiled egg. *Lots to do.*

The Latin dictionary sat beside a book on the rise and fall of the Roman Empire. Mira took it down and brought it to the same seat in the library she'd sat in two nights before and opened its index, getting the feel for it. It was old but fairly straightforward. She'd always been infatuated with how Latin root words shaped the English language. She supposed the interest came from her mother, who was the reader of the family. She'd tested Mira sometimes, asking her a certain word or phrase to see if she could glean the origin or base, giving a short explanation of the history afterward.

Now she opened the journal to the page containing the triangle and searched through the Latin dictionary, a handful of memories drifting back of her mother reading in her favorite chair beside the window with the best view in the house. Within a few minutes, she found the three words she was searching for.

Inanis — *empty.* Imple — *fill.* Fieri — *become.*

Simple enough. But what did it refer to? She frowned and started on the block of Latin on the next page. Gradually, she penned in corresponding English on a sheet in her notebook.

Initially, the journal had been interesting since it was obviously tied to the Wyndclyffe history, but maybe there was more to it, given Oliver's comment about Leland's odd behavior and beliefs. Something that might illuminate more about Allison's fears and help her understand the other girl better.

She paused at the end of the first paragraph, three familiar words leaping out at her from the text. *Mori et renovare.* The translation wasn't perfect, but it gave a good representation of the original text. Mira sat back and read.

Unto me a vision. Sleep into waking, still it remained. There are paths to thwart death. I break with the church forever. Damnation a lie. Freedom the illusion under which men labor. Metamorphosis through attrition, gratification, purity of mind. Those of weak souls utter false promises, and those just will rise. To die and renew.

To die and renew. Spider legs skittered in her stomach. She ignored the sensation until it went away, and started on the next page, reading it through when she was finished.

In sleeplessness dreams arrive to light the way. Lie upon the mouth of the dead so it may speak. Consume thy beloved. By fire's light the words are beacons. A shell placed atop the dead. A vessel to be filled. For death is a shadow unto the end of days and beyond. And in life more hells await than stars in the sky.

It read like some kind of manifesto. An ancient testament to a man's beliefs, or insanity. And written in the margins, more scrawl from Winston and Leland as well.

I understood today, Winston wrote on the second page. *What true possibilities await if I have faith. I am becoming.*

It's happening, Leland wrote beneath his grandfather's spidery script. *I can see the change beginning already. Someday soon she'll return.*

Mira swallowed, tasting acid. It seemed that both of them were delusional. Some kind of mania paired with hallucinations about . . . a metamorphosis? And this book seemed to be the foundation of their beliefs. This is what had driven the Wyndclyffes from England and most likely spawned the rumors surrounding their family and the island.

The next page revealed something new, not Latin but another language she couldn't identify. Its only defining characteristic was its repetition. The first two lines filled up the entire page and continued onto the next.

Unv jV nocw te xo fuh shton gou eth tun da \ Ts ga thera mon skl re na "lsh mun ta.

She was about to try sounding out the words but stopped short. *What if something happens?* The idea was ridiculous, but she didn't care for the look of the words. How they curled across the paper and smeared together the more she read them. Instead, she went back to the first page and studied it again. Below the triangle were the faint words *Caelum Ventustilla.* She flipped through the dictionary, and it took her a few seconds to realize this wasn't another phrase or instruction. It was a name which translated roughly as—

"Caelum Wind Drop," she said, sitting back in her seat. "Wyndclyffe." One of her hands slowly turned the pages, a finger running over first Winston's writing, then Leland's before turning back to the author's name.

An ancestor had written the journal and it had been passed down through generations. Passed down like mental illness waiting in the bloodlines for Allison to be born, to be exposed to abuse and tragedy, to reveal itself fully.

"Oh, God," Mira whispered. It was worse than she thought. *Allison didn't have a chance. Not in a secluded place like this with an untreated mentally ill parent.* No wonder the loss of her family had created a break. If the things in the journal were what Leland had tried teaching her, Allison's childhood had been a living nightmare.

"Mira?"

She started, hands jerking the journal and dictionary closed. Oliver stood at the library's doorway, leaning casually inside, eyebrows raised. "Sorry," he said. "Didn't mean to startle you."

"No, it's fine. Was just . . . distracted." She tucked the journal inside the dictionary, closing it tight.

"I was wondering if you could help me for a second. I hate to ask a guest for assistance, but Eleanor is busy, Gael has his hands deep in a batch of cherry tarts, and I cannot locate Jeffry to save my soul."

"No problem at all."

Oliver gestured down the hallway and she fell into step beside him. His shirt cuffs were undone and rolled up to the elbows, and there was a smear of something white and chalky on the knee of his pants. "It seems as the years go by, I need more and more help with things I used to handle on my own. Such is growing older, I suppose."

"I'm sure you've thought of hiring more staff."

"We have. Especially for the more hands-on household chores, but old habits die hard, and Eleanor and I are stuck in our ways. We both believe we're still thirty, unwilling to release any part of the mantle."

Reaching the T junction, they turned left. At the end of the hall, Oliver stepped into a rectangular room taking up a full corner of the wing. Its walls were lined with tall windows streaming late-morning sunlight. The floors were burnished hardwood, and dozens of canvases of different sizes leaned against the walls. Most were blank, but several held striking landscapes of ethereal quality—fog-shrouded grounds lit by moonlight, and whitecapped waters surrounding distant islands.

She was awestruck for a moment, the space and the light settling over her. Oliver must have noticed and said, "It's quite something, isn't it? This was Vanessa's studio."

"She did these?" Mira asked, moving closer to the paintings.

"Oh, yes. She was an accomplished artist." He picked up a small painting of a man and woman embracing in the middle of an open field beneath a flawless sky. For a few seconds, he stared deeply at it, one thumb rubbing the wooden frame. When he spoke again, his voice was faint. "Wonderfully talented. She had a dealer in the city who sold her work for her. It was quite popular years ago." He blinked and set the painting down. "And now I would assume the paintings would go for double their original price."

"My brother paints," Mira offered after a beat. Her gaze snagged on a canvas depicting a fairy ring of stones set in a forest. The view was from above, the woods surrounding the ring a perfect circle.

"Does he? Wonderful. Mayne I could give you the name of Vanessa's dealer. He might be interested in his work."

"Really? That would be amazing."

"Remind me to dig out his card. I should have it somewhere in the clutter I call an office." Oliver crossed to the corner of the room, where a tarp had been laid out. Part of the northern wall was torn down to the lath, and many of the boards were stripped away as well. "These two windows leaked early this spring and damaged the wall. Mold and whatnot began growing, and I didn't notice it until late summer. I don't come to this room nearly as much as years before." Two ladders were set up on either side of the hole in the wall, and Oliver climbed one while gesturing to the other. "I just need you to hold the other end of this tape measure, if you would be so kind."

Mira went up the first two steps of the ladder, grabbing the tape Oliver extended toward her, and like that, she was ten years old again, holding the end of a chalk line for her father in their garage. She could even smell the sawdust and feel the splinter she'd gotten beneath her fingernail when she helped him stand up the workbench they'd been creating.

"Good, and now the next," Oliver said, bringing her back to the present. They measured a half dozen gaps in the wall before he nodded and grinned. "Wonderful. That should keep me busy for the afternoon. My father was a carpenter. I never had his touch for detail, but the job always gets done anyhow."

He stood trancelike for a long moment, and she wondered where he'd gone to. When he continued to stare off into space, she cleared her throat and said, "Could I help you with anything else?"

Oliver blinked and looked at her for another span without speaking. Finally he smiled. "No, I'll putter around and make a mess until Eleanor tells me I'm needed elsewhere. Thank you for the assistance. And thank you for being here, for helping us. Helping Allison. You don't know how much it means. If she were to be taken away—" He shook his head. "Anyhow, we're very grateful."

"You're welcome, but I don't know if I've been that much help yet."

"It's the effort that means everything. I can tell you've got a kind heart."

Mira didn't know how to respond. "Dinner, then?" she said finally, heading for the door.

"Dinner it is."

She gave the paintings along the wall a lingering glance, then let herself out of the studio.

Questions circled her like lazy flies as she made her way back through the wing—Vanessa's painting of the fairy ring floating in her mind's eye clear and solid. Its location was very familiar, the only difference being the point of view.

It was the circular opening in the forest, it had to be, though she hadn't seen any small white stones as per the painting. But they could be hidden beneath years of growth and dead leaves, there amongst the other, larger rocks.

And so what? It appeared much of Vanessa's inspiration came from the island she apparently despised and wanted to leave. Why not the circular clearing in the woods? She thought again of the journal filled with the detached ramblings of not one but three Wyndclyffe men, and wondered if Vanessa's paintings had been some act of rebellion against her husband's control.

Stopping only to gather the dictionary and the journal within, Mira left the library and headed for the stairs, already forming a chain of questions for Allison that afternoon. She was so absorbed, she almost made it to the stairs without slowing and turning her head toward the photo. It was still the old picture of Yellow Bay's main street. Nothing more, nothing less. *You thought it was going to be different, didn't you? That it would be the photo of their wreck instead?* Yes. Without a doubt.

In a gesture of defiance, she studied the picture, then looked away as if it didn't bother her. She was almost to the stairs when she noticed something in a side hall she hadn't been down before. Mira angled toward it, a strange sense of detachment growing with each step until she was even with the painting on the wall.

It was one of Vanessa's. The style and tone were unmistakable after seeing the pieces in the studio. And not only did she recognize the work itself, the setting was familiar too. It was the clearing down by the river she'd visited on her first morning here. There was the dead tree overhanging the water and the rock shaped like a turtle. But it wasn't any of these things that caused her stomach to constrict in on itself. It was the subject of the painting itself.

It was the woman in the center of the canvas gazing out over the river.

It was the dark hair and curve of her face, the set of her eyes.

It was like looking in a mirror.

22

The breeze coming off the river and lake beyond held the first real bite of winter.

Mira shivered at the table in the garden, pulling her light jacket tighter around her. *Should've put on a thicker sweater before coming outside.*

Instead of seeking Allison out in the manor, she'd come here thinking it might be better to wait on neutral ground, but there'd been no sign of her. Mira hadn't seen so much as a shadow behind the windows in the half hour she'd been waiting. Given how their walk yesterday had ended, it wasn't surprising. Allison had retreated from the bridge they'd formed, and now there was a new divide between them.

And Mira felt something similar inside her now. There was before she'd seen the painting, and there was after. Just the thought of it made her woozy, as if the ground were shifting beneath her. This was no mistake of similarity in the dead of night. She'd stood in front of the painting, disbelieving but unable to look away. The likeness was uncanny.

What was happening?

If there was an explanation, she had no idea what it was. Vanessa died years ago, but somehow, she'd painted Mira standing in almost the exact spot she had been only days before. Possibilities rose and fell, each wilder than the last. The only one that seemed to hold water was the one she feared the most.

Whatever was broken inside her was worse than she'd thought.

Was there a faint slipping in her mind, like gears stripped of teeth? An uncoupling from the real and drifting into a void?

A flock of geese flew past overhead, wingtips whistling eerily. They were heading south. *Maybe I should do the same. Leave before the snow comes. Run away. Run. Run.*

She came back to herself and checked her phone again. Forty minutes had passed. She panned the device in a half-circle, experimenting if the service bars would rise in correspondence. They didn't. She tucked the phone away and pushed aside the painting as it loomed in her mind again before starting for the veranda.

She was almost to the steps when she noticed movement to her left.

A man was standing at the farthest corner of the building, attempting to peer into one of the lower windows. He wore a long peacoat over a gray suit and a dark briefcase dangled from one hand. He turned a round face with pinched features her way. His receding hairline was combed hard to one side. He seemed to notice her at the same time and froze. They stood facing one another across the distance until slowly he raised a hand and waved.

Hesitantly, she waved back. He smiled and started toward her.

Hands grasped her shoulders from behind. Mira stifled a startled cry as Eleanor appeared beside her. "Go inside," she said, steering her toward the door.

"What?"

"Go inside, please. Now." Eleanor gave her a gentle shove and headed toward the approaching man. Mira paused, then went up the steps and into the manor. She watched out the back windows as Eleanor intercepted the man and they began talking animatedly. *Arguing*. He motioned toward the manor, and Eleanor shook her head. He looked away and said something that caused Eleanor to cross her arms tightly. They remained in a standoff for a moment, then the man opened his briefcase and held out a sheaf of documents. Eleanor reluctantly took them, then gestured in the direction of Yellow Bay, leaving little to the imagination as to what she was suggesting. He stared her down, then gave her a dismissive wave before turning away to head back around the side of the building. Eleanor lingered, watching him go until he was out of sight before coming inside. She shut the doors and leaned heavily against them before glancing up to Mira. "I'm sorry."

"Who was that?"

Eleanor sighed. "Reginald Browning." The name rang a faint bell but Mira couldn't place it. "The lawyer for the trust. He's not supposed to show up unannounced; it's against the agreement. So I sent him away. Awful man." Eleanor spit the last part, then shook her head. "I'm sorry; he's definitely not your problem. I didn't want him badgering you about Allison, which he would have, given the chance."

Mira nodded. "I was actually waiting for her. Do you know where she is?"

"In her room, I believe."

"Thanks." She started away down the hall, a tinge of unease following her.

She was lying. There was no concrete reason to think so, but she did anyway. Mira didn't doubt the man was who Eleanor said he was, but shooing her inside felt completely off. And there was something else about the encounter she was having a difficult time putting her finger on. Something about the way Browning had looked at her. How he'd waved and smiled.

Her thoughts scattered and rearranged as she approached the door to Allison's room. It was shut, and Mira spent a beat realigning before rapping her knuckles on the wood. "Allison? Are you in there?" No answer. "Can I come in?" A sound from the other side of the door which could've been either a yes or a no. She chose to hear the former and turned the knob.

Inside, the drapes were pulled and only a single light burned in the far corner, illuminating a small desk. "Allison?" No reply. Mira made her way deeper into the sprawling space. When she got to the desk, she glanced around. The bathroom door was open to darkness. No one sat in any of the chairs. A few books were strewn on the desk's top, a single piece of paper covering them. She picked it up.

On it was a large circle drawn in what looked like black chalk, and in its center a triangle. While the circle was haphazard and elongated, the triangle was perfect. She got the impression if she were to measure its three sides, they would be equal. She set the paper down and examined a pile of white chalk, all short pieces with worn angles. Beside the chalk, one of the book's titles caught her eye. *Alice in Wonderland.* The top of a photo protruded from the novel, marking a page. Mira glanced around the room, feeling like an intruder but unable to help herself. She opened the book and drew the picture free.

It was of two young girls, both of them somewhere between eight and ten. Allison was easily recognizable with blond curls held back by two barrettes. The other girl was shorter with dark hair and dark eyes. They stood on the end of a pier it took Mira a few seconds to recognize as the one jutting from the island into the river. Allison held a small fishing rod, a sunfish dangling from its hook. Her expression was one of surprise and delight, while the other girl was more stoic, one hand reaching out to touch the fish. Droplets of water caught the sun of the day and became jewels falling to make dark spots at the girls' feet.

Mira studied the dark-haired girl, a pressure building in the air around her. Inside her.

The girl in the photo could've been her when she was ten.

"What are you doing?"

Mira spun to find Allison standing a few feet away. Mira's breath snagged in her lungs, and she found she couldn't reply. Shame lit her skin like sunburn.

"Uh, I was looking for you. I—" She fumbled with the photo and book, managing to drop them both. "Sorry, I didn't mean to snoop. I was just . . ."

Allison came closer, her eyes never leaving Mira's face. There was no reading the girl's expression; her features were flat and serene. Allison finally looked down at the photo protruding from the book and pulled it free. She studied it, then moved to the bed and sat down.

Mira didn't know what to do. She put her hands in her pockets, took them out, clasped them together, let go. "I'm sorry. I thought you were in here and . . . I shouldn't have gone through your stuff." Allison finally shook her head, whether to agree with what Mira said or to dismiss it, she wasn't sure. "I wanted to apologize for yesterday too. I shouldn't have suggested going to Yellow Bay. That was stupid."

Allison was quiet for a long time, then shifted on the bed. "No, it wasn't," she finally said. "I was thinking about it, and . . . I don't know if I could, but . . ." She swallowed thickly. "We could try, I guess."

"Really? You want to?"

"Yeah, if you're with me the whole time." Allison's gaze fell to the picture and she tapped it with one finger. "We used to go there a lot."

Mira seized the opening and moved closer, perching on the foot of the bed. "Who is she?"

"Isabelle." A fleeting smile crossed Allison's face. "My best friend. We basically grew up together." She tapped the photo again. "I remember that day." Mira took in Isabelle's features again, the color of her hair.

"It was spring and Oliver took us down to fish. We thought we'd really caught a trophy."

As Allison spoke, some of the disquiet from seeing Vanessa's painting began to fade, like fog lifting to reveal a hidden landscape. "Where is she now?" Mira asked, but Allison seemed not to hear her. She was lost in the past. Mira let her drift and studied the photo again. The carefree youthfulness of Allison frozen there in that moment struck her. Before troubles came calling and the world grew teeth. It was a crime for that innocence to be drawn so cruelly away. She thought of Aaron in the field at their childhood home, patiently following grasshoppers as they leapt and flew their stunted flights. Thought of him amongst the pale institutional walls of Village Gardens.

"We did everything together," Allison said, bringing her back. "I really miss her."

Mira started to ask what had happened to Isabelle again, but bit it back just as quickly. She wouldn't risk repeating the day before.

"Sometimes, there's this tightness, right here." Allison touched her breastbone. "It starts slow and gets worse and worse until it's not just tight, it's pain. Stabbing pain. Like an arrow in my lungs and I can't breathe all the way in." Even talking about it, Mira could see the panic rising. She scooted closer and took Allison's hand. Allison stared down at their intertwined fingers. "Last night, I couldn't sleep, so I went out to the garden. I might've dozed off in one of the chairs. When I woke up, it was still night, and I went back inside, but the clock said it was earlier than when I left. And . . . and . . ."

The wind gusted, skidding dry leaves across the window. Mira waited, feeling the skin on the back of her neck prickle and tighten. "What?"

"I saw myself in the hallway going outside. It was me but not me." Allison inhaled shakily.

Mira stared down at the floor. Let her eyes unfocus, everything beginning to blur. "The night my parents died, I was home with my brother. My mom had been at a yoga retreat and my dad went to pick her up. It was really windy. I remember the trees whipping back and forth. Aaron and I were watching a movie, just waiting for them to get home. But it got later and later, and then it was Aaron's bedtime. I called them—nothing. And I started to get worried. Not really bad, but it was there. Like some part of me already knew something was wrong. By the time my phone rang with a number I didn't recognize, I knew. I knew something terrible had happened. And I couldn't get myself to answer. It just rang and rang and rang." There were tears on her cheeks she didn't recall crying. Mira swiped them away and sniffled. "When I finally answered, it was the police and . . . they were gone. Just like that. I looked around our apartment and it was completely different. It was like I was seeing it through someone else's eyes. The front door looked strange because they'd never walk through it again. The kitchen table wasn't ours anymore because we'd never have another family dinner at it."

Allison squeezed her hand, and it was nice to feel the solidity of another person. Reminded her she was here and now.

They sat that way in their shared silence as the wind gusted at the window, asking to be let in.

23

Mira lay on her back in the middle of her bed, looking up at the high ceiling, trying to find pictures and meaning in the whorls of plaster.

She was tired and wrung out but lighter too, as if telling Allison about the most terrible night of her life had lifted something from her. Some small portion of the greater weight she carried. In retrospect, she knew why—because she'd told someone who actually understood her particular pain. Aaron knew their parents were gone, but he wasn't able to communicate the depths of his grief, so they couldn't really commiserate beyond looking at old photos or sharing a hug when they were both sad. And Shay was a good listener, but her trauma was of a different nature. Finding someone who could fully relate was freeing in a way she hadn't experienced before. On the other hand, she didn't know if she'd helped Allison feel any better about her own burden, but she had seemed less restrained, with more of the hidden girl underneath revealing herself.

She wondered for the first time if in setting out to help Allison emerge from her prison of grief, she hadn't stumbled on the key to her own.

Mira rolled over and looked out the nearest window. Now that she had a reasonable explanation for Vanessa's painting, she turned it over, examining it from different angles.

It was Isabelle in the painting—one of Allison's closest childhood friends. And given the likeness in the photo when she was younger, the idea she'd grown to look a lot like Mira wasn't farfetched at all. Everyone supposedly had a twin . . .

Even so, it was beyond eerie encountering a mirror image of herself here in this isolated place. And the fact that she'd been hired as a companion to Allison was a little too much to ignore. Was that why Eleanor had sought her out initially? As some kind of stand-in for Allison's absent friend?

Mira turned to her other side and eyed the Latin dictionary next to her phone. She hesitated, then opened it to reveal the journal tucked within. As she began paging through the small binding, there was a knock at the door. "Coming," she called, transferring the dictionary and journal beneath her pillow. When she opened the door, her heart gave a not-entirely-unpleasant flutter.

Gael stood in the hallway, looking impossibly handsome in a dark sweater and jeans. His hair was slightly mussed, giving him a just-rolled-out of bed look accented by his grin. "Hey, sorry if I'm bothering you," he said.

"No, no, not at all."

"I've got dinner under control and have a couple hours free, so I wondered if you were up for that tour now?"

"Yes," Mira said, realizing her lack of hesitation a second too late. "I mean, sure. That would be great."

"Cool." Gael nodded toward the stairs and she followed. She was so nervous and excited, she barely registered the grandfather clock as it began its chiming.

"You feeling okay?"

Mira pulled her fingers from her temple where they probed gently, trying to massage away the lingering headache she'd woken with. "Fine," she said, catching up to Gael where he stood at a set of huge double doors.

They'd been meandering through the manor for the last half hour after he'd shown her the kitchen with a notable tinge of pride, a delicious scent wafting from the glowing oven. Much of it she'd already seen either on her own or when Oliver had given her the initial tour. Gael seemed to sense this as he leaned against the doorjamb and said, "Guessing I've been rehashing a lot of stuff and you've been too polite to say anything."

Mira smiled. "Maybe a little." She'd also just been enjoying his presence, the timbre of his voice, how strands of his almost-white hair caught the light.

"Thought so. Well, I doubt you've seen this. It's my absolute favorite part of the house," he said, swinging the doors wide.

Beyond was a sprawling room with tall windows filled wall to wall with games.

There were four billiard tables in the far corner beside half a dozen professional dartboards. Next to them were two golden lacquered ski ball games along with a full-sized shuffleboard court. "Wow" was all she could say, turning in a half-circle to take it all in. A few ping pong tables filled up the opposite side of the room, and Mira could barely believe what lay past them, running along the entire western wall.

"A bowling alley?" she said, moving farther into the space. "Seriously?"

"Yeah; I mean, it's just one lane," Gael said, following her as she wove between two foosball tables. Mira picked up a bowling ball from the nearby rack and hefted it, set it back down, and picked up another, all the while eyeing the pins at the end of the lane. "Don't tell me you're a bowler."

"Not really. My dad belonged to a league for a few years, and I'd tag along with him sometimes. He'd set me up a lane or two over from his team and I'd goof around while he played."

"Sounds great."

Mira slowly replaced the ball she was holding. "It really was."

Gael looked from her to the pins and back again. "So, ten bucks if you can knock down more than half of them on the first try."

Mira grinned and chose a dark gray ball with deep purple striations. Without pausing, she took two steps and sent it down the polished wood in a graceful curve, clipping the lead pin with the rest toppling behind it.

Gael gaped. "Mistakes have been made."

Mira cocked her head and faced him. "What do I get for a strike?"

"You get a challenge. Winner has to tell the most embarrassing thing that's ever happened to them."

Mira smiled as her ball was returned and the pins settled into place. "Can't wait to hear yours."

"So, I'm running about five minutes behind schedule and I'm rushing with the pan of lasagna. The instructor's waiting at the table along with a few other chefs, and he's got these ridiculous white leather boots on; don't ask me why," Gael said, sitting forward, his eyes alight with the memory. Mira nodded, giggling, and leaned back in her chair at the little bar in the corner of the game room. "And the whole time I'm like, this didn't bake long enough, it's too watery, I'm totally going to lose a ton of points on one of the most important exams, and I fail to see the puddle of water right next to the table someone spilled earlier."

"Oh, no."

"Oh, yes. Suddenly, my feet are at eye level and I'm falling, holding this enormous pan of molten-hot underdone lasagna. I come down on my back and all I can think is *Try to save the dish, try to save the dish*. So, I keep from losing the pan completely but it comes down perfectly flat on the floor, and a stream of sauce and noodles goes shooting out like missile—right onto the instructor's boots."

"No way!" Gael nodded, eyes closed. "What did he say?"

"He glanced down at his boots and said, 'Monsieur Danforth—this sauce looks thin.'"

"Oh, my god."

"Yeah. So, the upside was since I fractured my elbow, they let me redo the exam, and I aced it the second time." Gael shook his head while Mira's giggles gradually subsided.

"That's amazing."

"It wasn't at the time, but now it's pretty funny." He raised his glass of iced tea. "Speaking of amazing, here's to your bowling skills."

She clinked glasses with him. "It wasn't really a challenge, honestly."

"Wow. That sounds like a rematch talking. Then maybe I can hear your most embarrassing story."

"Doubt it." They grinned and fell quiet. Gael glanced out the windows and Mira found herself studying him, wondering if there was anything to his subtle flirting or if he were just being nice. "So, why here?" she asked.

"What do you mean?"

"You graduated from a prestigious culinary school and you could've gone anywhere, right? What made you want to work at such an isolated place?"

He sobered, clearing his throat. "My mom got sick while I was away. It was . . . uh . . . really fast."

"You don't have to—"

"No, no, it's okay. I came home to be with her, and Eleanor approached me about the job. It was a good fit. She and Oliver did a lot for us near the end." He cleared his throat. "It had always just been

Mom and I. My dad left before I was even born, so he's a complete stranger. She willed me the house in town." He gestured around at the walls. "But I guess this felt more like home afterward."

"You seem more like the city type. I can picture you lording over some fancy kitchen in New York."

He laughed. "Not really. I'm kind of an introvert. Lots of people make me nervous. I like the island. It's beautiful, quiet. I have an amazing kitchen and the pay's good."

"Sounds perfect."

"Not perfect. It can get lonely. Oliver and Eleanor are great, but . . ." He glanced around with mock caution and whispered, "They're old." They both laughed, and for a few seconds, their eyes met and held. Mira's stomach lifted again in a sweetly sick way, and she had the sudden urge to lean toward him, which only made her insides squirm more. She looked to the side, scrambling for something to say. "What about Allison? Do you guys hang out?"

Gael sat back, something flickering behind his eyes. "Uh, no. Not a lot. She's pretty private. How about that rematch?" He stood and started away.

Mira hesitated at the bar, wanting to call him back and apologize, to rewind ten seconds and not say anything about Allison. It had been so nice, so *normal,* to just sit and talk with him. But the moment had slipped away.

She grimaced and rose to follow him back toward the game she no longer wanted to play.

SEPTEMBER 2021

Her father's voice woke her.

Allison thought it might be a nightmare, but then she was looking around her room, seeing the moonlight streaming through the window, feeling the fullness of her bladder, and hearing the edge in his voice carrying down the hall. He wasn't yelling, not yet, but that blade in his tone was a warning of what was to come.

A frantic bird beat its wings within her chest as her mother responded more quietly. She wondered, not for the first time, which was worse—to be afraid for yourself or for others.

Allison swung her feet to the floor and crossed the room, easing her door open. The volume of her parents' voices increased.

"You didn't think I'd notice?" her father said.

"I told you I don't know what you're talking about."

"You were trying to poison me."

"Poison you? Listen to yourself—"

"I found the pills. You put them in my food. Drugged me."

Allison stepped into the hall, heart beating harder. The floor was cold against her bare feet, and she suppressed a shiver both from the chill and from the possibility of being caught out of bed. She took two steps toward her parents' room and felt a hand reach out from the dark and grasp her own.

Allison bit back a scream and turned to look into Isabelle's wide eyes. She stood in her pajamas, hair askew, rocking from foot to foot.

What are you doing? Allison mouthed. Isabelle nodded down the hallway as Allison's parents began talking over one another again. "Go back to bed." Isabelle shook her head and gripped Allison's hand harder.

She considered shoving Isabelle back down the hall and depositing her in her room. They could turn on the radio low to drown out the argument. Isabelle could sleep with her tonight like she had so many other times when they were younger. Allison had become used to the feeling of the blankets being drawn back and the bed shifting in the middle of the night as her friend crawled in with her. Even then, she'd known it wasn't healthy behavior, but she also couldn't bear sending her back to her room alone. Allison had sensed that the delicateness and vulnerability in Isabelle was something more—a marker of some deeper instability that was still evolving.

Isabelle let go of her hand and started down the hall despite Allison's whispered protests. Allison gave the safety of her room a last glance, then followed.

They crept closer and closer to the door in the hall that was open several inches, spilling soft light onto the floor. Years before, it had been a game to sneak around the manor and listen in on the adults' conversations. It had been fun and exciting before they began to understand what some of the harsh and acidic words meant. What violence sounded like. Now they crouched near a mahogany table holding several tall vases, hands finding each other in the dark, and listened.

"You're why she lacks the will," Leland said. His voice had gained volume and timbre, like an orator readying for a flourish to a well-practiced speech. "You undermine me every chance you get."

"Do you realize what you're doing to her?" her mother replied. She sounded breathless, like she was moments away from crying. Allison swiped one hand on her pajama bottoms, still feeling the repulsive edges of the thing she'd found under her pillow before bed.

At first, she hadn't been able to understand what it was, since there was no reconciling something like it being in the place she slept. But then she'd picked the gray-white thing up and turned it over, seeing the dull shine of silver and realizing it was a dental filling and she was holding a human jawbone. She'd thrown it across the room out of reflex, one of the smaller teeth leaping free when it hit the floor. After realizing who had put it there and why, she picked it up using a towel from her bathroom and deposited it in the nearest garbage, then washed her hands until they were red and raw.

"I'm creating the way," Leland said slowly. "She has a destiny."

"Your mother is dead. She's dead and not coming back."

A heavy silence filled the air. Allison held her breath as Isabelle's hand tightened on her own. The other girl leaned closer and put her lips close to her ear. "I'm sorry," she whispered.

Allison tore her attention away from the doorway. "What?"

"I tried to help," Isabelle said. "I put some of my medicine in his food. I thought it would make him better." Allison found her friend's luminous eyes in the dark. "If he was better, then you could stay."

Allison wanted to scream at her. To hit her. But her attention was pulled back by her mother's voice finally breaking the quiet. "I want you to talk to someone. Please."

"You always say that. Talk to someone. Talk to who?" There was a deadly pause. "Who have *you* been talking to?"

"What do you mean? No one."

"Have you told someone about the becoming?"

"Who would I talk to? I never leave this place. I just want to help you."

"You're hiding something. I can see it. You disappear sometimes for hours. Where do you go?"

"I'm not hiding anything. I want you to get better."

"Do you remember what I told you the night of our wedding?"

Allison felt Isabelle trembling against her. Her mother made a sharp cry of surprise and said, "Stop, please."

"I promised I'd always be with you and you promised the same."

"Yes, I remember, I remember."

"There's nowhere in the world I wouldn't find you if you tried to leave. You know that."

Her mother made another muted cry of pain and Allison rose to her feet, untangling herself from Isabelle even as her friend tried clinging tighter. She was going to do something, stop him somehow. Most of her life had been lived in a shadow of fear. Fear of his volatility, of his anger. A shadow only lifted by brief highs when he would shower her with love and praise, his face beaming while he talked of a future so bright with possibility, it was almost easy to forget nights like this.

Allison managed to free herself from Isabelle and was taking a step toward the bedroom when a pair of hands grasped her firmly by the shoulders. They spun her around and she was suddenly looking into Eleanor's shadowed features.

"What are you doing?" Eleanor hissed. She didn't wait for Allison's response, only hauled Isabelle up from where she crouched on the floor, and began steering them both back down the hall. Allison tried twisting away, but Eleanor's grip was like iron. "Don't" was all she said, and the word was enough to take the fight out of Allison. Because there was compassion there, and a resignation which resonated in her center. There was no fixing this, no finding a magical cure to what ailed her family, only escape with the hopes of finding something better elsewhere.

Allison stopped in her doorway. Eleanor only looked back for a long second before urging Isabelle farther down the hall. There was still the wild impulse to run to her parents' room and try to stop what was taking place inside, but it was a dampened coal now instead of the flame filling her before.

Slowly, she closed her door, knowing she would lie awake for hours in the dark, knowing that was all she could do. As the door clicked shut, she could just make out the last thing her father said, his voice quieter now, rage finally spent.

"We'll always be together. We promised. And I keep my promises."

24

That was wonderful, Gael, even for you. Bravo."

Oliver clapped politely and leaned back from the table, placing a hand on his belly.

"Roast is my specialty," Gael said.

"It was delicious," Mira added. Gael gave her a brief smile, then began clearing the dishes. She withered inside.

Their bowling rematch had been awkward with stilted conversation, the earlier ease of Gael's charm replaced by politeness that made her cringe internally until he'd finally excused himself to go finish dinner. Mira had wandered back to her room and thrown herself onto the bed, wanting to sink into it and disappear. Why had she brought up Allison? And more importantly, why had it affected Gael so much? Did the two of them not get along? Had something happened between them? While pondering everything, she'd drifted off until it had been time to eat. On the upside, the nap had cured her headache.

Eleanor tossed her napkin to the table and stood up. "I believe I'm in the mood for a walk to help all this food settle. Anyone care to join me?"

"Not I, said the pig," Oliver said.

"You definitely ate enough pork to qualify. Mira?"

She considered it, then stood as well. "Sure. Only so many days before the snows, right? Should enjoy the weather while we can."

Eleanor smiled. "I couldn't agree more."

They left the manor, bundled in coats and a pair of hats Eleanor produced from her office on the way out. Mira's was rough wool and smelled of cedar and dust. They walked with the great house at their backs and made their way to the view of the river and the lake beyond. The sun spilled its lagging light across the water in orange and reds. After a time, Eleanor continued down the path into the woods, and Mira followed, appreciating the lack of conversation, the solitude of the walk, the refreshing chill against her skin.

The woods were quiet and the thought of the mountain lion arose only once as the path first darkened in the trees' thickest point before brightening again on the other side. Soon they stood at the top of the steps leading down to the concrete tongue jutting into the water. Eleanor took a seat on the top step and patted a place beside her.

"Probably my favorite spot on the island," Eleanor said after a while. The evening had taken on the look of a pastoral painting with Yellow Bay's lights winking on until the town could've been some model on a hobbyist's workbench. "More so than the view up by the house. Mostly, I think because this one wasn't planned. I like watching the town and how it cycles through the seasons."

"Do you ever miss—" Mira said, gesturing to the opposite shore.

Eleanor gave her another smile, this a different species from the one in the dining room. "It's the oldest story in the book. You always want what isn't yours after a while. No matter how content or happy you are, it just takes time."

Would she eventually yearn for New York once she and Aaron left? Was that what fueled her longing for the country—an absence needing to be filled, only to empty again once they'd reached their goal? How much of it was simply wanting to turn back the clock, to fix what was broken? To take away the question of why in Aaron's eyes? She carried the same feeling in her heart, the desire for home.

"What about you?" Eleanor said, breaking her from her reverie. "Aching to be back over there and gone soon?"

The question threw her off guard. "No; I mean, I miss my brother."

"I bet. Oliver mentioned he paints." Mira nodded. "You know, I was Vanessa's liaison regarding her work in the city. The broker who she dealt with was a former friend of mine. Lover, actually," she added after a pause. She gave Mira a conspirator's smile before tilting her head. "I'd be thrilled to see some of your brother's work sometime."

"Really? Well, here," Mira said, drawing out her phone. She opened the pictures app and began to page through. After a minute of searching, she frowned. "I know I have a few shots of his recent ones."

"It's okay; you can show me whenever," Eleanor said, turning her attention back to the glowing town.

Mira continued to scroll through her pictures, going back over a year. Nothing. No shots of Aaron's work anywhere. She swallowed, some of her meal trying to rise to the back of her throat, and began a new search, this time going slower.

"You get used to it," Eleanor said. "Even with the others around and the occasional vacation, there's a sense of isolation. We all knew what the job was when we took the positions, but there's definitely a period of acclimation." She paused. "Maybe it never stops."

Mira heard and didn't hear her. She'd stopped scrolling and tucked her phone away. Not only could she not find any pictures of Aaron's art, she could only find one of Aaron himself. It was from the prior Christmas when he'd donned the new sweater she'd given him with the smile that never failed to melt her heart. *That's not possible. There are dozens and dozens more of him.*

Then where are they? She was drawn back again by a question from Eleanor, one she had to ask the older woman to repeat.

"I said, are you feeling all right? You seem distracted."

"I'm fine. Just . . . maybe a little homesick."

Eleanor appraised her. "Not to pry, but do you have anyone else waiting for you besides your brother?"

"Well, a friend."

"But no one special?"

"Oh, no. Not like that."

"That surprises me, a beautiful girl like yourself and whip-smart to boot." Mira didn't know what to say to that, so she stayed quiet. "Well, relationships can be wonderful, but they're work, too. Anyone who tells you different is lying. My marriage started with such passion. But over the years, it became something else. Something deeper. A promise."

"And you just had the one daughter together?"

"Yes. She had dreams of living in the city, but it wasn't for her. She says she wants to be a writer someday. She does have a flair for the dramatic." Eleanor shifted. "I wanted to say I'm sorry again for upsetting you the other night. Oliver and I felt terrible about it."

"It's all right. I normally don't get that emotional. It's been years since they passed, but sometimes, it seems like yesterday." She saw her mother again, standing at the window, watching her and Aaron play.

It could've been a digital shot for how clear it was, all except for her mother's face. It was a blur as if time had blotted it out to gray. For a long, painful moment, she struggled to bring her face into focus.

"Some things never get easier, do they? Losing Vanessa . . ." She paused, expression darkening in time with the failing light. "And Leland."

"I can't imagine . . . what you had to do. I'm so sorry."

"It was the worst moment of my life." Eleanor stilled, only her eyes roving the water below. "Pulling that trigger. I thought Ollie was dead. I knew Vanessa was, and I knew Leland wouldn't stop until—" Her voice cracked, and she shook her head when Mira put a hand on her shoulder. "I wish he would have accepted help. Maybe things would've been different. We loved him the best we could."

Mira thought for a moment. "I think some of the worst things are done for love."

When she looked back Eleanor was studying her closely. "I apologize again for the scene earlier with Browning."

"That's okay."

"It was upsetting, seeing him there all of a sudden, unannounced. He has such a sense of entitlement. I noticed it the first time I met him almost twenty years ago. I hope he wasn't rude to you before I intervened."

"No, he didn't say anything." *But I think he was about to.* A second later, Eleanor stood and offered her a hand.

"We should get back; it's nearly dark."

"Before we go, I wanted to ask you something." Eleanor paused, eyebrows raised. "Um . . ." Mira shifted in place, then gestured to the lights across the water. "I was wondering if it would be okay if Allison and I went shopping in Yellow Bay?"

A strange half-smile crept onto Eleanor's face. "Well, it would be if she were able to leave the island."

"She said she'd like to try."

"She did?" Eleanor blinked. "When?"

"This afternoon. I brought it up to her yesterday, and she thought about it and said she wanted to go." When Eleanor didn't reply or move, Mira hurried on. "I mean, I thought that was good, right? It's progress?"

"Of course; I'm just shocked, is all. That's wonderful news."

"So, Jeff can take us across in the boat?"

"I don't see why not. I'll let him know."

They walked back to the manor in silence, saying their goodnights once inside. As Eleanor made her way down the hall, Mira found herself starting to ask about Isabelle and the likeness they shared, then stopping. It was what she'd opened her mouth to say down at the river, but instead, the request to go to the mainland had come out. At least Eleanor had been receptive if not a little caught off guard.

Readying for bed, she decided she'd ask Eleanor about Isabelle the next chance she got. There had to be some reasonable explanation about their likeness. Until then, there was Allison's progress to be happy about.

But lying there in bed with faint moonlight staining the walls and floor, she couldn't help feel lingering unease. It was slight but there. All of the oddities of her stay so far creating an underhum buzzing unpleasantly in her nerves.

Leave.

The thought came unbidden and strong, as if someone else had spoken in her ear. Mira rolled to her side and closed her eyes, ignoring the sudden urge to rise and pack her things and go. But that was foolish. Nerves were just nerves, and if she ran away now, she'd never forgive herself.

It was the chance of a lifetime, and she wasn't going to let it slip away.

25

Isabelle listened to the night sounds.

At first, there was nothing, then the wind pushing against a window somewhere, a groan of stone still settling even after a hundred and fifty years, the faint dripping of moisture in some hidden place.

She always listened at night when sleep wouldn't come. The sounds kept her company, kept the darkness from consuming her fully. It would be easy to slip away if she weren't careful. In the dark, she had no compass, no way to tell what she was looking at or who she really was. In the dark, she could be anywhere, be anybody. It was terrifying and freeing all at once.

Her mind drifted into what was to come. It frightened her to no end—the future. It always had. Change was her oldest enemy, and she'd been fighting it as long as she could remember. There was a good possibility they would have to leave the manor soon, and she thought she would rather die than have that happen. The idea was oddly comforting. At least she had an option, which was something the outside world denied her just by being the way it was.

In the meantime, she could watch and hope. Because there was also the possibility that things would remain the same. The same was a warm blanket on a cold day. The same was safe.

In the dark, Isabelle smiled.

26

"We played down here a lot," Allison said.

They sat in the morning sun on the same rock Mira had stood on her first day on the island, not far from where Vanessa had painted Isabelle. The river flowed by as if late to an appointment with the sea, and the air held the humid promise of a storm.

"You and Isabelle?" Mira asked. She picked at the stem of a dried water reed, which came apart in delicate strands and curled as soon as they were free of the whole. She kept her eyes averted from the light-planished water since she'd slept badly the night before, plagued by nightmares, and her headache was back. Maybe there was something really wrong with her. Like brain-tumor wrong. But if it were something like that, she guessed there would be more warning signs other than intermittent headaches and terrible dreams.

"Yes," Allison said. "This was our favorite spot. We built a little shelter over there under the overhangs of the trees. It was secret and we thought we were so clever, but Oliver knew it was there. So did Mom."

"Not your father?"

The question stopped her. "No. Well . . . I don't know. He may have, but he never said anything about it. Never found us there."

Never found us. Mira stripped more sections of reed away. "Would he have been mad?"

"Probably. He was mad a lot."

Allison stood and made her way to the water's edge. After a beat, Mira followed. They stood side by side, looking out across the river. In the distance a sailboat skimmed past, one of the people on board raising a hand to them. They waved back.

"I miss things from before, like Mom reading to me and family dinners. But I don't miss how he was and what he made me do. I'm glad he's gone."

Mira's throat tightened. It was as if she were stepping out onto a wire over a vast drop. "What did he make you do?"

"You know," Allison said so low, it was nearly lost in the sound of the river.

Mira paused in stripping another length of the reed. "I don't."

Allison appeared to go away for a moment, receding until she was like another fixture on the bank of stone. "He made me stand in the circle and say the words."

"Which words?"

"The weird ones. From the book."

There was a second of disconnect, then realization. "What were the words supposed to do?"

"Help make me empty. And call to someone." She paused and looked at Mira "There's a type of wasp that lays its eggs in a living host. When the larvae hatch, they start eating." Allison's voice grew soft. "They eat the host's inside, hollow it out, and hatch from its body. That's what he wanted. He wanted her hollowed out so something else could grow there."

A flock of blackbirds perched in nearby tree took flight in a blast of wings and Mira flinched.

"She was supposed to leave who she was behind. She was supposed to forget." Allison's face had gone slack, her voice flat. She looked at Mira, but her gaze was somewhere else, far beyond the shore they stood on. "He made her stay awake for days. In the circle. He said without sleep, the way would open. For the emptying. It was so dark out there. So, so dark." Her jaw loosened and her eyes glazed. "She found hair in her tea. Corpse hair. Dead and gray." Allison's head tipped to one side. "He didn't love her. Not really. He wanted her to be someone else."

Mira's scalp tightened, hairs rising with the deadness in Allison's voice. The ground shifted and the horizon shuddered, began to tip.

Allison blinked and life flowed back into her eyes. "Do you think we should still go today? It's starting to look like rain."

Mira drew in a shuddering breath. For a second, she'd been sure she would pass out, but the faintness was fading as abruptly as Allison's trance.

"What?" Allison asked when Mira didn't respond.

"N-nothing."

"You look really pale."

"Just . . . maybe something I ate."

Allison started up the trail toward the manor and paused when Mira didn't follow. "Coming?"

Mira got her legs to move after a moment of revolt. "Yeah," she said as brightly as she could. "Let's go."

The door to the boathouse was a wide rectangle of darkness, a clank of metal on metal coming from within. As they neared the threshold, Allison slowed, then stopped.

"What's wrong?" Mira asked.

Allison nodded toward the sounds coming from inside. "Jeff. He creeps me out."

"Oh. I mean, I get it." Mira noticed Allison had started wringing her hands and shifting from foot to foot. "I'll just go ask him, okay?" Allison nodded thankfully, and Mira gave her a reassuring smile before moving to the open doorway.

There were no overhead lights on and the dank air washed over her from within. After a moment of letting her eyes adjust, Mira recognized the shape of a boat lift and the craft she'd arrived on within its cradle. The boat was hoisted into the air and a work light on the floor illuminated Jeff's bulk hunched over the motor.

"Um, hi," she said, stepping fully inside. The groundskeeper looked up from his work, hands stained black with grease, a wrench gripped in one of them. "Allison and I . . . we were wondering if you could take us to town."

Jeff gave her a lingering look, then returned his attention to the outboard. "Would if I could, but I can't. Motor's busted."

Mira stepped farther into the cool air of the boathouse, feeling it seep up from the concrete floor and chill her instantly. "How long will it take to fix?"

"Don't know. Parts are getting delivered later today."

"So, this afternoon?"

"I said—" Jeff turned to face her again, and not for the first time, Mira noticed how tall and wide he was. How hard and gnarled his hands were—how scarily strong they looked. "—I don't know," he finished. His eyes were two polished stones beneath the bill of his hat. He turned back to his work. "I'll let Eleanor know when it's done."

Mira gave him a long stare, but when he remained as oblivious as a statue, she turned and made her way outside.

Allison was waiting on the lowest stair, turning a dead leaf over in her hands. Mira stopped a few feet away. "I guess the boat motor isn't working. He said he'd let Eleanor know when it's done." She paused, taking in Allison's frown. "Sorry."

Allison stood and dusted herself off before starting to climb the stairs. "It's okay. I'm actually a little relieved." She threw Mira a sheepish look.

"I totally get that. It's fine." Except there was an added layer to their cancelled trip Allison didn't seem to grasp or care about.

They were stranded.

Mira swallowed a metallic taste in the back of her throat. There had to be another boat somewhere on the island, a kayak or canoe at least. But wouldn't it have been stored down in the boathouse too? *No way my only real connection to the outside world is an old boat with a broken-down motor.*

She was about to ask Allison if she knew of anything else when a rumble of thunder came from the east. Heavy clouds roiled like silt disturbed on a river bottom. Lightning forked between them and vanished.

"It's really going to storm," Allison said as they stopped to watch the approaching weather. Ahead, the manor grew from the landscape in its dark gray lines and angles. Sometime in the last few days, it had lost its hypnotic grandeur. Now it felt different. Now it seemed to be waiting.

She recoiled as Allison touched her arm. "We should go," Allison said, hurrying on as distant rain swept down onto the river, pebbling its surface. Mira jogged after her, pushing away the thoughts about the manor.

It was a just a house, like Eleanor said.

A big house.

On an island I can't leave.

27

A minute after they closed the door, it started to rain.

Big dollops of water splashing the windows, soaking the grass, and raking some of the last leaves from the trees. Everything outside looked dark and shiny and cold. Like a fresh oil painting.

They sat in the staff dining room, eating sandwiches Allison had retrieved from the kitchen. Mira had looked for Gael among the prep tables and storage shelves, but he was nowhere to be seen. She chewed thoughtfully, savoring the meal while studying Allison across the table, where she slouched in a chair, picking at a pile of potato chips. A part of her wanted to ask about Gael and see Allison's reaction while another shouted the idea down. *Why are you so worried about Gael's personal life? You're not here to make a connection with him; you're here to help Allison.* And given her earlier—what? Trance? Fugue?—there was still a long way to go.

For a second, Mira was back on the shore, watching Allison recede. It was like she'd witnessed her split into two people, then merge to one again. What she'd said still echoed in Mira's mind. How Leland had wanted to change "her". Not "me"—"*her.*" Almost like Allison was speaking about someone else.

It must've been a glimpse inside her depersonalization. Just thinking about it turned her stomach—how awful it must be for Allison. There were a few bites left of Mira's sandwich, but she wasn't sure she could finish even though it was delicious and Allison's appetite didn't seem to be affected—

Mira stilled, realizing they were eating together for the first time. Until then, Allison had always dined alone. Mira watched her take a last bite of a sandwich, unsure if she should comment on the fact or leave it be. She decided not to say anything that might make Allison self-conscious or cause her to retreat again, and finished off the last of her iced tea.

Allison belched loudly and covered her mouth, eyes going wide. Mira burst out laughing and Allison joined her a second later. "Sorry."

"It's a sign of a good meal, right?"

Allison nodded. "Gael makes the best food. It doesn't hurt he's super hot, too."

"Uh, yeah . . ."

Allison grinned. "Admit it. I don't think you would've spent so much time with him in the game room otherwise."

Mira squirmed in her seat, scrambling for something to say. Then she stilled. "How do you know that?"

"He told me." Allison dabbed absently at some chip crumbs with the pad of her finger and licked them away. "He also said he likes you. You guys would make a cute couple."

"I don't think—"

"Hey! I know what we can do since it's raining outside—hide-and-seek!" Allison stood from her chair, features alight. "The manor is the best to play in."

Mira opened her mouth to say no. She didn't want to play hide-and-seek; she wanted to lie down. Her head was buzzing strangely and she still felt a little sick to her stomach. But Allison was practically vibrating with anticipation.

"Okay, on one condition," Mira said, rising. "I hide. You seek."

"Thirty-four, thirty-five, thirty-six . . ."

Allison's voice followed Mira up the stairs to the second floor. She'd left Allison sitting in the dining room, hands pressed to her eyes like a child, counting loudly to a hundred. Mira's heartbeat quickened as she tested doorknobs on her floor, moving from room to room when they proved to be locked. She stopped at the corridor's T and glanced each way, trying to decide which direction to go.

"Fifty-seven, fifty-eight, fifty-nine . . ."

Mira doubled back as thunder exploded directly over the manor, the thick walls barely muffling the blast. She could hide in her room, since Allison might overlook it as too obvious, but the only place to conceal herself would be in the small closet. The goat's head was still in there, and she wasn't going to shut herself in a dark, cramped space with it.

"Seventy-one, seventy-two, seventy-three . . ."

She paused, mind leapfrogging ahead, then hurried up the stairs to the third floor, knowing exactly where she was going.

The library was cool and dark when she stepped inside, a few curtains drawn against the gray stormlight. The last numbers she'd heard drifting up the stairwell were in the nineties. Allison would be on the move soon, and Mira didn't know if she'd bother searching the first floor. Quietly as she could, Mira crossed the wide space and found the hidden room's panel. A stutter of lightning threw her shadow against the false wall and she paused. Was it really a good idea to go inside again? It obviously wasn't a reading nook or a place intended for guests, but what could it hurt? They were playing a game.

Mira slid the door aside and stepped in just as Allison called out from down the hall. "I'm going to fiiiiiiiiiind you!" Her voice oscillated eerily, as if it were far away and then almost in the same room. For a second, the game was lost and a rush of goosebumps covered Mira's body. She quickly resettled the door in its place and stepped back, wondering how Allison had known to come directly to the third floor. But would she search the library, since she had an aversion to it? Mira hadn't considered that. Now it seemed almost unfair.

She was lost in her thoughts, debating whether or not to give up and start over when Mira realized there was a draft in the room. And with it came the scent from the first time she'd been there—the subtle stink of decay. But now it was stronger. Slowly, she turned around.

The single lamp still burned just as she'd left it, illuminating the small space. Lightning flashed outside the triangular window, flaring book spines into relief. Everything was as it had been before.

Except now there was a new doorway in the opposite side of the room.

It took her a long moment to believe her eyes. She blinked, rubbing them, and looked again. The door was still there, a black rectangle slightly smaller than a typical entrance. Within the darkness, a single step of an ascending stairway was visible.

"Mira?"

Allison sounded much closer, maybe right outside the library. Part of her was already retreating—leaving the odd little hidden room that had somehow grown another doorway to rejoin Allison out in the hall where the air didn't reek of something dead.

Instead, she moved to the doorway and examined it. It looked like it had been cut perfectly between two other wooden panels, a tiny handle folded up that blended well with the rest of the scrollwork in the trim. The closer she came, the more of the stairway was revealed. The treads were bare wood and very old with rimes of dust covering their edges. But the centers were clear where regular footsteps had cleaned them.

And there was a light above.

"Mira?" Allison was farther away now, but her voice lingered in Mira's ears, as if there were an echo in her head. Mira placed a foot on the first stair and wobbled as a wave of vertigo swept over her. She put a hand against the wall, feeling rough wood and tasting dust in the air as well as the unpleasant undertone drifting down from above. Her stomach lurched and she shut her eyes again, but the dizziness only worsened. She opened them and took another step up, only then seeing she was no longer alone.

A head and shoulders peered down from near the top of the stairs.

It was only a vague outline, but its sudden appearance caused her stomach to plunge down so far, it seemed to press against her bladder, which threatened to give way.

The person swayed there as if searching the darkness where she stood. Mira tried to turn, tried to flee back through the passage, but she was paralyzed—a bird watching the hypnotic dance of a snake. Slowly, they came forward, their shadow growing and growing, elongating monstrously until she was sure they were not human. No person was that tall.

Her body was frozen, feet growing roots, skin trying to crawl away from what was coming down the stairs. The thing stopped a tread above her and bent forward. A hand came out of the dark, reaching toward her.

"You shouldn't be here." The voice was like wind in a hollow tree.

Everything was wrong.

The stairs were incongruent now, running sideways as well as up and down.

The light behind the figure was too harsh, forming a corona around it, darkening the body into a black hole.

Her head swam sickeningly and she flew apart from herself, dislocated and floating.

"You aren't ready."

Mira wrenched free of the paralysis and fell back into the hidden room, catching herself before she sprawled fully on the floor. Then she was up, careening through the short passage and clawing at the outer door. Her hands fumbled, pressing instead of pulling, and she imagined she felt the soft touch of fingertips grazing her shoulders.

Then she was out, stumbling past bookshelves as lightning flared the room white and thunder pursued her out of the library and down the hall.

28

"Tell me again, this time slower."

Mira rocked on the edge of a chair in Eleanor's office, arms wrapped tightly around herself as if to keep from falling apart. Some of the tension had eased, though her head still sloshed like a fishbowl if she moved it too fast. Eleanor sat across from her, leaning forward, brow furrowed. The older woman had found her curled up in the corner of the second-floor staircase landing. Mira didn't know how long she'd been there. In her panic, she'd only been able to relay bits and pieces of what had happened as Eleanor guided her down to her office. Allison had been nowhere in sight.

"We were playing hide-and-seek. I went to the library and hid in the secret room," Mira said. She gauged Eleanor's reaction to the mention of the hidden space, but she only nodded and motioned to go on. "I'm sorry; I just stumbled onto it and thought it would be a good place to hide, but there was something else inside . . ." The memory was a dark kaleidoscope—everything shifting strangely and melding with itself. Keeping it from collapsing completely caused a painful tightening in her skull. ". . . and I started feeling really sick. Then someone else was there with me."

"Who?"

How to explain the encounter when what little she recalled was even now trying to slip away? "I don't know; I couldn't see their face. They said something . . . but now I can't remember what it was."

A soft knock came from the doorway, and they both looked up as Gael entered with two cups of steaming tea. Eleanor had called the kitchen with the order upon sitting down in her office. "Here we go," Gael said, setting Mira's cup at her elbow. She kept her eyes down, blood heating her face until it felt like it could glow in the dark.

"Thank you, dear," Eleanor said.

"Everything okay?" Gael asked, pausing in the doorway. She could feel his eyes on her and hear the gentle concern in his voice, and she wanted nothing more than for him to go away.

"We're fine. Mira and I were just having a little chat." Gael nodded and headed off down the hall. Eleanor waited until his footsteps had faded before sitting forward. "Are you taking any medications? Anything that could've brought something like this on?"

"No. Nothing."

"And I hate to ask this, since it was part of the contract you signed, but you haven't indulged in any substances while you've been here?"

"Substances? No, of course not."

"Please don't take offense, but our overall concern is for Allison's well-being." Eleanor straightened. "How have you been feeling—emotionally?"

"I mean . . ." She considered the turmoil over the past days, how the past seemed to be closer than ever before. "Okay, I guess."

"I wonder if all of this might be too much, given your loss. I thought it could be a connection between you and Allison, but maybe it's too fresh. If you feel like you can't handle it, please say the word and we'll get you home."

Mira tried considering it, weighing how she felt, but she was too exhausted to think clearly. "I think right now, I just need to lie down."

"Of course. Let me help you to your room."

"That's okay; I can make it," Mira said, standing. For a second, she wondered if that were true as the floor tilted then steadied. But once she got moving, it was better.

"And if you ever need to talk," Eleanor said before Mira stepped into the hall, "I'm here."

She fell asleep almost as soon as she crawled into bed. There was the constant tap of rain against the windows and some halfhearted thunder, which retreated as she dropped deeper and deeper into sleep, then nothing. She woke later to the last murmurs of the storm, the rain now a silver mist—everything outside spun from spider's web.

She sat up and assessed herself. She felt . . . much better. Her head was clearer and there was no strange liquid shifting if she turned it too fast. The nausea was gone too and her hands didn't tremble when she held them out.

How have you been feeling—emotionally? Eleanor's question had caught her off guard. Was it that apparent she was struggling? Probably, since her father had always been able to tell when she was upset. It didn't matter how hard she tried hiding it; he would always find a quiet time when it was just the two of them and ask what was bothering her. Now she picked up her phone and opened their message string.

I don't know what's happening.
I thought I could handle things.
I've been trying to think what you would do.
But it's been really hard.
And I'm scared.
I hope I'm not disappointing you.
I love you.

Before she could stop herself, she hit Send. The progress bar grew and grew and finally flashed fully across the top of the screen. It had sent to his number, now disconnected and without a device associated with it. But her plea had flown across the airwaves to . . . somewhere. It was better than any prayer she could think of.

After splashing water on her face to wash away the tears, she checked the time. She'd missed dinner. That was okay; she wasn't hungry. And she didn't know if she could face anyone at this point. Eleanor surely would've told Oliver and Allison what had happened. At least, as much as she'd been able to relay. Now the memory was a vague echo. A story she'd told herself and barely remembered secondhand.

Her eyes fell on the Latin dictionary and she picked it up. The journal still felt strange in her hand as she paged toward the end and slowly began translating the final paragraphs. When she was finished, she read them, then looked out the window and let her gaze dissolve and become a part of the falling gray.

Follow and believe. In the void of faith lives folly. The way is made through flesh, through blood. Two can exist as one. Empty. Fill. Become.

And below that Winston Wyndclyffe had written:

In the end death is conquerable. It is a gauzy curtain we can look through. And if we know how, it can be drawn back to let the ones on the other side return.

I am ready.

Her hand shook as she set the journal down, and it rattled against the table. She sat staring at the little book and wished there was a fireplace in her room. If there had been at that second, she would've built a fire and tossed it in. Winston Wyndclyffe hadn't just been into collecting oddities of the occult; he'd been a believer. He'd lost his son Rasmus, and it had driven him to seek out some way to bring him back. She recalled what Allison had told her, how Leland had forced her to stay awake for days in the circle and recite the words from the journal. He'd put something in her tea; what had she called it . . .

Corpse hair.

Her stomach rolled. If Winston had been a believer, Leland had been something else, something more. A *practitioner.* Someone willing to submit his daughter to extreme psychological and emotional distress in an attempt to . . . what?

He wanted her hollowed out so something else could grow there.

No wonder Allison had moments when she seemed to be someone else. No wonder she was terrified of the outside world. With Leland's untreated illness hanging over her entire childhood like a smothering shadow, it was amazing she was still here at all.

Someone rapped sharply at the door.

Mira jerked. She'd been drifting deeply in her mind, unmoored in a sea of disturbing thoughts. The knocking came a second time, and she started for the door, hoping and dreading it was Gael.

Allison stood in the hallway, holding a dinner tray and looking apologetic in the dim light. "You weren't at dinner, so Eleanor asked me to bring this up."

Mira let her in and Allison set the tray on the nearest table, where she'd eaten breakfast yesterday, or was it the day before? Falling asleep so late in the day had skewed her sense of time. "Thanks. I can't believe I slept through dinner."

"No problem. Eleanor said you weren't feeling good."

"Yeah, sorry I . . ." How to explain what had happened, and how much to say to Allison? "I got sick and came back to my room. I couldn't find you," she finished lamely.

"More like I couldn't find you." Allison clapped her hands against her hips in twin little gunshots and smiled. "Where'd you hide?"

"Uh, the library," Mira said, sitting down in the loveseat.

"Oh." Allison blinked. "I never would've looked there."

"Yeah, sorry. I didn't think about it until after—"

Allison waved her apology away and paced around the room. "It's fine. It was just a game." Mira glanced down at the tray, took in the grilled chicken breast and mixed vegetables, the butter still softening and melting on a warm roll. It smelled heavenly but only partially aroused her appetite. She was reaching for the glass of ice water when Allison said, "What are you doing with this?"

She held up the journal and Mira's stomach sank.

"Oh, I—" Her mind whirred for a reasonable explanation, but after a second of taking in the creases on Allison's brow, she settled on the truth. "I found it and wondered what it was, so I started translating it."

Allison gave the book a look of disgust and tossed it down again. "If you already knew about the words, why did you ask?"

"I didn't—I mean I didn't know there was any connection, that your dad did that to you and this was what was guiding him." Allison shook her head and turned away, moving to the window. Mira squeezed her eyes shut. "I'm sorry." When Allison didn't reply, Mira rose and joined her at the window.

Evening had fallen and the shine of mist was duller. Dirty. Mira searched for something to say, some way to tell Allison she hadn't been snooping into her past, but realized that wasn't the truth. She had been. She'd gotten carried away by the mystery and sheer weirdness of it all. But now she'd alienated a friend.

Friend.

She hadn't stopped to think about it, but somewhere in the last few days, she'd begun to consider Allison one.

"I was wrong. I shouldn't have read it when I didn't know what it was and how it might affect you. I'm sorry." It felt like she'd done nothing but apologize the last few days.

Allison pressed her forehead against the window. Her breath fogged the glass. "You don't understand how he was," she finally said. "How *terrifying* he could be. You don't know what he wanted."

"What?" Mira heard herself ask. "What did he want?" They were close to the edge again, and she didn't want to do anything to push Allison over it.

Allison continued to stare out at the grounds, looking through the twin reflections of her own eyes. Then she stepped back and took Mira's hand. "I'll show you."

29

They came to a halt in front of the tall hedges.

Allison hadn't said a word since leaving the room, only beckoned her to follow as they went downstairs and out into the brisk evening air. Now she gestured at the wall of growth and waited while Mira looked it over. She shook her head and shrugged. "What?"

"You don't see it, do you."

"See what?"

Allison took two steps and vanished.

Mira jolted. "What the hell?" A second later, Allison reappeared, seeming to materialize from the hedges themselves.

"Crazy, right?"

Mira stepped to the left and slowly saw the hedges had been grown in a way so their lines overlapped, creating a narrow passage between. Allison gave her a smile that didn't touch her eyes and disappeared into the hedge again. After a second's hesitation, Mira followed.

The passage was so slim, it forced her to sidle along with the foliage scratching at her clothes and face like small, reaching hands. Allison was only a few feet ahead, but Mira lost sight of her every so often in the dense growth. Then Mira was free, stepping into the open and gathering her bearings.

The space was large, at least twenty yards square and hemmed in on all sides by the looming hedges. Shaggy grass grew around the feet of a wrought-iron bench near one edge. The only other features were a circle of statues and pillars protruding from the ground and a round stone dais situated in their center. A faded triangle was emblazoned on the dais's top. The clearing had a familiar empty, ominous feel she couldn't place. Leaves covered the ground in a carpet of faded red and gold. Allison stood off to one side, watching.

Mira considered her, then moved toward the middle of the space, leaves crackling under her feet. The sound was muffled in a strange way, the hedges devouring any noise she made. When she was close enough to the nearest sculpture, she stopped and regarded it for a time, a coldness seeping into her belly and making it tighten.

It was an effigy carved out of graying stone, anomalous overall, its shape resembling a man. But the proportions were wrong. It was as if the figure had been melted by a powerful heat, then molded into something distorted and inhuman. It hurt her eyes to look at it for too long. Below the sculpture was faint chiseling worn by time and weather.

Winston Wyndclyffe
1853 – 1920

She turned away from the carving fast enough to leave afterimages trailing behind. The next stone held another Wyndclyffe family member's name along with their birth and death dates. The same was true of all the rest of the circle.

This was a cemetery.

The earth over three of the graves was noticeably fresher—Leland and Vanessa's. But who was the third? "They buried all the family members here?" Allison nodded. "Why?"

"Tradition. But Winston and . . . my father used it for the becoming. This is where it was supposed to happen." Mira turned in a slow circle, taking all of it in once again. "This is where she was supposed to come back."

"Who?" Mira heard herself ask. The world had taken on a sickening watery quality again, and she rubbed the webbing between her thumb and forefinger, an old trick supposed to quell nausea.

Allison pointed to the third disturbed grave. "His mother," she finally said, spitting the words. "He thought he could bring her back."

Mira froze like she'd been struck. In a way, she had been. Struck by sudden clear understanding. Leland had found his mother dead by her own hand. What had that done to him? Done to his already-ill and troubled young mind? And when had he happened upon the journal? The one written by a relative who might've shared his same mental instability and annotated by a great-grandfather crushed by the loss of his own son. All the forbidden promises within, whispering of something impossible.

"He was going to bring her here at the equinox. He'd dug up his mother's coffin. He was going to put . . . put her inside. Make her stay until she . . . changed."

Mira moved toward the dais. It was raised six inches from the ground, its top beginning to pit from weather. She knelt at its edge and ran a hand over the cold surface, thinking of candles in the dead of night with the wind moaning across the grounds and shadowed figures huddled here, hoping for a dark miracle.

She drew her hand back and wiped it on her pants, yet the stain was internal—a mental oiliness. She took in the hidden cemetery again, finally seeing it for what it truly was. A place of hope for broken minds. A place that broke others.

"I didn't know," Allison said in a tear-choked voice. "I didn't know what he'd do." She stood with her head lowered, hands twitching at her sides.

Mira went to her then and held her. The other girl stiffened for a moment, then sagged, gasping a quiet sob into Mira's shoulder. "It's okay. It wasn't your fault."

"I didn't mean for it to happen. I swear."

"Shhh, it's okay. It's gonna be okay."

They stood there, swaying to the sound of Allison's grief, as the day lost the last of its light and darkness closed in around them.

SEPTEMBER 2021

Allison's bedroom door was open when she came back from the kitchen, a sandwich and fresh vegetables on a plate in one hand.

She slowed, then stopped in the hall. Her door was never open. She always kept it shut when she was inside and made sure she closed it behind her whenever going somewhere else in the house. A tingling flowed across her skin and tightened her scalp, the urge to turn around and go back to the dining room almost too strong to deny. Or maybe she could just walk out the front door and never come back. Start her escape now instead of waiting.

She had almost run the night after her parents' last fight. The next morning, after making sure they were completely alone, she'd asked her mother to leave, right that minute, but her mother had only gotten very quiet and said they couldn't. That certain arrangements weren't complete. This, paired with Isabelle's meddling, had almost driven her over the edge. She wanted to grab Isabelle and shake her; the only thing holding her back was the understanding of why she'd done it. She was trying to fix things, make them tolerable enough to keep from losing her best and only friend. Allison realized now she never should have told Isabelle they were leaving. As cruel as it was to run out on her with no explanation, it was worse wondering what she would do next to "help." Allison wanted to tell her this place was like Chernobyl or Three Mile Island, somewhere toxic that seeped into your bones and made you sick. They all needed to get out soon. The comparison to a nuclear meltdown haunted her. Not only because she could feel the radiation of her father's sickness but also because she felt the disaster hadn't fully arrived yet. That the worst was yet to come.

Allison gathered herself and stepped into her room.

Her father stood at her dresser, his back to her, head lowered. She could see his reflection in the mirror mounted to the dresser, how vacancy permeated his eyes, could see her hairbrush gripped in one white-knuckled hand.

"Dad?"

He set the brush down and turned to her, and for a brief second, the emptiness remained in his gaze. Then he blinked and smiled, his entire expression changing. He became someone else, the person she still loved.

"Hi. Was looking for you."

"I made a snack."

He crossed the room to her and there was a bounce in his step. *Manic,* she thought absently. *On one of his highs.* She saw a rollercoaster car poised at the very top of its track, a vertiginous drop plunging away into obscurity.

He gripped her by the shoulders and stared into her face. "Look at you. Can't believe how old you're getting. It was yesterday I was walking up and down these halls with you in my arms, trying to get you to fall asleep. I swear it was."

"That was a long time ago." She couldn't think of anything else to say. His fingers had increased their pressure. It was starting to hurt.

"Yes" was all he said, staring at her. His eyes had become hollow again.

Allison shifted, turning slightly to break his grip. "Dad, can I eat?"

He came back from wherever he'd gone. "Sure." He stepped past her, pausing at the door. "I'm going into town. I'll be gone for a while. Do you need anything?"

"No. That's okay."

He gave her one last look that took all of her willpower to endure, then was gone, his footsteps echoing down the hallway.

Allison sank to her bed and set the plate down on a nearby table, no longer hungry. She'd become accustomed to her father's alternating moods but still thought the highs were almost as bad as the lows. These times were filled with hugs and praise and activities he knew she enjoyed. They would watch movie after movie until her eyes ached, or go down to the pier and fish well into the early-morning hours. There was no denying him during these times; it was as if their family were being dragged behind a horse that had spooked. It was when his beliefs would bleed through the clearest, when he would insist that death wasn't the end, that it was just a thin barrier. That the departed were only inches away, waiting to be called back. She thought of him making her recite the terrible words from the journal, staying awake for days until it felt like what he was suggesting wasn't fantasy at all. Debilitated when he would call her by another name, hoping he would see someone else behind her eyes.

Thumpthump!

She was yanked so suddenly from her thoughts, she jumped. Someone had knocked on the door. At first, she was sure it would be her father again, but when she opened it, Isabelle's face appeared in the gap.

"Can I come in?" When Allison didn't answer, she swallowed thickly and said, "Please?"

Allison caved, making room next to her on the bed. Isabelle sat and they stayed that way for a minute, neither looking at one another. Finally, Allison offered her the sandwich and veggies, but Isabelle blanched and shook her head as if the sight had made her sick. Up close she was very pale. "Your dad's gone," Isabelle said, after another uncomfortable silence. "I watched him go down to the boathouse and across the river."

"Yeah, he was going into town."

Isabelle nodded, looking out one of the windows. "I'm really sorry," she whispered. When Allison looked at her, there were tears standing in the other girl's eyes.

She sighed and readjusted herself so she faced her friend. "I know. But do you realize what you did?" Isabelle was still for moment, then nodded. "You can't do anything like that again."

"I just . . . I don't know what I'm going to do without you."

"You'll be okay. Someday soon, you'll leave here too. You'll go on to other places and things, meet new people."

But Isabelle was shaking her head. "You don't understand. I can't. I—"

"Your mom will help. She's been looking into a new remote therapy." Allison halted, realizing what she'd said. She wasn't supposed to know Isabelle's last treatment plan had been a failure. "I mean—"

Isabelle's tear-filled eyes narrowed. "It's easy for you, right? Just run away and start over. You can go make new friends anywhere."

"Izzy, I'm sorry—"

"Don't call me that!" Isabelle stood and pressed her fists to her sides. Her complexion became blotchy with anger. "I won't be okay. But who cares, right?" She turned and went to the door as Allison rose.

"I'm sorry."

Her friend stood with her back to her for a long beat. When she turned, Allison expected the anger to be gone and the tears to have returned. But what she saw instead made her retreat a step.

Isabelle's face was as blank as one of her mother's virgin canvases. It was as if she'd taken a fast-acting sedative and was about to go under. She stared at Allison. *Through* her. "Maybe it will be okay. Maybe it will. I guess we'll see."

Then before Allison could reply, Isabelle slipped through the door and was gone.

30

I *didn't mean for it to happen. I swear.*

The cold cramp of fingers touched her throat and begin to squeeze as she struggled, up, up through black liquid until a ceiling materialized beyond the darkness, and it wasn't fingers but a sheet wet with sweat, drawn taut against the skin of her neck as she rolled over and pulled it away.

Mira sat up, legs hanging over the edge of the bed, and tried breathing deeply, but her lungs hitched and she struggled to regain control. Gradually, her galloping pulse slowed and the nightmare's grip loosened. She'd been drowning. She could still see the dark water over her head, miles of it separating her from oxygen. And she hadn't been alone either; there'd been someone else there in the deep with her.

Allison.

She'd been floating beside Mira, pale and lifeless, but her voice had spoken in Mira's head just the same, repeating what she'd said in the hidden graveyard the night before.

Mira went to the bathroom and tried showering the dream away. But even the near-scalding water sluicing over her skin couldn't erase all the chill she'd felt in the fathomless depths. She couldn't recall ever having so many vivid nightmares other than right after her parents passed away. In the weeks following the crash, she'd dreamed of the accident—the buckled steel of her parents' car, broken glass glinting in the harsh glare of emergency lights, the smell of scorched metal and hair. And the phone. Ringing and ringing and ringing. Each time, she'd woke sick and sweating, a cry for her parents barely held back.

As she dressed, she decided it was stress along with being in the manor itself fueling the nasty dreams. The place was getting to her, slowly revealing its cracks and blemishes like any house with a long and troubled history.

Still feeling as if she'd been chiseled from a block of sleep, she made her way downstairs toward the dining room, stopping short to listen to the low voices coming from the kitchen's open door. She hesitated, then inched closer, taking care not to make a sound.

"It's not what you told me." Gael said, an uncustomary edge to his voice.

"It wasn't what I wanted, but think about what's at stake," Eleanor responded. "Think of what will happen to her if we don't follow through."

"I don't know."

"You already agreed." Eleanor's voice dropped lower. "Don't forget that."

A clatter of dishes came from the dining room and Mira's insides shriveled. She waited to hear more from the kitchen, but the silence stretched out, and it felt like Gael and Eleanor were listening too. Slowly, she crept away toward the dining room and walked in as naturally as possible. Oliver was leaning against the far doorway, eating an apple. He nodded to her as she came in.

"Good morning," Eleanor said a moment later as she swept in behind Mira. "How is everyone? Well rested, I hope."

"Definitely," Mira said, taking a seat at the table as Eleanor set a cup of steaming coffee before her.

"Wonderful. I noticed you and Allison were out for a while last night."

Mira nodded, drinking deeply. "She . . . showed me the cemetery."

Both Oliver and Eleanor visibly stiffened. "Really?" Eleanor said, turning around. "I'm sorry about that. Did it upset you?"

"Yes," she said, deciding not to be polite.

"Understandable," Oliver said. "Not common these days."

Mira hesitated. "Allison told me what Leland used it for."

Eleanor sighed and lowered herself into a chair. "I see. I suppose you have questions."

"Well, yes, but I think I mostly understand."

"You'd be the first," Oliver said. "His parents failed in getting him help, and then those strange . . . *beliefs* took hold."

"He never got over his mother's death. He would've believed

anything to ease the suffering," Eleanor said. "Ollie and I approached Vanessa about putting a stop to it, but she was afraid of what Leland would do." She paused, studying Mira in a way that made her want to squirm in her seat. "I'm surprised Allison was able to talk about it."

"Me too. She—" How to form the thought she'd been wrestling with since the night before? She didn't want to betray Allison's confidence, but these were the two people who cared about her the most. "She kept saying it was her fault. I think she was talking about what Leland did, but—"

"She's always felt guilty," Eleanor interrupted. "I've told her over and over it wasn't her fault, but she still blames herself."

"Why?" Mira asked. Oliver had paused in eating his apple and only held it loosely in one hand, his gaze introspective.

"Because she was going to run away right before it happened. Vanessa had made plans for them to disappear, but Leland found out somehow and . . ." She let the rest of the implications hang in the air. "I still believe he would've done the same thing even if he hadn't been ill. He was deeply possessive, and his wife was attempting to leave him and take their child with her. And like many men, he reacted with violence."

Mira digested this. It made sense now. Allison's disassociations, her catatonia, her fear of leaving the island. She believed she'd been responsible for setting her father on the course which killed both her parents.

The silence in the room was broken as Oliver cleared his throat and glanced at the remainder of his apple with a look of disdain before throwing it in the garbage. "Well, if you'll both excuse me, my mistresses—lath and plaster—await my company on the third floor." He left the room, his footsteps echoing down the hallway in short clips.

"It's hard for him," Eleanor said when he'd gone. "As far as guilt goes, he harbors a lot himself. We all do. You wonder if you could've done things differently. You wish you had."

Mira flashed on the night her father had gone to pick up her mother. So many small choices were the seeds from which ruin grew.

"Would you like more coffee?" Eleanor said, bringing her back. Mira glanced down into her cup.

There were coils of gray hair at the bottom.

She threw the cup away from herself. It skidded across the table, tipping over and splashing dregs of coffee as it rolled. Eleanor snatched it before it could fall to the floor. "What's wrong?"

"There—there was something in the cup."

Eleanor gazed into it, then turned it toward her. Mira couldn't get herself to look for a moment, the image of the *(corpse hair)* floating in the coffee made her want to scream.

But when she finally brought her gaze up, the cup was empty except for a few splashes of coffee. There was no hair. Nothing.

"I'm—I'm sorry. I thought there was . . ." Eleanor waited, watching her quizzically. ". . . a bug. I thought I saw a bug or something."

"Well, nothing there now. Would you like me to fix another cup?"

"No. No, I'll get it."

Eleanor appraised her again. "All right, then. Will you be needing anything else before you begin the day?"

Her mind freewheeled, then caught. "Do you know if Jeff was able to fix the boat motor? I was wondering if he could take us to town."

"I'm not sure. See if you can track him down. It would be a major step for Allison." She flashed a brief smile and left the room.

Mira remained for a time where she was, listening to the sounds of the manor, listening for the stealthy footsteps of someone in the hall. After another hesitant inspection of her cup, she counted the fruit. Counted all the bananas, the apples, every grape. She went to the fridge and looked inside. She wasn't hungry at all but thirsty. A glass of cold water, drained in four long swallows.

When she stepped outside a short time later, the sun was hiding behind a shawl of clouds stretching from horizon to horizon. Mira tried using the landmarks around her as much as she could and positioned herself in what she thought was the right spot, then pulled out her phone. There wasn't a single bar until she'd moved a dozen yards to the north, then it only flickered briefly as she hit Shay's contact and listened as static growled in her ear. Faded ringing. Louder, gone again. Silence. She turned slightly and the quiet changed in the earpiece. "Hello?" she said.

An intake of breath. "Wow, —at's how you start? —ello?" Shay said.

She wasn't ready for the rush of emotion at hearing her friend's voice. Mira had to swallow thickly before replying. "Hey, the connection's bad here. How's it going?"

"—oing? You send me that emai—how it's going?" The connection picked up and dropped, chopping Shay's voice every few words.

"What was that?"

"—ome nerve, girl. Seriously, I don't—at all. Never thought I'd be called smothering in my life."

Mira squinted into the bright gray horizon. "What the hell are you talking about?"

"I can only hear every other word, so—enough in the email. You wait this long to call—guessing you need something?"

"I don't know—"

"—worth my time. When you come back, hit me up—more yourself."

The line went dead.

Mira blinked and looked at the screen. Still one bar. The connection had dropped. Or Shay had hung up on her. "What the fuck?" she whispered, and punched Shay's number again. There was the same static crackle, then Shay's voicemail telling her to leave a message if she wanted.

Mira hung up, a strange hollowness in her center. The call had been spotty, but she knew her best friend's tone of voice, had heard Shay annoyed and full-blown pissed before. This had been somewhere in between.

You wait this long to call?

This long . . . a week, ten days? How long since she'd spoken to her? Mira swiped a hand across her face. The emptiness within her had taken on a weight, and it sank as Shay's voice continued ringing in her ears.

When she opened up her email, she ignored Unread and went straight to the Sent file. Inside she scrolled through dozens of messages over the last three weeks, quickly at first, then very slow.

None. There were none to Shay. Why send her an email when they texted?

She stared at the phone for another beat, then found Village Garden's contact and rang it. A moment later, a woman's voice bloomed out of the static.

"Hello, Village Garden Care Center, —isty —eaking."

"Hi, Misty? Can you hear me?"

"—llo? The connection's really bad."

"Yes, sorry." Mira moved a desperate step to the left. Static crackled, step to the right, it faded to a loud whisper. "How about now?"

"—hear you —ittle better. How can I help you?"

"This is Mira Caine, Aaron's sister. I was wondering if I could speak to him?"

"—rip. —ot sure who. Maybe call ba—."

Mira swore under her breath. "Okay, I'll try later. But could you do something for me? Do the 'shave and a haircut' knock for him? He'll know it's from me."

"—aking up."

"'Shave and a haircut'; he'll do the other half."

"Sorry, you—ception's better. Bye."

The line went dead.

She held the phone out, wanting to throw it, wanting to cry, not doing either.

The better part of her was already back in her room packing, hauling the bags down the stairs and telling Oliver and Eleanor she was leaving. She was in the boat with Jeff piloting across the water to Yellow Bay. She was in the car, heading south through hills toward the city.

She let it play out in her head until the end, until she was hugging Aaron and he was smiling at her and then she was apologizing to Shay and trying to make up for whatever the hell she'd done to piss her off.

Then she was back in her tiny room with its thin walls and cold floors, not really any closer to leaving the city. Nothing had actually changed. Her parents were still gone.

She was still alone.

31

"I'm not really sure I feel up to it."

Allison lay on her side in the middle of her bed while Mira perched on the footboard. She had been quiet and morose since Mira knocked on her door, the room dark and cool as if reflecting the other girl's mood.

"It's a pretty nice day out. Kinda cloudy but warm," Mira prompted. There was a small stab of guilt in urging Allison off the island, but it was overshadowed by the need to know she wasn't trapped here. Wasn't being held by hidden shackles. That it was only her imagination telling her she couldn't leave. "Eleanor said it was fine. We just need to find Jeff and ask him."

Allison's eyes traveled slowly around the room as if searching for something before she rolled over, facing the opposite wall. Mira grimaced and thought for a moment, then rounded the bed to sit on the other side. She put one hand on Allison's ankle. "Hey." When she finally looked up Mira said, "If you're worried about last night, don't be. I know you feel responsible, but you aren't."

Allison was quiet so long, Mira thought she wasn't going to respond. Then she shifted and sat up, wrapping her arms around her knees. "You don't understand," she said in a near-whisper.

Mira weighed something, measured its heft. Like all heavy things, it felt almost harder to set down than to keep carrying. "I might." When she felt Allison's eyes fully on her she let out a long breath and said, "The night my parents died, Dad was running late—he was answering emails from his boss on a Sunday night, and he was in a hurry. I remember him putting on his coat at the door and slipping on his shoes and—" She smiled but still felt the tears surface anyway. "We were out of my favorite ice cream and I almost asked him to stop to get some, then I didn't. I could see he was stressed and Mom was waiting to be picked up from her yoga thing, so I didn't ask. But that's what would have saved them. Not even him actually stopping to get the ice cream. Maybe just pausing to tell me no. That would've done it; that would have been enough."

Mira swiped at her eyes and tried smiling again but it wouldn't stay. Allison watched her, pale and still. "But what I realized later is anything could have changed things, not just me. Dad could've blown off his emails until Monday and left earlier. Mom could've stayed for one extra class. Even the drunk that killed them could've had another round before leaving the bar—but it all lined up just right." She focused on Allison. "That's how life goes. It comes together to make a miracle, or it takes everything away. But blaming yourself when you're only a small part of what happened isn't fair."

Allison was still for so long, Mira imagined her as a statue—stone instead of flesh and blood. Then the spell was broken as she sat forward and reached out, and Mira was there, holding her again.

This time there were no tears, only a long embrace that felt like an understanding. A promise.

When they parted, Allison stared down into her lap. "I'm sorry about your mom and dad. I don't think I ever said that."

"Thanks."

"I guess when it's your pain, it feels special. Like it's the only kind in the world." Allison sniffled once and glanced around. "You said it's nice out?" Mira nodded, giving her a half-smile. "Then let's go find Jeff."

Catchuk. Thunk.

Catchuk. Thunk.

The sound carried across the grounds, echoing off the trees. Jeff hadn't been in front of the manor or down at the boathouse where they first searched. The rear grounds had been empty as well but held a lingering scent of mown grass hanging in the air. He was somewhere close.

Catchuk. Thunk.

There it was again, louder now. Mira and Allison headed for the garage, rounding the corner of the building, and the groundskeeper finally came into view.

Jeff stood with his back to them, holding something Mira had only seen in movies before. He pointed the crossbow down and put one foot through the ring at its front while cocking the weapon's string with both hands. Then he slid a compact arrow into a groove at its center and put the stock to his shoulder, gazing through a scope at a life-size foam deer target at least fifty yards away. After a moment's aim, he pulled the trigger.

The crossbow's string snapped forward. *Catchuk.*

Quicker than Mira could track, the arrow zipped downfield and buried itself in the deer's foam side among half a dozen others. *Thunk.*

Mira turned to see Allison's reaction, but she was no longer beside her. She must've stopped prior to coming within sight of Jeff. Slightly annoyed, Mira stepped forward and said, "Hey, Jeff?"

"Yeah?" The groundskeeper didn't startle or even look at her. Mira hadn't made a sound approaching him, yet he seemed fully aware of her presence.

"We were wondering if you could take us to town."

Jeff cocked the crossbow again. "Told ya, motor's busted."

"I thought you said you were getting parts." Mira heard the distress tinging her voice but couldn't help it.

Jeff glanced at her before nocking another arrow. "Weren't the right parts." He shouldered the weapon, aimed, and fired. The arrow lodged itself in the deer's neck and shoulder joint.

"Any idea when it'll be fixed?"

"Maybe tomorrow."

"Could you let us know when it is?" Jeff gave her a long blank stare, then turned away and cocked his weapon again.

She almost started to say something else, something she knew she might regret. Instead, she bit the words back and let them burn and dissolve on her tongue like bitter medicine. At the front of the garage, she found Allison waiting in the shade of the overhang. "Sorry, I just couldn't get myself to talk to him. Especially when he's shooting that thing."

"He said the boat isn't fixed yet," Mira said once they'd started walking again. "He's such a grumpy bastard."

"For real."

"I'm surprised Eleanor puts up with him."

"Oh, he's not like that with her. It's all 'Yes, ma'am' and 'No, ma'am.'" Allison giggled. "I think she's the one person on the island he's afraid of."

Mira threw a last look over her shoulder as they neared the manor, but the grounds were empty except for the sound echoing across them.

Catchuk. Thunk.

32

Feeling okay, Mira?"

She looked up from her half-eaten dinner at Eleanor across the table. Took in her concerned eyes. They were alone in the dining room, since Oliver had wanted to put the finishing touches on the plaster job. It was the first time they'd eaten without him, and his absence was tangible. "I'm fine. Just have a headache."

"Fresh air's always the best cure," Gael said, sweeping into the room. He was carrying the dessert course—a picture-perfect cherry pie—and when he looked at Mira, his gaze lingered. "At least, that's what my mom always said."

"Would you like some aspirin?" Eleanor asked.

"No, that's okay. Thanks."

"Let me know if you change your mind. No need to suffer."

Gael gave her a last look and left the room as quickly as he'd entered. Mira watched the door swing shut behind him, pulled back from her thoughts when Eleanor cleared her throat.

"How was the afternoon? Do anything fun?"

"We went for a walk and watched a movie."

"Wonderful. And how was she feeling?"

"Fine, I think." Mira replayed the afternoon, Allison's mood continuing to rise until she was laughing so hard at something Mira had said, tears sprang from the corners of her eyes. "Yeah, she's good."

"Great to hear. And how about you?" There was a lot unsaid in the question. Mira thought of throwing the coffee cup that morning and pushed the image of the gray hair away.

"I'm okay. A little tired."

Mira reached for the pie, unable to resist the smell wafting from it. She cut herself a piece, then offered it to Eleanor, who waved a hand.

"I couldn't possibly." She wiped her mouth with a napkin and rose. "I should go check on Ollie, see if I can be of any help."

When she'd gone, Mira ate her pie, not intending to wolf it down but not being able to stop once she started. Before she could tell herself she shouldn't, she ate a second piece. When she'd finished, she made her way out to the front entrance, checking the kitchen on the way, then continuing outside.

The night had cooled, and a breeze drifted up from the river, carrying its alkaline scent. The moon hung behind wisps of a cloud, and she tried recalling when it had begun to wane. Something caught her attention along the manor's side and she headed that way, stopping when she was a dozen steps from the corner where the tall shrubbery grew. The ember of a cigarette she'd spotted flared again.

"Headache better?" Gael asked from the darkness.

"Much." She tugged her jacket tighter around her shoulders.

"Told you." The cigarette tip blossomed again, revealing his face, eyes dancing in the glow.

Mira's stomach fluttered as if a feather were sliding across it, and she looked up at the sky. "It's really pretty tonight. My mom knew all the names of the full moons." She paused. "I can't remember any of them."

Without replying, Gael began moving toward the river. She fell in step beside him as more and more stars bloomed to life above. When they reached the overlook, they stopped, the twinkling lights of homes across the river and the greater expanse of the lake unfurling before them. Gael finished his cigarette and tucked away the butt.

"I didn't know you smoked," she said.

"I don't. Not really. I have about one a week. Calms the nerves."

So, he was nervous too. It wasn't only her whose heart was picking up speed and who was deeply aware of how close their shoulders were, how their hands dangled only inches apart.

"Dinner was really spectacular," she said, needing to say something. "Especially the pie."

"Thank you."

Mira waited but he offered nothing more. Somewhere a bird called, saying goodnight to the world as the breeze lifted her hair and nudged the clouds from the moon. She was about to comment on the night for something to say when he spoke instead.

"Your brother, he lives in an assisted facility, right?"

It caught her off guard. "Yes."

"The two of you . . . you're close?"

"He's—" *the only person I have left,* she almost said. "He's very, very special."

"Anyone else? Another special man?" He hesitated. "Or woman?"

She smiled a little. "No, no one at the moment."

Gael seemed to absorb this as the wind danced a flurry of leaves around their ankles. Talking to him out here when she could be inside in the warmth and light was uncharacteristic of her, strange and a little wild, and it felt . . . good. His arm was pressed against hers, and there were nervy twists in her center she tried mentally to smooth out. He was just a guy—a shockingly handsome one—but still a guy. She'd dated before, been in love, or thought so, and felt the ragged tear of heartbreak. But there was no denying the promise of something new and exciting. "How about you?" she finally managed.

He was a long time answering. "No, not anymore."

He turned to her then, moved a little closer. One of his hands found hers and her heart stumbled, then sprinted. His breath puffed in the cool air, and she could feel his warmth. The moonlight was strong enough to see he was looking at her in a way that was both hypnotic and unnerving. Like a judgement. As she started to lean closer, he said, "I think you're a lovely woman. Really kind, as far as I can tell."

"Thank . . . thank you."

"I want you to understand something. It's . . . complicated. Difficult. I haven't been completely—"

He turned his head as if he'd heard something. She listened too but there was only the wind. "What is it?"

Gael was still squeezing her hand and now he gripped it tighter, almost to the point of pain. He leaned close again and for a horribly wonderful second, she knew he was going to kiss her. She wasn't ready, but was anyone ever really ready for a first kiss? Wasn't that what made it so beautifully frightening? So real?

She closed her eyes, waiting for his lips to press to her own.

Instead, the smoothness of his cheek brushed hers and he whispered, "You should leave here. Now."

Then he let go and moved swiftly away into the dark, a shadow one second, gone the next.

She was so stunned, she didn't call out after him. Only stood there wavering between anger and confusion. It had to be a joke. He'd reappear out of the dark with a smile and a laugh, and they'd pick up where they left off, even if his sense of humor and timing was odd. So, when the sound of footfalls headed her way, she was ready to laugh along with him even if it wasn't really funny. But then she realized the footsteps were coming from the direction of the manor, opposite the way he'd gone.

She was frozen in place, torn between standing her ground and hiding. Then adrenaline overshadowed reason and she ducked, hurrying low and fast to the trail leading toward the river. When she reached the first trees, she left the path and hunkered low behind an oak's trunk, listening over the rush of blood in her ears.

There.

Heavy, plodding footsteps. Familiar enough she wasn't surprised to see who it was when he appeared.

Jeff materialized out of the gloom and passed by her hiding spot without stopping. His boots scuffed loudly on the paved path and he coughed, hawking and spitting into the underbrush a few feet from where Mira crouched. Then he was trundling out of sight, the night darkening as another layer of clouds slid across the moon.

She remained completely still, an irrational fear overtaking her. *What if Jeff's hiding and waiting for me to move so he can grab me and haul me off into the woods?* But when she stepped back onto the path, it was empty and the night was quiet except for the faint sound of the groundskeeper's passage.

Mira took a step in the direction of the river. Then another, and another, until she was creeping steadily downward through the trees. She didn't fully understand why she was following him instead of returning to the manor. It was a reflexive urge, like scratching a maddening itch. *What's he doing, and why is he out here so late?* Mira picked her way carefully along the path, stopping to listen every so often to make sure Jeff hadn't paused as well and she'd stumble into him around the next curve.

Gradually, the river came into view along with the stairs leading down to the pier. Jeff wasn't at the top, and when Mira sidled to the edge and peered down, he was nowhere in sight. With hesitant steps she made her way down, pausing every so often until she was at the bottom. Small waves lapped and chuckled around the pier, and the clouds slid free of the moon, illuminating Jeff standing a few yards away off the path to the boathouse.

Her center turned to frozen lead, every muscle seizing. Any second, he would stride forward and grab her, do something terrible to her. And she would be powerless, locked in place. Jeff hummed something off-key that sent a silent shiver through her, and then she registered the shine of his eyes fastened on the moon as if in a daze.

Without daring to breathe, she inched backward until a tree blocked him from sight and she crouched again, making herself as small as possible. Everything seemed to slow, the night gelling until she felt as if she were underwater. The faint sound of crickets elongated into a grating rasp.

Then Jeff was moving again, huffing away down the path toward the boathouse. Mira stood and wobbled, a swirl of vertigo in her head. She slunk after him, staying well back and hidden in the shadows on the side of the path.

Jeff reached the boathouse and went inside, slamming the door behind him. She crept a few more paces and froze again as a sound echoed out of the structure's open end, loud and unmistakable in the night air.

A moment later, the boat appeared in the river before its engine rose to a howl and sped away from the island into the darkness.

33

The night breathed around her.

She was caught inside a set of giant lungs, everything contracting and expanding sickeningly. Mira lurched up the last of the path and out of the trees, the manor's lights coming into view. At first, she'd thought it was the adrenaline crash, but as she moved, the sensation only got worse.

She tried calming her heart rate with several deep breaths, but the air tasted strange and made her head swoon more. She needed to get to the manor, needed to tell Eleanor Jeff was lying about the boat being broken. Needed to—

She stumbled and fell, a rock biting into the skin of her knee. She pushed herself up and pressed on, trying to beat back the nausea foaming in her stomach. She felt like she had while playing hide-and-seek, only worse.

The manor's steps loomed and she made it up them, swaying and nearly falling backward at the top, then she was inside and moving down the hall to Eleanor's office. The door was shut tight and locked. She knocked and the sound hurt her ears. Part of her wanted to move along the corridor and find Eleanor's bedroom, but a stronger urge turned her toward the stairs, toward her room. She needed to lie down, needed to calm herself because there was something wrong—Gael had said . . . he'd said . . .

But there was only an image of his face there in her mind and the softness of his cheek against hers. She so wished she would have kissed him, felt the warm press of his lips and his body so close and real.

She found herself in front of the large painting of the woman's displaced features. As she watched, they slowly aligned themselves. The face became whole. Familiar. Mira swayed and put one hand out to steady herself. When she touched the painting, it was back to its original state, the face scattered once more. Her eyelids fluttered and she staggered away and up the steps.

The stairs were fading in and out. First they were there, then they were something else. They were smoothing out, no longer steps at all but a road she was walking up. And she knew this road. Knew it so well.

It was a driveway she hadn't seen in years.

She wore no shoes or socks and the gravel bit the soles of her feet, but she didn't pause or move to the grass strip beside the drive. It was early morning and dew slicked every surface, muting the vibrant greens of the brush and purples of the blooming alfalfa. It dripped from oak leaves overhanging the driveway of her childhood.

Wind blew across the fields, ruffling her hair and clothes, and it was such a pleasant sensation, she closed her eyes, knowing she could walk all the way to the house in the distance without needing to look. She was home.

The yard opened up and she took it in, memories of playing catch and tag with Aaron rising and falling away, of her father guiding her and her bike without training wheels for the first time along the sidewalk, his hand steady and then gone. Of her mother standing in the picture window, looking out as they played in the snow, one hand clasped near her chest as if to hold her heart in place.

Mira moved to the window and looked in.

They were there, gathered around the table in the soft morning light. Her family.

Aaron sat on the far side of the table, head down over his bowl of cereal, eating with the mechanical efficiency she always marveled at, his spoon never spilling a drop of milk. Her mother was to the right of him, sipping a steaming cup of coffee, both hands holding the mug, looking across to the man who sat there. Mira's father. He was reading a newspaper flattened on the table, absently chewing a piece of toast. And beside him, with her back to the picture window, was Mira herself.

Mira pressed against the glass, fingers and breath leaving foggy smears on the surface. There was a reason she was here, if she could remember. Then it came unbidden and she felt the bottom drop out of her stomach.

She could warn her, warn her younger herself. Tell her to ask her dad to stop for ice cream years down the road. She could ask her mother to skip her yoga retreat. She could change everything.

She tapped on the glass. Gentle at first, then harder until she was pounding and saying her own name. Her father and mother looked up, but she needed her own attention; otherwise, it wouldn't work. Slowly, young Mira turned her head toward her, looking over one shoulder, and Mira's breath hooked in her chest, refusing to move.

It wasn't her.

It was some other girl at the table eating with her family. Except when Mira looked again, her mother and father were different too, strangers. Aaron was older, longer hair—not Aaron at all, not her brother. This was another family, not hers.

Mira stepped back from the window, arms and hands held up as if she were still pressing against the pane, and she felt like the glass was all around her now. Like she was trapped inside a box she couldn't see and it was closing in. Getting tighter until it pressed against her chest, constricted her lungs as she fought to draw in air that wouldn't come.

Her foot caught on something and the world tipped.

The house fell away along with the morning light.

She landed hard on her stomach, the last of her breath whooshing out, blowing dust from the stair treads she'd fallen on.

She was partway up a set of stairs and it was dark, only faint light seeping down from somewhere above. Mira tried pushing herself up, but her muscles were weak and watery. After a struggle, she was able to get fully upright and swayed there in the dark.

She was two parts. One was her body, taking in and sending out information to the second: her mind. Except the connection between them was faulty. Her thoughts were fluid and running, soaking through the fabric of her brain and bleeding outward. She couldn't control them, so she tried just feeling instead.

Cold. She was cold and her feet were bare. She should move. Find somewhere familiar, somewhere to rest. Half-falling forward, she climbed, instinctually moving toward the light rather than away from it. As she went, she tried recalling how she'd gotten there. A moment before, she'd been at her old house, at home, but that was impossible because . . . Her memory betrayed her again, ending in a gray wall.

What had she been trying to do? Had it been a dream? Two more stairs, then she emerged into a large room.

It was long with high ceilings. To the left was a tall stack of storage bins and old lumber. The rest faded into shadow. To the right, a steel ladder angled upward to some kind of hatch in the ceiling. And straight ahead was a lamp illuminating two chairs.

One of them was occupied.

"Hello?" Mira croaked. The scene before her brightened, then wavered, a mirage in the desert, and for a second, the view through the picture window was there again. Not her family looking out at her, other people. Then she was moving forward, falling and catching herself before she hit the floor. "Where . . ." She trailed off as she looked around again, trying to make sense of where she was and why. Her memory was a road dead-ending in a towering gray wall that went up forever.

The person in the chair hadn't moved, and Mira wondered if she were speaking aloud or in her head. She tried again. "Hi, I . . . I don't know where I am." For a terrifying moment, she didn't know *who* she was. Then a semblance of self came back. She was . . . Mira. She was trying to help someone, here to help . . .

What was that smell?

For some reason, the scent hanging in the air made her think of a mountain goat with staring black eyes. Dead eyes. She made her way unsteadily into the pool of light. The person—it was a woman with dark hair she could see now—was looking away to her left. Mira sidled around between the chair and the light, the woman's face slowly coming into view.

Her features were smeared, and Mira blinked, trying to focus. "Sorry, I—" she began, but then her eyesight cleared. Mira staggered to the side and fell, trying to catch herself on the lamp, but it toppled with her.

The lamp bounced off the other chair and hit the floor.

The bulb burst in a hiss and went out.

But not before she saw herself sitting in the chair.

Her knees unhinged and she sat down hard on the floor, scooting backward until her shoulders bumped something solid and she let out a quiet moan.

She was sitting in the chair.

She was sitting on the floor.

All she could see was the outline of herself there, staring off into the dark.

Then her head turned, facing her fully.

Mira skittered away, away from the chair and her twin watching her in the dark. She could feel eyes like fingers, touching, probing. And soon she'd feel hands, grasping and pulling her back. In her mind, images played on an endless reel.

A car crash.

A boy drawing.

Her family at the breakfast table, all of them strangers, staring at her coldly.

Hands came out of the dark and grabbed her shoulders.

Mira screamed, but she was already being hauled to her feet and hurried away.

"How did she get up here?" a voice said to her left.

"No idea."

"Do you think—"

"Hush."

Mira tried scrambling away, but her equilibrium was gone and she only managed to tip sideways again. The hands steadied her, but she was falling, falling toward a wall the color of smoke building itself higher and higher into eternity.

34

A tapping brought her up out of the gray.

Mira opened her eyes to see a bird flitting from the alcove of her bedroom window. A faultless blue sky burned outside so brightly, she had to look away. The middle of her skull throbbed like a toothache; her mouth was sour and dry.

She tried sitting up, waiting for the repercussions, which came in gradient waves of pain that slowly became manageable. She slid from the bed and swayed, meaning to go to the bathroom, but there was something wrong. It took her a few seconds to realize she didn't remember going to bed the night before. In fact, she didn't remember anything of the prior evening. The last recollection she had was eating dinner, and then . . . nothing.

She took the downcast puzzlement with her to the bathroom and relieved herself before washing her face. She felt hungover but more so than she'd ever been in her life. Had she been drinking? No, she wasn't much for booze in the first place, and she definitely wouldn't have sneaked any here with so much at stake. She wasn't going to disappoint . . .

Her mind grasped at empty air. Names and faces floated just out of reach. Tension ran through her chest to the middle of her back like an arrow. Why couldn't she remember the people's names who were here on the island?

"It's okay, it's okay, just calm down and go back," she whispered aloud. Speaking did some good, and gradually her mind quieted. She was at the Wyndclyffe estate to help . . . Allison. Eleanor and Oliver, they were the caretakers. And Gael and . . . Jeff.

An uncomfortable swell came and went with the thought of the groundskeeper, but she couldn't say why. She concentrated on it for a moment before letting it go. She was okay, she was safe, she'd just—

Just what? Had a mental break?

She sank back onto the bed, reeling internally. Could she have hit her head? That might explain the pain, but when she probed her skull gently, there were no bumps or lacerations anywhere. Just as she was attempting to get up again, a knock came at the door, Eleanor's voice floating through a second later.

"Are you awake?"

"Um . . . yeah."

"May I come in?"

She glanced around, noting she was still in her sleeping clothes but not able to summon the will to change. "Sure."

Eleanor entered, carrying a tray with a lid over. "You weren't at breakfast, so I decided to bring something—" She stopped short when she caught sight of Mira. "Are you all right?"

"I think so; I'm just—" *What? What was she?* "I didn't sleep well."

Eleanor set the tray down and came to sit beside her. "Are you sick?"

"I don't know."

Eleanor placed a cool palm against her forehead and Mira shut her eyes, leaning into the gentle touch. For a second, she was twelve again, sick in bed, and her mother had just brought her soup. One of her hands was on Mira's forehead, checking her temperature, and she was saying that she was already getting better. That everything would be all right.

"You don't have a fever," Eleanor said, breaking the illusion. Mira opened her eyes and looked away from the older woman's concerned gaze. "Maybe you should rest for a bit."

Before she could protest, Eleanor was tucking her back into bed and smoothing the quilt over her. She tried to sit up again but she was very tired. Maybe that was all it was, pure exhaustion.

"Your food is over here if you get hungry. Come down whenever you feel up to it," Eleanor was saying. But Mira was already drifting again, the softness of the bed and pillow enveloping her in intoxicating warmth. She was slipping down, down into cottoned silence no matter how hard she tried keeping her eyes open.

The last thing she heard was the door clicking shut and the faint voice of her mother saying everything was going to be all right.

* * *

Isabelle listened to them talking inside the room.

She stood to one side of the door in the second-floor hallway with her head cocked at an angle. She couldn't make out any actual words. Then someone was coming toward the door and it was opening. She stepped back as Eleanor entered the hall, startling at the sight of her.

"What are you doing?" Eleanor said in a low whisper.

"Is she all right?"

Eleanor grasped her elbow lightly and Isabelle let herself be guided toward the stairs. "Yes. She doesn't seem to remember what happened."

"Do you think it's working?"

"Yes. She's almost ready."

"And Gael?"

"Gael is . . . fine. He's fine." She considered something, pausing on the landing. "Where's Oliver?"

"With Allison," Isabelle said, motioning upward. "He was cleaning up the broken lightbulb and making sure the lamp still works."

They stopped in the main hallway beneath the skylights high above. The house was silent. Peaceful. So peaceful. And safe. Isabelle breathed the safety in. "Thank you for this. For everything."

Her mother smiled, and it transformed her. Eleanor cupped the side of her face. "You know I would do anything for you. Anything."

35

She stood on the island's shore, looking toward the mainland, but there was only empty water as far as she could see.

Mira had once seen a picture of the salt flats in Bolivia. Endless white fields with dramatic mountains in the distance. At certain times of the year, the flats would flood, covering them with a thin layer of water, which reflected the sky and turned the world into a mirror, and that was what it looked like now as she stared from her place on the shoreline.

In every direction, there was only water and sky. Clouds above and reflected below. No other land. Nothing.

Wait.

There was something out there. A small sliver of wavering blackness like a burnt match on the horizon. It was a person walking on the water, slowly coming into focus until she could make out a head, torso, arms, legs. They were coming toward the island and her heart surged. *They were going to save her! Save her from this place and take her away. Take her back to her mother and father and brother and their life that was paused and waiting if she could just leave here.*

The person stopped and became a featureless point. Mira waited, sure they couldn't miss the island in all this water. They would come get her and they'd leave this place forever.

The figure raised a single arm . . . and waved.

Before she could react, they turned and began to shrink. To lessen until they were only a point of shimmering darkness, like a black flame guttering in the wind.

"No! Come back!" Her cries were quiet even in her own ears, as if her voice were caught underwater. And even as she screamed again, the person winked out and the mirror was flawless once more.

"No!" She sat up in bed, clutching at the blanket, sweat coating her body. Mira glanced around the sunlit room, cheerful, quiet, unthreatening. She let out a long, slow breath and tried holding on to the dream because it was important even if it was terrible. But it was thin parchment in liquid, disintegrating into tattered pieces and floating away. Gone.

She was thirsty. Beyond thirsty. She lurched out of bed, nightclothes clinging to her, and grasped the tall glass of crystal-clear water on the food tray and drank the entire thing down. Panting, she relished the coolness on her throat. Better. Much better. Despite the headache, she felt more rested than she had upon waking that morning. And it was now—she looked at her phone—nearly noon.

The large room felt claustrophobic, the air thick. *Outside. Being outdoors will help clear your head.*

She dressed and left the room, stopping once to watch a bird soar past her window, envy burning in her center like a hot stone.

She sat watching the river flow by from the turtle rock. A portion of her dream had returned upon sitting down and taking in the view. Something about the water and the sky going on forever without land in sight. Except there was land now, solid and real as anything.

Staring into the distance, she turned over the blank spot in her memory from the night before, approaching it from different angles. Tried moving through every step from the prior afternoon leading up to dinner. But no matter what tactic she used, the result was the same.

Blankness. Terrible blankness.

She'd never really considered what it would be like to lose grip of reality, but now with a smoking hole in her recollection, she realized how truly terrifying it was. How helpless she felt.

There had to be an explanation. Maybe she had hit her head. It was the most logical cause. Maybe someone could fill in last night so this feeling would go away.

"What's the worst thing you've ever done?"

Mira startled, nearly falling from the rock. Allison sat a few feet away, perched on a large piece of driftwood, gaze distant across the water.

"What . . . Where'd you come from?" Mira said, eyes searching the path and the trees to either side.

Allison glanced her way. Her face was devoid of expression, then she smiled. "What are you talking about? I've been here the whole time."

"No, I was alone. I—" *Wasn't I?* "I was . . ."

"You were talking about last night. How you couldn't remember what happened."

Mira blinked, placing a hand against her forehead. The ache there was fading but a familiar swimminess was taking its place.

Allison rose and stretched, lacing her hands behind her head as she resumed staring toward the Canadian shores. "The strange thing about the worst thing you've ever done is you don't know it's the worst thing until you've done it. Beforehand, you might even think it's good. Then after—" She dropped her hands to her sides, where they hung motionless. "You begin to realize it's bad. Really bad. And there's no taking it back."

Mira blinked. The light on the water was too bright. It was shining into the back of her skull. She looked away. "What are you talking about?"

"I killed her. I didn't know what I was doing, but I killed her anyways. I ruined everything." She retreated to the driftwood and sank down to it. "I didn't think there'd ever be a second chance. Then you came, and now everything's different."

"I don't know what you're talking about," Mira breathed. Her stomach churned and sweat had sprung into beads on her forehead. She closed her eyes. "I'm really sorry, but I think I might have to go home. I can't stay. There's something wrong."

The wind rose and with it came a chill that slid beneath her clothing. She shivered, squeezing her eyes more tightly shut, trying to force out the swirling images in her head.

A person standing on water.

Twisted metal and broken glass.

A woman in a chair.

"You belong here," Allison whispered in her ear.

Mira startled and looked around.

She was alone.

36

The grounds were silent, quieter than they'd ever been since her arrival.

Mira hurried across the sun-drenched expanse toward the manor, deeply aware of the day's gorgeous contrast to what was going on inside her.

What's happening?

She'd gone to the river alone, had been sitting there by herself when Allison appeared. Just as suddenly, the other girl had vanished. And not for the first time. The already-strong sinkhole of dread in her center widened.

Something's wrong.

It had been there as an undercurrent since coming to the island, but this morning, it had hit a crescendo. A sense of having forgotten some important piece of information, something crucial, and a feeling of a building wave at her back, rushing down to sweep her away.

She glanced over a shoulder to see if Allison was following her, if she'd hidden as some kind of joke, and the movement sent her off balance. The dizziness was back and it was growing.

When she stepped inside, she was comforted to hear familiar voices coming from the staff dining room. She found Eleanor and Oliver sitting across from one another at the table. Both of them noticed her at the same time, and their expressions changed as one.

"What's wrong?" Eleanor asked.

"I'm . . . still feeling a little strange," she said, taking a seat. The room was the same as every other day, the fresh fruit and coffee bar already set out minus the steaming carafe. "Do either of you—" She stopped, struggling for a moment. "Do either of you know what I did last night?"

The two of them shared a look. "Well," Eleanor said. "We ate dinner, then I spent some time with Ollie. You said you were going to get some fresh air for your headache."

Something tried rising in her memory—a darkened stairway and a room at its top, then it slipped away as Eleanor set a cup of coffee before her, turning the handle so it lined up on her right side.

"Here, this might help brush away the cobwebs a bit," she said. "Do you want cream?"

Mira blinked at her. Finally nodded. Eleanor brought the container to her. "Thank you." She poured some cream into the steaming coffee. Watched the dollop of white swallowed by the black. Her eyes tracked to the fruit bowl. She started to count.

The room was quiet for a time before Oliver stood and touched her shoulder lightly on his way to the door. "Hope you feel better." She watched him leave, and it was a beat before she realized Eleanor was saying something. "Sorry, what?"

"I said, 'Did you get any rest this morning?'"

"Yes. Yeah, I think so."

"But you can't recall what you did last night?"

"I . . . I don't know. I think something happened. I . . . went somewhere."

"Where?"

"I don't know."

"Are you sure it wasn't a dream? A nightmare?"

"No. It was . . . I don't know." She took a breath. Her heart had adopted a strange off-beat. She took a long sip of the coffee. It burned all the way down. "I'm sorry, but I think I need to go home."

"But you're doing so well here."

"I know, but I'm not—" She lost the thread of what she was saying, the gray wall in her head building again. The idea of going home was prominent, a need, yet she couldn't picture her room or apartment or wherever she lived. Just a window looking out at the city; that was all.

"It's okay; take your time," Eleanor said.

Mira gulped the coffee. It was almost too hot but she drank it all down anyway. "Something's not right. I need to leave." Her gaze roamed the room, as if seeking out an answer to her spinning thoughts, and landed on an apple core in the wastebasket. Its dark exposed seeds gleamed. "Why do you do the same thing every morning?" she heard herself say.

Eleanor paused in bringing her own cup of coffee to her mouth. "What?"

Mira gestured at the surroundings. "This. Every day, it's the same. Oliver's eating an apple and you offer to fix me coffee and ask if I want cream. You turn the cup's handle to the right. Day after day, you ask the same questions, use the same words." She picked up speed as she went, her voice gaining volume while beginning to flutter with emotion. "There's exactly the same amount of fruit on the table, the same number of grapes—I've counted them. What's happening?"

Eleanor sat completely still, then lowered her cup to the table. "They said it might be this way."

"Who said? What are you talking about?" There was a frantic bird in her chest, beating its wings against the cage of her ribs.

Eleanor glanced down and reached out to take one of her hands. "Does the manor seem familiar at all to you?"

"Familiar?"

"You don't recognize anything?"

"What? No. I need . . . I need to go home now." She tried to rise and managed a few inches, then dropped back into her seat. Her body was both weightless and a thousand pounds. "What's . . . what's happening to me?" Eleanor said something but it was drowned out by the bass drum of her pulse. "What?"

"I said, 'You're remembering.'"

Mira clenched her teeth, fought to filter her words until they made sense. They didn't. She shook her head like a dog clearing its ears of water.

"There are instances, so terrible, so horrific, we can't accept them," Eleanor continued. "Things we hide from ourselves so that we can go on."

The room was shuddering in time with her heartbeat. Mira licked her lips, but her tongue was rough and dry. "Why are you doing this?"

"We're trying to help you. We've been trying for a long time."

Mira managed to turn herself to the side. She was going to leave. She would go down to the boathouse and take the boat herself if she had to. "You suffered a mental break years ago," Eleanor said, rising and coming around the table to kneel at Mira's side. She had taken something from her pocket, a folded newspaper clipping. "You spent six months in a mental health facility because of what you survived. Because of your guilt, you created a new life for yourself, a new reality, something your mind could accept."

"No," Mira whispered.

"You tried to forget," Eleanor said, the words catching in her throat. "You *did* forget. But now you're here." She unfolded the clipping and placed it in Mira's lap. Mira stared down at it. Eleanor waited as tears rose in Mira's eyes, beginning to cloud her vision. "Now you're home."

The clipping was an article she'd read before, the one outlining the Wyndclyffe tragedy. But now it was different. Her eyes skimmed the words.

Reclusive couple dead in murder/suicide.

Two others injured.

The tragedy leaves behind the couple's daughter, Allison—17—who could not be reached for comment.

The single picture beside the report was nearly the same. It was the shot taken from a distance and magnified, the one of the manor's façade, the gray wall. But now the person in the window was recognizable.

It was her.

Eleanor brushed away a tear that had crept onto her cheek. "You're finally home, Allison."

PART 3

FIERI

37

Silence fell around them like a shroud.

It flowed outward from the room until it enveloped every inch of the manor. Mira felt bound by it, like she would never be able to speak again. Fighting against the weakness flooding her body, she pushed the clipping away and watched it flutter to the floor. "No."

"Look inside yourself. You know it's true," Eleanor said softly.

Mira shook her head. "No. I'm not Allison. She's here. She was with me at the river this morning."

"You've been spending time with Allison for the last week, but answer me this—has anyone seen the two of you together?"

Mira opened her mouth, then slowly closed it, wracking her memory for a moment when the two of them had been with someone else.

"It's because you've been alone." Eleanor tried taking one of her hands again but she pulled away. "The dissociation, the PTSD, the catatonia—all of it has kept you from facing the truth. And this other family you created along with a tragedy to explain your trauma was another barrier of protection."

"I have a brother. His name is—" For an agonizing second, it wouldn't come, then it floated up to her out of the gray. "Aaron. My brother is Aaron."

Eleanor grimaced and sat back on her haunches. "The doctors warned us bringing you here might only reinforce the delusion. But we thought the familiar surroundings would be good for you."

"Stop!" Mira stood from her chair and the room swayed. She swallowed bile and dug for her phone. "I'll prove it." No signal.

"Allison, please—"

"Stop calling me that." Mira hurried from the room, moving as fast as she could. The walls flexed with each step and the taxidermied eyes followed her, animal heads seeming to turn to watch her go.

"Allison!"

She managed to run, stumbling into the main foyer and going left. Down the hall to Eleanor's office. The door was open and she flung it closed behind her. Locked it. A second later, the handle jiggled. "Open the door. Please," Eleanor said from the other side. Mira backed away, clocking the ring of keys on the desk before her gaze fell on the telephone.

Her fingers fumbled the receiver and it clattered to the floor. Eleanor knocked on the door. Hard. Harder. "Open it, please."

Drawing her cell out, she mentally fumbled for the name of Aaron's facility. *What is it, what is it? City, no, town. No, that wasn't it either. Village! Village Gardens!* She located the number and punched it into the landline.

Eleanor pounded on the door and it rattled in the frame, the sound so loud, it hurt her ears. Mira turned her back to it and strained to hear the ringing in the earpiece. As she listened, her eyes fell upon something above the desk.

The picture on the wall was different.

It was no longer summer inside the frame like the first time she'd seen the office. The sky wasn't open and cloudless, nor did the grass grow lush and even. There were no flowers. Now it was winter in the photo. Tall drifts of snow lay against the manor's front, and ice crusted the window frames. It was the same angle and tone but the wrong season.

Mira stared at the picture, waiting for it to change. For it to shift back to what she'd seen before. She jerked as the ringing in her ear became a voice.

"Village Gardens Care Center, this is Mary, how can I help you?" Mira tried to speak, but for a second she only produced a short wheeze. "Hello?" the woman asked.

Bang! Bang! Bang! Bang!

"Allison? Please open the door."

"Hi, sorry." Mira cleared her throat. "This is Mira, Mira Caine; I'm calling for my brother Aaron."

There was a low humming on the line, then the woman on the other end inhaled, long and slow. "Aaron, Aaron, Aaron. Same last name?"

The question dumbfounded her. "What do you mean?"

"I mean do you share the same last name? You said *Caine*, right?"

"Yes." Mira's chest was constricting, cinching tighter and tighter against her lungs. "Is there a problem?" she managed, then had to steady herself against the desktop as the room tilted slightly.

"She's locked herself in," Eleanor said outside the door. "Get something to break through."

There was a long silence from the other end of the line and Mira was sure the connection had broken. Then came the rattle of a keyboard. "C-A-I-N-E?"

"Yes, that's . . ." Mira inhaled shakily. "That's it."

There was another pause, this one stretching centuries. Even more concerning was the quiet outside the door. They would break through any second. A tremor slid through her and she leaned harder on the desk as dark petals unfurled in the corners of her vision.

"I'm sorry," the woman finally said, the clacking of keys going quiet. "But I'm not seeing any record of an Aaron Caine here."

"What?" was all she managed to say.

"I'm not seeing anyone by that name. Possibly you're mistaken about the care facility?"

Mira tried to speak but it came out a strangled wheeze. The room had grown smaller while she'd been looking down at the desk, and now the walls were crowding in. She was sure of it. That was why she couldn't breathe. "No," she managed after a second. "Check again."

"I did, ma'am, just now. There's nothing."

"Look him up under my name. Mira Caine. He's been there for years."

"Like I said, there's no one listed under Caine. Now, if there's nothing else I can help you with—"

"I want to talk to my brother!" The shout startled her and only made her more angry, more afraid. "Put Aaron on the phone, goddamnit!"

"I'm sorry, but I won't stand here and be verbally abused."

The line went dead.

"No," Mira said, and it was a half-sob. A sound of something wounded. "No, that's not . . ." She struggled as a tsunami of lightheadedness washed over her. Small black birds glided across her vision and began to flock, blotting out the room. She staggered to the side and rebounded off the wall, tried catching herself on the desk and missed. Her vision became cut reels of film.

A flash of the floor coming up, the ancient wooden planks beneath her hands.

Dark.

Lying flat, staring under the desk, dust covering everything.

Dark.

Crawling to an empty corner where she curled tightly in on herself.

Dark.

A harsh bang and splintered wood flying across the room.

Dark.

Then just her breathing, in and out. The dryness of her mouth and a sound coming closer and closer that she thought was her heart until hands grasped and turned her over.

An outline of a face above, features shadowed.

"Daddy," she said.

She was picked up and carried. Her neck lost its strength and her head lolled, the upside-down hallway the last thing she saw before closing her eyes.

38

There were voices in the dark.

Some familiar, others alien. They were background noise to her dreams, the words softened and lost amongst the static of images flickering in the auditorium of her mind.

She was five years old and walking hand in hand with her father along a dirt road. When she looked up, he towered so far above her, his face was lost in the clouds.

A boat bobbed in the water of a misted lakeshore, and she was afraid to board it but more afraid not to. She dipped her hand in the water as she sat down near a gunwale, and it bit her fingers with deep, cold teeth.

A rainstorm lashed against a window, water beading and slithering in long silver trails to where her hands pressed against glass and her breath fogged a reflection of herself to gray.

"Allison?"

The voice was clearer, more insistent than before. The sodden weight of sleep pulled at her, but a hand shook her shoulder gently and she opened her eyes.

Her room. It was late afternoon or early evening, the sun slanting down and drawing long shadows on the floor. A woman stood beside the bed, looking at her cautiously. *Mom?* No, that wasn't right.

"Eleanor," she rasped, and she nodded, holding out a glass with a straw in it. She drank.

"You've been sleeping awhile," Eleanor said. "It's good you're resting. You need it." She tried to move, but the weakness in her limbs was all encompassing. "No, don't try to get up. Not yet," Eleanor said, helping her lie back down. "You're not ready yet, but soon. Soon."

She attempted to keep her eyes open, because there was something she'd forgotten, some task that needed doing right now. But the fatigue was a physical thing, forcing her down, down into the soft embrace of the mattress and pillows. Down and away from the lengthening light.

"You're safe," Eleanor whispered. "You're safe and you're home. You're finally home." She was gliding downward on a warm draft of air, drifting on the sky's tide, and in the haze of clouds, she knew no more.

By degrees, she became aware someone was in her bed.

A hand found hers and interlaced their fingers. She rolled with some effort to the left and found herself face-to-face with a girl.

She was slight and blonde with large luminous eyes that seemed to drink her in. They lay only inches apart, and she could feel the faint puff of the girl's breath on her cheek. "You . . . You're . . ." she said, but the words lost their intention the moment she spoke them, lost their meaning. She was so tired.

"Isabelle," the girl said softly. "I'm Isabelle, your best friend." She tried absorbing this, but before she could begin, Isabelle went on. "You were gone for a while. But now you're back."

"I . . . I don't remember."

Isabelle shifted, bringing herself closer, almost close enough to kiss. "We used to walk in the garden and swim in the river."

"I'm so tired."

"We did everything together."

"I want . . . want to go back to sleep."

Isabelle fell quiet for a long time. When she spoke again, her words vibrated the air between them. "Everything's going to be okay now. You won't leave me again, will you?"

She was a long time answering, and when she replied, she wasn't sure if she said the words or dreamed them.

"No. I won't leave you."

39

The days became weeks became months.

40

She walked with Isabelle along the melting path leading down to the river.

Isabelle moved slightly ahead, wearing heavy boots made for the colder weather of winter, which had finally passed. The sun was out full and strong with warmth she hadn't felt in a long time. It had softened the last of the snow so that you could pack it into snowballs and fling them at your best friend. She did so now, tossing one lightly enough so it wouldn't hurt but hard enough to register.

Isabelle squawked and gathered her own snowball. They exchanged throws until she was out of breath and dizzy and had to sit down. She still got this way whenever she exerted herself too much. Isabelle sat by her until she felt better, then they went along the path through the trees to the steps and looked at the river.

"It's completely open," Isabelle said. The ice was gone along the waterway, its former white road littered now with only a few bobbing pieces of ice, some of them eddying with the current. Spring was here and the water was free to flow out to the sea.

Thinking of its freedom created an ache in her center she didn't have a name for. Something about the fragments of ice making their journey away from the island pulled at her and made her want to wade into the frigid water and slide beneath it.

"Come on; let's have tea," Isabelle said. They returned arm in arm to the manor. She only looked back at the river once.

The afternoon was like all the others. Tea before the fire in the great hall that had come back to life since her homecoming. Gael served vanilla macarons on fine china, and Eleanor joined them, talking animatedly of subjects she couldn't keep track of after they were said.

The fall and subsequent winter on the island had blurred into a long, ever-playing dream. Sleep and waking were distinguishable only by the cold bite of air when they ventured outside or the warmth expelled by the fire as they watched snow fall in lazy curtains beyond the windows. Most mornings, she woke to Isabelle asleep beside her, their fingers interlaced—her own bloodless from how hard her friend grasped them. She felt she'd watched the pond freeze an hour at a time as the weather turned and dreamed of the fish down deep in the darkness, cold and sluggish in their movements while they waited for the sun and the warming of their bodies to rise again.

Isabelle said something to her, asking about some memory from years before, and she nodded. Yes, she remembered. It was easier to agree than to fight the gray wall that went upward forever. She'd quit trying months ago.

The staircase. It took the place of memories when she relented. It hung alone in the dark air when sleep wouldn't come. And still she didn't know why she thought of it. It was there whenever they went to the library or when she answered Mr. Browning's questions in the receiving area off the main hall. He'd come twice since she arrived back home, and their talks had been short, always with Eleanor standing by if she got too tired. Whenever he left, he seemed both relieved and irritated. Otherwise, there had been no visitors. And the winter had been long.

"Do you think it's time you have separate rooms?" Eleanor said over the rim of her teacup. "You could stay down the hall from each other like when you were younger."

"We're happy where we are," Isabelle said. "Aren't we?"

"Yes. Happy."

For a while, the only sound was the crackle of flames in the big room, then Oliver appeared in the doorway. He was pale and as thin as she'd seen him. Eleanor noticed him there and motioned to an empty chair by the fire. "Ollie, come join us."

"Maybe in a bit. Have some more work to do first." He gave them a tired smile and disappeared from view. Eleanor sagged a little in her seat.

"Do you think he'll ever come around?" Isabelle said quietly.

"Yes. He's adjusting. He needs more time," Eleanor replied.

"Does he blame me?"

"Of course not. He loves you. Very much. He knows we did the right thing; he just doesn't like it."

"Do you think—"

"I think," Eleanor said, her voice sharp, "we should talk about this later."

Isabelle nodded and turned away, and in profile, she looked like someone else. Someone she'd laughed and danced with. Someone with earrings that sparkled and shone like the lights of a city.

"Would you both like to go fishing tomorrow? We could take a lunch down to the river and spend the afternoon. It's supposed to be warm," Eleanor said, breaking the quiet.

"Yes, let's go fishing!" Isabelle said. She sat upright with excitement. "Do you want to?"

She shifted in her seat and looked at Isabelle. Isabelle in the photo on the concrete dock with Allison. Isabelle with the dark hair. She looked at her friend. Looked at Isabelle. At Allison. No, *she* was Allison.

The entire room shifted slightly as if it had been nudged by some enormous force.

Gael appeared to retrieve the cups and plates. He brought the tray holding the macarons over to her and held it out. "Have you had one?" There was a hint of something behind Gael's eyes. Sadness.

She stared down at the airy cookies he held out for a long time before gathering the notion to eat one. It was crumbly and light, the vanilla sublime on her tongue. As she chewed, another flavor invaded her palate, and she grew still, gorge rising. Then it was gone and she swallowed.

"Fishing it is, then," Eleanor said, standing. "I'll have Jeffry gather the rods and tackle. What's for dinner this evening, Gael?"

"Pork ribs braised in cranberry sauce."

"Excellent. Can't wait."

"Why don't you both lie down for a nap?" Eleanor said. "You got up so early this morning."

"Come on," Isabelle said, pulling her to her feet.

They walked side by side down the hall toward the bedroom. They were almost to the door when the subtle unease in her stomach turned suddenly violent. Her throat clenched and she staggered.

"What's wrong?" Isabelle said. "Are you dizzy again?"

She couldn't answer, didn't dare open her mouth. She hurried down the hall to the waiting bathroom. On her knees before the toilet, and then everything was coming out of her. Again and again her diaphragm heaved upward. Her eyes bulged and the room pulsed. Faintly, she registered Isabelle holding her hair back.

Sweaty and shaking, she sagged against the wall. Isabelle was gone and then she was there with Eleanor in tow. They tried helping her up, but she was sick again and had to purge once more before leaving the bathroom. Down the hall to the master bedroom. Her head lolled and she saw the staircase supported by nothing, then they were helping her into bed.

Lying down in cool sheets with Eleanor's equally cool hand on her forehead. Isabelle's frightened eyes floating in the gloom.

She closed her own.

41

She surfaced to consciousness in momentary bouts of confusion.

Whenever she woke, nausea tormented her. At one point, Eleanor appeared beside her bed with a tray of food. She managed to shove the tray with one hand, slopping some soup from a bowl.

"You have to eat," Eleanor said. She could only shake her head. "Then at least drink some water." Eleanor held out a crystalline glass, which sparkled so sharply it hurt her eyes. The thought of putting the straw between her lips made her gag, and Eleanor pulled the glass away.

Low murmuring somewhere near the doorway, then she drifted again, needing to get away from the roiling in her center. At some point later, Isabelle sat on the bed beside her and brushed her hair.

Darkness.

She woke to a sting in her arm and opened her eyes to Eleanor inserting an IV into a vein. "Don't want to get dehydrated," she said, checking the translucent bag hanging from the head of the bed. Coldness flowed into her arm. "You'll be right as rain in the morning." Eleanor's hand soft and cool on her brow once more, then gone.

She was beginning to float again when someone emerged from a shadow in the corner of the room. For a moment their features were only darkness, then they gained definition and became a thin, handsome face. A sad face.

She watched numbly as Gael pinched off the IV with a small plastic clip. He was moving fast, his body leaving after-trails in the dark as he drew back her covers. There was something in his hand, a plastic tube of some kind. He flipped a cap off one end.

"Wha—" she tried, but the word died on her tongue.

With a single motion, he jammed the tube down onto her thigh.

A sharp, biting pain as if she'd been stung, accompanied by a deep ache flooding outward. He held the tube there for several more seconds, then pulled it away.

"You have to listen to me," Gael said in a whisper. Coldness tingled through her leg and upward into her torso. "You need to wake up now. You have to remember. We're going to have to run."

She shivered, then jerked. Her eyes widened and she inhaled deeply. Something was plowing through her veins, moving quickly as her heart picked up speed, faster and faster. A pressure built in her head, and she squinted against the pain she knew must come, but it didn't. Instead, a cool clarity washed across her mind, washed away the muddy confusion of her thoughts, and they began to sharpen.

Remember. He wanted her to remember. Remember fishing with Isabelle. Remember walking with her father. Remember her mother painting and standing at the window, watching them play.

Them. Watching them play. Who, who was she with?

Her stomach lurched upward and she gagged, remembering something else. The last time she was sick like this, the memory tied deeply and beyond the gray wall, intertwined with the sense of taste that transcended almost all else.

The taste of nutmeg.

She was ten and at a friend's birthday party, eating cake. The flavor soured her tongue on the first bite. Made it numb by the last. And on the way home, her father had to pull over for her to be sick.

She moaned, both on the roadside and in the bed with its soft sheets. Gael put a finger to her lips and steadied her. "Shhh, quiet. We have to be quiet. Can you stand?"

"I . . . I don't know." She looked around, the darkened room becoming clearer with each second. "What's happening?" Gael gently drew the IV from her arm, then helped pull her legs to the side of the bed as she sat up. "What are you doing?"

"Something I should have months ago." He dropped to one knee and slid a pair of socks on her feet as the room tried tipping on its side. Except it wasn't the room; it was her. She'd almost fallen over but caught herself and stayed upright, barely. A second later, he was lacing a pair of shoes onto her feet. Her heart continued to hammer but she was feeling . . . better. No, not just better, good. *Great.*

"What did you give me?" she asked, holding one hand out in front of her face. Even in the dark, she could see every crease in her palm, every hair on the back of her hand.

"Epinephrine," Gael said, standing. "Come on; we have to hurry."

She stood up and was surprised to find her legs held her. Only a few minutes had passed since Gael had appeared, but things were sloughing from her mind like a child discarding winter clothes after coming inside from a blizzard.

She was at the Wyndclyffe estate.

She'd been here since last fall.

She'd come here to help Allison.

She was Mira.

Mira Caine.

"I'm Mira," she said, gasping her name.

"That's right. Now come with me." He grasped her hand and began guiding her toward the door, but she pulled away.

"You were . . . You helped them. Helped them do this to me."

"Please, we don't have time." When she didn't move, Gael held out his hand. "I'll explain, but we have to move. *Now.*"

Mira hesitated, indecision tipping her first one way, then the other.

She took his hand.

42

The hallway was empty.

The wall sconces were half-lit and shadows drenched the far end of the opposite wing. Gael squeezed her hand tighter and the clarity of her thoughts increased. The epinephrine continued to shoulder aside whatever they'd been drugging her with. And they had been drugging her; she knew that now. The stupor of her mind and memory over the last months was a curtain being swiftly drawn aside.

They had lured her here and Isabelle had masqueraded as Allison Wyndclyffe, had accepted her friendship as they slowly increased the dosage of whatever they'd given her. *But why? Why lie to me?* And where was the real Allison? Her lookalike? And something else invaded her racing thoughts as Gael eased them both from the room and started down the hallway, hugging the wall closely.

"Where's Isabelle?" she whispered. The girl had barely left her side since last fall. She'd been staying in the main bedroom with her, most times sleeping in the same bed.

"Eleanor made her stay in another room while you were sick," Gael replied, pausing near a small table in the hall. He surveyed the great entry, which was another dozen paces away. It was empty, with only the suggestion of gray beginning to seep through the skylights. A fire burned low inside the huge hearth. "They should all be sleeping and the boat is ready in the boathouse. When we get outside, we have to run. Can you run?"

"Yes."

"Okay. Let's go." He started forward, low and quick, pulling her with him. They were ten steps from the front door.

Five.

Three.

Light bloomed down the hall from Eleanor's office.

They skidded to a halt, freezing in the center of the entry. The office door was opening. The light clicked off.

Someone's coming.

Without pausing, Gael swung them to the left and started down the hall toward the back garden but stopped suddenly. Light bled out from the open doorway of the staff dining room. A dish clattered quietly.

Mira dragged Gael to the side toward the staircase and hurried upward. He faltered for a split second, then followed as footsteps echoed from the direction of Eleanor's office.

They made the first landing and turned out of sight just as someone appeared in the entryway. Mira nearly fell, taking two stairs at a time, but caught herself and continued on as someone spoke from the base of the stairs.

"What are you doing up?"

For a horrible second she thought they'd been spotted, then Isabelle's voice came from the direction of the back hall. "Couldn't sleep. It's uncomfortable alone."

Silently, Mira reached the second floor and surveyed the hallway ahead. Empty. Gael stopped beside her and stared back down toward the voices.

Eleanor sighed. "She needs to get feeling better. You can sleep alone for one night."

A long pause. Gael caught her attention and brought his hands together, then drew them apart. He pointed in the direction of the entry and raised his eyebrows to see if she understood. *Wait for them to go their separate ways, then we go down and out. Yes?* She nodded.

"Can't I at least check on her?" Isabelle said.

Mira's already-speeding pulse thundered. Gael shook his head. Another drawn silence and Mira willed Eleanor to deny her, just this once, please, only this once.

"If you must," Eleanor said. "But don't stay. Check in, then on to bed."

"Thanks, Mom."

Mom?

Footsteps echoed in the hallway, and Gael grasped her hand and she squeezed it back. She could feel him shaking. He held out three fingers and began folding them into his fist.

Three.

Two.

One.

A sound came from the bottom of the stairs, and a second later, Eleanor's faint shadow appeared, thrown forward on the treads from the light below.

She was coming up.

Mira spun, searching for a place to hide. She ran toward the nearest room and twisted the knob but it wouldn't turn. The second door, *my first room,* she thought wildly, was also locked. Gael was still at the head of the stairs, frozen in place.

Mira rushed back and grabbed his hand, dragging him to the right, into the alcove holding the grandfather clock. There was no space behind the clock's bulk to hide, and on either side, they would be completely exposed. With a frantic movement, Mira grasped the edge of the clock's oblong door and pulled. It came open, exposing its softly ticking guts, but there was a space to either side of the machinery, and she eased inside, pulling Gael with her. They pushed gently against several counterweights and wedged themselves tightly together. As Mira pulled the door closed, she caught a glimpse of Eleanor appearing at the top of the stairs.

Had she seen them?

Mira waited, breath held, heart slamming in her ears, trying not to move any of the counterweights or, God forbid, trigger the chimes. Maybe thirty seconds passed. It was hot inside the clock and she could smell old grease and their stale breathing. Gael nudged her arm. "I think she's gone."

"Okay."

"We have to be fast. Isabelle—"

Mira responded by shoving the door open. The alcove was empty, as was the head of the stairs. She listened for a beat as Gael clambered silently out of the clock. No sounds from below. Not yet.

They grabbed one another's hands automatically and rushed to the stairs. *Should we go out the back way instead since Isabelle is closest to the entry? And what if we're stopped? Could I hurt someone?* She thought of Isabelle watching her from across the table in the garden. Them laughing together. Crying as she relayed memories and feelings that weren't her own. Betraying her trust.

Yes, Mira decided as they reached the stairs. *Yes, I could hurt someone.*

She'd placed one foot on the first tread when a cry came out of the semi-darkness below. It bellowed past them, echoing up to the third floor above and back again. Even though she'd almost been expecting it, her stomach clenched painfully at the raw panic in Isabelle's voice.

"She's gone!"

43

Gael cursed and yanked her to a halt. She tugged him forward but he broke her grip.

"Come on," Mira said, starting down the stairs.

"She'll lock the doors."

"What?"

"Electronic locks. She'll lock them from your room." As if on cue, a soft humming came from downstairs, followed by a faint electronic beep. Gael sagged. "We're locked in."

"We'll break one of the windows. Come on." She grabbed his hand again and started down the stairs but froze.

Someone was coming up. More than one person, by the sound of it. There was a murmur of conversation and she thought she heard Jeff's voice. Mira retreated and turned, intending to find a window on the second floor and jump if she had to. Gael's hand suddenly tightened on her own and he drew in a breath.

Eleanor had appeared at the far end of the hallway and stood staring at them. She and Mira locked eyes for a long moment, then Eleanor started forward, holding out one hand as if to keep her in place.

Mira spun and started for the third floor even as Gael hissed a protest. But she wasn't stopping. Not now. Not after the long months of the winter spent mired in a swamp of muddied memories and drug-laden half-dreams. She thought of Aaron opening the sweater she'd given him the prior Christmas, the look of joy on his face as he pulled it over his head, how it had felt when he hugged her. She had a life, her own life she remembered fully now, and it had nothing to do with this place. *I'd rather die than stay here*. The thought gave her a sense of peace. No matter what, she would escape.

They made the third-floor landing and sprinted down the corridor, doorways flashing past. Where to hide? Where wouldn't they look first? They had to at least get back down to the second floor; a drop from the third would break bones or kill them. She paused at the first T in the hall, lungs burning.

"Where should we go?"

Gael was looking back the way they'd come, eyes flat and staring. Mira slapped him.

His head snapped around, and he touched his cheek where her white handprint was flooding red. "What?" he said.

"We need to hide."

Footsteps pounded up the stairs. Almost there.

Gael blinked and pointed to the left. "This way."

They rushed down the western wing, took another left into a shorter hallway that dead-ended. Mira was about to ask what the hell he was thinking when he stopped next to a set of double doors and dug out a key ring from his pocket. Gael unlocked the doors and shoved the keys into her hands. "Unlock that one," he said, motioning to a single door directly across the hall. He didn't wait to see if she would follow orders, only disappeared inside the room.

It took her three tries to insert the key in the lock and turn it. When the door opened, it was to a simple room with almost no adornments inside. A stack of moldering cots leaned against one wall along with several folded canvas tarps. There was one window, absurdly narrow, opposite the door. No way out.

Mira ran across the hall to find Gael tying the last of three sheets together in the center of a sprawling bedroom. Tepid light revealed an enormous four-poster bed between two soaring windows and another set of double doors leading off to an attached bath. "What are you doing?" Mira whispered. Muffled shouts and several metallic *clack*s came from the hallway.

Gael armed away a sheen of sweat from his forehead, unlocked the closest window, and swung it inward. With deft movements, he knotted one end of the makeshift rope around the bed's nearest post and tossed the rest out the window. Mira stepped to the opening and looked down.

The knotted sheets hung barely halfway to the ground. Beyond the end was another thirty-foot drop.

"We'll break our legs," she said.

"No, we won't." Gael grabbed her arm and guided her back across the room and out the door. Without pausing in the hall, he pulled her inside the room she'd opened and swung the door closed, turning the lock without a sound. He gave her a long look and placed his finger across his lips.

A sound came from down the hall—a rattle and snap. Then a *clunk*.

They were checking the rooms.

Mira glanced around. Her vision was still crystal-clear but her head was becoming heavy. Still so tired. She pinched herself on the inner forearm, and the pain was bright enough to brush some of the fatigue away. She motioned at the narrow window and held up her hands questioningly. Gael shook his head and nodded at the hallway.

The sounds grew closer and closer. If she had to guess, they were only a few rooms away now.

"Here!" The voice startled her by how near it was. It was as if Isabelle had shouted in her ear. Padded footfalls rushed toward them. Shadows glided past in the narrow gap beneath the door. "They're in here!" Isabelle called. A moment later, another set of footsteps approached, then paused in the doorway across the hall.

"They're outside," Eleanor said. Her voice was high and tight.

"How did he wake her up?" Isabelle said.

"Let's go. We'll find them."

The two women hurried back into the hall, and Mira could almost feel the heat of their bodies through the wood of the door.

"I . . . I can't leave again. I won't." Isabelle again, but faint. They were hurrying in the opposite direction now. There were barely restrained tears in her voice.

"That's not going to happen. We'll fix this. Come on."

Then they were gone.

She waited a beat, then searched Gael's face as he listened. He finally nodded and reached down to unlock the door. Cracking it open, he gazed through the gap, light striping his face, and nodded again. He led the way out of the room, pausing every few strides to listen. Mira followed a step behind like it was some kind of child's game, moving when he moved, listening when he did. There was nothing to hear. The manor was silent as if nothing had happened in the last half hour. Without much effort, she could believe it was all a dream, that her entire life had been imagined before this moment.

They reached the first junction in the hallway and stopped, peering around the corner.

Empty.

Sweat slid in a steady stream down the middle of Mira's back, pooling wetly in the waistband of her pants. Her heart kept up its heavy throb, and the injection Gael had given her continued filing her nerve endings to points. After another ten seconds of waiting, they moved again, exposing themselves in the center of the main hall. At the far end of the east wing, darkness shrouded the doorway to Vanessa's studio. Someone could be standing there watching, waiting for them to look away before rushing forward. But no one revealed themselves. Nothing moved except them.

At the central T, they stopped again, taking time to catch their breath. "They should all be outside now," Gael whispered. "It'll give us enough time to go out the front door. Once we're out, don't stop for anything. Understand?" She nodded, her hands clenching and loosening over and over. "Ready?"

"Yes."

"Go."

They set off around the corner, jogging at first, then sprinting. Gael ran a few paces ahead, his shoes hissing on the deep carpet with each step. Mira tried controlling her breathing even as lightheadedness assaulted her. She couldn't pass out now, not when they were so close. So close to leaving this place forever.

Catchuk. Thunk.

The noise came from somewhere ahead of them and sent a fleeting cramp of familiar revulsion through her mind. Gael slowed to a jog, then stopped completely. He stood in the center of the hallway, shoulders heaving from exertion before turning toward her.

"What is it?" Mira asked. Gael opened his mouth, tried to speak, but nothing came out. Instead, he looked down. Mira followed his gaze.

The shaft of an arrow protruded from the right side of his chest.

44

Blood ran in strikingly red rivulets from around the arrow down the front of his shirt.

Gael tried to speak again but only coughed out a mouthful of blood that spattered Mira's face in a hot shower.

She yelled his name as he took a step and collapsed. She caught him partway down, easing his fall. When he was fully on the floor, she could see all the way to where Jeff stood on the landing, his crossbow dangling from one hand. He started toward them, nocking a fresh arrow as he came.

Mira hooked Gael beneath the armpits and began dragging him back the way they'd come. He was surprisingly light. Any second, the bow would make its terrible sound again and the arrow would pierce her.

But Jeff hadn't aimed his weapon at her yet. He was walking, *strolling* toward them as if there was no reason to hurry. One of Gael's legs kicked weakly, trying to help propel them along.

"You can put him down," Jeff said, continuing to close the gap. "He's lung-shot. He'll be gone in a minute or so."

Mira heard an animalistic keening and knew she was making it but couldn't stop. Gael looked up at her from beneath his sweat-soaked hair, eyes pools of panic. The wall brushed her left side and she threw a glance over one shoulder before easing Gael down.

"There you go," Jeff said.

She turned and opened the library door and grabbed Gael again, hauling him inside before kicking the door shut. The last thing she saw before it closed was the grimace on Jeff's face as he lurched into a run.

She let go of Gael again and twisted the heavy deadbolt on the door just as Jeff hit it from the other side.

The door rattled in its frame but held.

"Goddamnit! Open it!" Jeff said and the door shook again.

Gael made a hoarse choking sound and more blood drooled from the corner of his mouth. Mira searched the space frantically before rushing to the nearest loveseat to grab two of the ornamental pillows. She placed both of them beneath Gael's head and shoulders, propping him up, which quelled the terrible croaking sound he was making in his chest. His breathing was heavy and slow and had a liquidity that turned her stomach. His eyes rolled in their sockets, first to the door that shook again with Jeff's efforts, then to her.

"It's okay, it's okay, it's okay," she whispered, her hands fluttering over his chest to his shoulders, not knowing what to do. "We'll get you out."

Gael shook his head. "My mother's . . . house," he wheezed. More blood ran over his lower lip like water over a spillway. "The . . . oven vent."

"Shhh, don't talk," Mira said.

"I'm . . ." His voice was quieter now and possessed a dreamy quality. "Sorry."

"Open. This. Fucking. Door!" Jeff yelled. Each word was punctuated with a kick that rattled the door in its frame. But the wood was old oak, the lock heavy black iron. It held.

"It's going to be okay," Mira said, starting to gather Gael up again.

He cried out weakly as she tried pulling him upright. He peeled one of her hands away and she settled him back to the floor. "Go." The effort for him to speak seemed monumental. "Get away." His chest hitched soundlessly. Once. Twice. Then he was still.

Mira stifled a sob climbing up her throat. She swiped at the tears flooding her eyes and attempted to stand. Her legs wouldn't lift her the first time. The second, they held, barely. She drew in a deep, shuddering breath and started across the library as a voice came from the hallway.

"Allison?"

Mira stopped and stared at the door, imagined Eleanor standing directly on the other side of it.

"Allison, it's me. I know you're very frightened and confused. I want you to listen to me. Gael was mistaken. He didn't know what he was doing. Please open the door and we can talk. That's all we want."

Mira hurried away, leaving Eleanor's voice behind as she started speaking again. At the far corner of the room she pushed on the wall panel, and it shifted, sliding away to reveal the hidden room. Inside, she slung the door shut and searched for a way to barricade it, but it was smooth and featureless. Nothing to brace or lock.

Lock.

Eleanor would have a key for the library door's lock. It would only be a matter of time before they were inside. And they would come directly there.

She rushed to the desk and dragged it in jerks to reinforce the door, knowing it wouldn't do much, knowing this was the end. She retreated to the opposite wall and searched for a weapon, anything to defend herself with, but there were only the books and bookshelves.

Some of the remaining strength left her legs and she knelt. Gael's blood was sticky on her hands and she wiped them on her pants, beginning to rock back and forth.

"Allison?"

They were inside the library.

Her breath burned in her lungs and one of her hands stole to the nearby wall. Her knuckles rapped against it. *Shave and a haircut.*

The wall moved.

Mira stilled, then pushed on the wall again. A narrow panel shifted slightly, and when she leaned closer she noticed a seam in the wallpaper. A door. Another door. Yes, she faintly remembered now. There had been another hidden door open when she'd been here before. Her hands danced around the frame, finally catching on a small lever built into the trim work. She pulled it down and the wall swung inward. She moved cautiously, half-expecting someone to burst out toward her, but there was nothing except a cool, dank draft and something else . . . a faint smell.

Inside, she could make out the first treads of stairs. As she started up, the door leading to the library ground against the desk. Someone grunted from the other side.

Mira stepped fully onto the stairs and swung the second door closed. She fumbled around its frame in the dark, and her heart gave a cry of triumph as her fingers found latches on both its top and bottom. She snapped them into place and hurried up the stairs mostly by feel as her eyes slowly adjusted to the lack of light.

A faint impression of openness ahead. The sense of a vast space. A soft *thud* came from behind her. They'd entered the hidden room. Gradually, she felt the air shift and knew she'd reached the top of the stairs.

The room materialized around her. It was long with high ceilings; that much she could see. To the left were a tall stack of storage bins and old lumber. The rest faded into shadow. To the right, a steel ladder angled upward to some kind of hatch in the ceiling. Straight ahead were two chairs and a lamp.

I've been here before, she thought, taking a step forward. The lamp threw enough light to see someone was sitting in one of the chairs.

I've seen this. And there was something else, a scent permeating the air that brought back the terrible sound of the arrow burying itself in Gael's chest.

She made her way unsteadily into the pool of light. The person—it was a woman with dark hair she could see now—was looking away to her left. Mira sidled around between the chairs, the woman's face slowly coming into view.

There was a moment of pure unreality, a heartbeat where she questioned her senses—her sanity—then she was stepping back, a hand coming up to cover her mouth.

It was her sitting in the chair.

She was looking at herself. The woman's hair was swept to the side, revealing blank features, but they were hers.

And not hers.

The initial likeness was beyond shocking, but there were subtle differences even in the low light. Something—some *otherness*—she couldn't name was in the woman's face. She had time to think it was because of her own perspective, that you never saw yourself from a side profile other than in pictures, that you could never experience seeing yourself in real life this way. After another teetering moment, her mind reclaimed an amount of balance and she realized who it was in the chair.

Knew her name.

"Allison?" she said quietly, not wanting to startle the other woman. It didn't appear she'd heard Mira enter the room or even noticed her presence at all. Mira sidled around so she could see more of the woman's face, so eerily like her own, it was uncanny, and took a step closer. Allison hadn't moved, hadn't blinked. *Catatonic.* She realized maybe

Eleanor hadn't been lying about *everything*. Allison, the *real* Allison, apparently did suffer from catatonia, and they'd sequestered her up here in this hidden fourth floor for some reason. Kept her out of sight and presented Isabelle in her place instead.

Mira swallowed, listening for more sounds from below, but they'd ceased. She guessed the locked door wouldn't hold them off for long but maybe long enough to hide or find another escape route.

"Allison? My name is Mira, and I need help," she said, coming a step closer. The woman didn't move, didn't respond. "Can you tell me if there's another way to get outside?"

Nothing.

Allison continued to stare at waist level, stare through her. Mira knelt, coming even with her gaze. There was something unsettling about looking directly into her eyes, like looking into a slightly warped mirror. Mira reached out to gently touch one of her hands, to try waking her from the trance she was in. "Can you hear—"

Her hand met Allison's, and something in her center curdled.

The other woman's flesh was cold and . . . *hard*. Stiff and unyielding, not like skin or flesh should feel. Mira's jaw loosened as a core-deep revulsion sank into her.

Horrific truths were lining up and snapping into place. She saw them in flashing images.

The animals hanging from the walls, jutting from their posts.

Jeff's workshop and the deer he'd been mounting, how his fingers had pressed the yielding skin into place.

The human-shaped mannequin on the shelf.

The mountain goat's staring eyes, so much like the ones looking back at her now.

A scream tumbled free of her as she ripped her hand away and fell backward, sprawling hard on the floor. She crab-crawled away from what sat in the chair, away from the sickening scent of decay hanging in the air. The struts of her sanity began to crumble, and she let out another cry of horror and retched, trying to stay conscious as motes of darkness swarmed her vision.

A hand grasped her shoulder.

Mira screamed again and spun on her back, kicking at the figure looming over her. One of her feet connected, and Oliver stumbled to the side, clutching his stomach where she'd struck him.

She scuttled backward until her shoulders met a pile of lumber. Her eyes rolled as she searched the rest of the room, but there was only Oliver, holding his hands out before him. "Please, I just want to talk to you."

"What . . . What's . . ." was all she could manage. She shot a look at the woman in the chair, at Allison Wyndclyffe, or what was left of her, and swallowed bile.

"I know you're frightened and confused, but let me explain," Oliver said. He'd straightened and moved closer to the floor lamp. He was haggard-looking, as disheveled as she'd ever seen him, and there was a glaze in his eyes that might've been exhaustion but looked more like shock.

Mira gathered herself and managed to stand. Every muscle was traitorous and threatened to give out at any second. She needed to get out of here, get away from this . . . whatever this was . . . away from the smell. She was sure if she stayed much longer, she would lose her mind.

"Oliver," she said with as much calmness as she could summon. "I need to leave."

His gaze lingered on Allison, then drifted back to her. "I'm sorry, but that won't be possible."

Two shadows materialized out of the gloom. Eleanor and Isabelle, hands linked. Blocking the stairway.

"You're too important," Oliver went on, gesturing at the two women. "My family and I need you."

45

She was adrift for a second.

Untethered and floating. Mira looked from Oliver to Eleanor and Isabelle and back again, more pieces attempting to fall into place.

"It's true," Eleanor said, moving to the center of the room, stopping beside Oliver. "I'm going to be honest with you now, and I hope you'll listen. I know you have no reason to, given what we've done, but I promise to tell you the truth."

Mira said nothing, only swallowed and furtively searched her surroundings for a weapon, tried gauging the distance to the stairway and wondered if she could make it past Isabelle and down the steps without being caught.

Eleanor nodded, accepting her silence as agreement. "You know the story of what happened the night Allison lost her mother and father. You know Leland shot Oliver and then killed Vanessa before trying to kill Allison. But you don't know why." She gazed at Oliver who took her hand. "We loved Allison like our own. For years, she was our daughter's only friend." Isabelle stepped closer but gave Mira only a fleeting glance. "When Leland discovered the journal handed down through the Wyndclyffe bloodline, his illness took on a new shape. One bent on destroying the rest of Allison's life. Ollie and I knew she had to be off the island before the equinox, so we helped Vanessa plan their escape. But . . ."

"I told him," Isabelle said, her voice low and shaking. "I thought he would just make them stay. I didn't know . . ." Tears streamed from her eyes.

"So, you tried making me her. Why did you try making me Allison?" Mira said, moving slowly to the left.

"Please, you have to understand, it was out of necessity. Leland kept us all hostage here." Eleanor faltered, glancing at her daughter. "Isabelle can't leave the island. She has terrible agoraphobia. We found out when she was young and tried to go on holiday. It was . . ."

"The worst days of my life," Isabelle finished quietly. "I thought I was dying."

"We wanted to have therapists come here for treatment, but Leland wouldn't allow it. He was too paranoid." Oliver said. "So, we did the best we could, but the medications weren't effective, and any time we tried bringing Isabelle off the island . . ."

Mira continued to shift around the edge of the room. The epinephrine was waning. Weakness was seeping back in, draining her. She had to make her move soon. "But why this?" she said, motioning to Allison. "What happened? Why did you do this to her?"

Eleanor looked down, composing herself. "Allison was never the same after her parents died. She dissociated and suffered long bouts of catatonia." She paused, her mouth moving without sound. "One night about a year ago, she overdosed on sedatives. We think it was an accident. Ollie found her." Oliver stared at the floor blankly. "We were all utterly destroyed. But beyond the grief, there was something else to contend with. If the board learned Allison had died, we would all have to leave the island. It . . . forced us to make a decision."

She let the statement hang in the still air. The implications of it. Dizziness washed over Mira and she swayed but steadied herself. "You . . . you had Jeff *preserve* her."

"It was the only way. The lawyer, Browning, knew of her catatonia. We kept the lights low whenever he visited, and it bought us time."

"Until we saw you on the news," Isabelle said. "You look so much like her. It was like destiny."

Mira made her move and bolted toward the stairs but skidded to a stop as Eleanor stepped in the way, a hypodermic needle appearing in one hand.

"We're sorry," Eleanor said. "We were going to lose everything."

Mira gritted her teeth, backing away. The immensity of the lies, the treachery, the layers of deceit fell upon her like a physical weight.

But beyond that was something worse. The time. The months she'd spent here, months away from Aaron. *He's been alone, wondering why I abandoned him.* The thought broke something inside her and rage spilled out.

"You tried to make me believe I was someone else. Ripped me from my life."

"Please, we have money," Eleanor said, swiping away a tear that had fallen to her cheek. "If you'll agree to continue playing the part, we'll pay. We can make this work; just tell us what you want."

Mira looked at Eleanor and Oliver, at the naked pleading in their faces, then at Isabelle.

"I want . . ." Mira let the words hang and die in the room. ". . . my life back."

Eleanor took a step forward and Mira grasped the floor lamp, heaving it at her as hard as she could. There was a pop as the bulb shattered, and someone cried out. She spun and rushed to the farthest corner of the room where the steel ladder ascended to what she hoped was the roof. Eleanor bellowed her name as she yanked herself up the narrow rungs and pawed at the hatch's handle in the ceiling, praying it wasn't locked.

For a terrible heartbeat it wouldn't budge, then it turned and the hatch door swung up and out and she was scrambling onto the manor's roof. She threw the hatch closed, a last glimpse of Oliver helping Eleanor to her feet, then she was running.

Cold light illuminated the roof in a maze of old brick chimneys and newer HVAC equipment. Mira hurried past a low air-conditioning unit, hearing the sound of the hatch banging open behind her. It took a few seconds to figure out which direction she faced, then she raced toward the far roofline, where a four-foot-high ledge lined its border.

Her vision thudded with each heartbeat and footfall. The vertigo was back and her lungs had caught fire.

She stumbled, kept going.

Then she was at the ledge and climbing onto it. The open morning air surrounded her, filled her up.

She shivered, watching the family make their way across the roof, slowing as they neared.

"Please, come down," Eleanor said, stopping a dozen feet away. Mira inched a little closer to the edge and looked down, immediately wishing she hadn't. The sheer height sent a lightning bolt of fear from her feet to the top of her head, and she felt the intoxicating pull of the drop. She'd been here before, near the edge with another girl, but now she was the one contemplating jumping.

Eleanor held one hand out. "Come down and we'll talk."

She eased backward, feeling open air beneath her heels. Her stomach climbed into her throat and she resisted the urge to step onto the safety of the rooftop. She'd already made her decision.

"Don't make this hard," Eleanor said, equal parts desperation and resolve in her eyes.

"Or what? You'll kill me like you did Gael?" Oliver's brow wrinkled and he shot a look at his wife. "Jeff killed him," Mira said, her voice breaking.

"It was an accident," Eleanor said. "Jeffry misunderstood. We'll deal with him."

"Ellie, maybe we should—" Oliver started, but Eleanor ignored him, stepping forward.

"Come down and we'll make this right," she said, holding out her hand. The other gripped the hypodermic tightly.

She surveyed them, mind shying away from what was coming, skittering over every possibility to avoid it. "It wasn't all an act," Mira finally said, staring at Isabelle until she looked up. "You were honest with me sometimes. I saw you. The *real* you."

Eleanor took another step closer. "Think about it, Mira. Financial security."

"We were friends," Mira continued. Isabelle blinked, lips opening and closing as if she were trying to respond. "We *are* friends."

"You and your brother will never have to worry again. You'll be able to provide for him for the rest of his life. It's what your parents would have wanted." Eleanor said. "Stay here with us. You'll see; it's—"

"Let her go, Mom," Isabelle said.

Eleanor stared around as if she didn't know who'd spoken. "What? What do you mean?"

"We can't keep her here." Isabelle raised her head, eyes shining with tears in the early-morning light. "I made that mistake with Allison."

"Honey, you don't know what you're saying," Eleanor said. "If she leaves, it's all over. Everything. We'll have to leave the island forever."

Isabelle didn't respond, only looked away toward the growing dawn.

Eleanor surveyed them both, something changing in her posture.

Mira stood above them, the breeze lashing her hair, and knew what was about to happen. She let it settle over her.

The rising sun was strong on her face. It flared everything into stark relief. She'd been in places like this before, high places where she could see for miles both beyond and within. She'd sat with her brother on the roof of their old house and looked at the stars and told him their stories. She'd brought a girl back from an edge just like the one she stood on now, helped give her a second chance. She'd wavered in a high, dangerous place after her parents died and left her to care for her brother. Somehow, she'd found her way down safely. But now was different. Now she knew what she had to do.

There was a swelling second of hesitation, then Eleanor sprang forward, reaching out to grasp her, to pull her back.

Mira Caine turned in one fluid motion.

And jumped.

46

Terror gripped her so fiercely, it bordered on exhilaration.

Within it she said a quiet goodbye. Goodbye to her brother and Shay. Goodbye to the life she'd had up to this point. Flawed as it was, it still held times of purity and joy so clear her heart ached for more of them. The second before she hit, she recalled the last time seeing the ocean beneath a clear blue sky and felt the pull of the saltwater in her veins.

The pond met her. Hard.

It smashed into her bare feet and slammed up through her legs and back, since she'd tipped slightly in the fifty-foot drop. Then the water closed over her head in a static howling and she speared downward into the cold dark.

Something touched her foot as she decelerated, the hard slap of the water finally filtering its way through her nerves, and she pictured a fish frightened out of its senses as she passed. Mud somehow even more frigid than the surrounding water squelched between her toes, and she finally opened her eyes.

Murk drifted by, the water churning with her impact. Bubbles floated up from her nostrils and already her lungs throbbed, calling out for air. Mira pushed off the bottom and swept her arms out, stroking for the light-dappled surface.

It was a long time coming. So long, she began to think she would inhale a breath of water, but then she was five feet from it.

Two.

One.

Her head broke through. Glorious air rushed into her lungs along with some water vapor, and she coughed and choked, but the oxygen flowed through her bloodstream along with a pure shot of adrenaline.

When she turned her eyes up to the rooftop, three faces peered down at her.

Mira swam the fifteen feet to the pond's edge and gradually stood as the bottom came up to meet her. She'd leapt just far enough out to land in the deepest part of the pond. The air nipped at her, and her clothes clung to her body.

A quick glance around the grounds for Jeff, then she was out and onto bare ground. Slow at first, her pace gradually picked up until she was running, feet stinging against the cold concrete path, eyes watering, heart thundering a song of escape.

Down the path and into the trees.

Shafts of spring sunlight cut across before her and she soared through them, the cold acting like fuel now, spurring her onward. She imagined she heard footsteps other than her own echoing off the trees and ran harder. Past the bench with its engraving and wild laughter trying to bubble up through her as she sped on, the Latin ricocheting in her skull.

She crested the last small rise and the river came into view, the concrete pier jutting into its dark skin, and it was a beautiful sight. So much beauty so suddenly, and she thought she might be losing her mind a little, but that was okay. That was just fine as long as she could get to the boat.

Mira pounded down the narrower path to the boathouse, each intake of breath beginning to stab painfully in her side. Her feet were numb and the feeling was spreading upward into her legs. She couldn't run much farther, but she wouldn't have to. Across the river, Yellow Bay was coming to life. A car horn honked in the distance, and it was like a voice calling out to her, calling her home.

The first fear that the door would be locked dissolved as she met it, barely pausing to turn the handle. The second, that the boat would be absent, also fell away as her eyes adjusted to the dimmer light and its shape formed in the lapping water. A single rope from a nearby piling was tied to the gunwale, and she set about loosening it, fingers cold and fumbling. Her eyes kept straying to the open doorway. Any second it would darken with someone's shape, and she would have to fight them, fight until she couldn't move anymore, because anything else was to succumb to a lifetime composed of the last few months. She struggled with the rope and nearly had the knot loose when a set of hands came over the side of the boat and grabbed her own.

Mira screamed. The hands were strong and callused and ground the bones in her fingers together as their owner slowly appeared from the boat's bottom.

Jeff stood to his full height and stared down at her.

Mira fell and he lost his grip, her fingers twisting painfully as he tried to hold on. She wheezed, crawling backward, mind in freefall and finding no purchase. Jeff climbed over the side of the boat and started toward her.

"Pity it came to this," he said. "Figured they'd fuck up one way or another. Told them, too. But that's rich folk for you. If you're not their equal, your opinion is only worth as much as they're willing to pay for it." He stepped toward her as the sound of footfalls came down the path outside. "Come on. Let's get you back to the house."

She shook her head, unable to form words, and managed to climb to her feet. Behind her, the wooden walkway led to the river, the boat no longer an option. A quick glance told her there were no weapons within reach, nothing but a small coil of rope and an old pile of life jackets.

A second later, Eleanor appeared in the doorway holding the hypodermic in one white fist. They approached like she was a wild animal.

"Mira, please," Eleanor said. "You're going to hurt yourself. Come inside with us and we'll talk, just talk. I swear it." Mira retreated two more steps and the back of her thighs touched the low railing between her and the water. There was nowhere else to go.

"It can be a good life. A comfortable one," Eleanor said quietly as Jeff took another tentative step forward. "You'll have everything you need." A thought seemed to occur to her. "Aaron will be fine. The payments for his care are already in place."

At the sound of her brother's name, Mira stiffened and found her spine slowly straightening. Her chin came up, and the advancing cold in her limbs retreated. She quit shivering and was still. She looked at them in the low light and they saw her looking at them, saw her *seeing* them, and they halted as if she'd suddenly produced a weapon. Slowly, her gaze tracked over their shoulders and her eyes widened.

"Isabelle! Don't!" Mira cried.

They turned as one—to the empty boathouse behind them.

Mira lunged, grabbing one of the closest life jackets, and leapt over the railing into the river.

Her ears were filled with the deep thrum of water for a second time, then she surfaced, already stroking from beneath the boathouse's canopy into the morning light. She'd landed on the life preserver, and it buoyed her enough for her head and shoulders to stay above the waterline, but her body felt as if it were encased in ice. The day she and Aaron had swum in the great lake upstream filled her mind, but this time, the biting needles of the water were sharper, so much worse. There was no safety of a sailboat to climb onto now, no mother and father waiting to wrap her in warm, fluffy towels. She paddled harder, legs and arms flailing as she sucked in huge, whooping lungfuls of air. *I won't die in this river.*

Yellow Bay gradually panned to her right even as she swam toward it, the river's current drawing her inexorably downstream. Above the slamming of her heart came another sound, one which jerked her head around hard enough to send a stinger of numbness streaking through her neck and into her tongue.

Jeff was starting the boat motor. She caught a flash of him at the craft's outboard, triggering the starter, the hard rasp of steel cranking in an echo across the water. Mira tried swimming faster, but something strange was happening to her arms and legs. She was telling them to move, but they were responding slower and slower, as if she were a fly caught in ointment. The most alarming thing was that she was becoming warm. It seeped in from the bottoms of her feet upward through her calves. There was mist on the water now, floating only inches away—so thick, she thought she could feel it sticking to her face. Somewhere far away, a boat motor flared to life.

Mira bit hard into her lower lip and tasted the brine of blood but barely registered the pain. She kicked feebly. It would be so easy to quit moving, to give up. She could rest then and they would take her back to bed and she could sleep. Another stroke and her neck lost the strength to hold her head up. Water washed across her nose and mouth and she coughed, trying to keep moving, but it was no use. She was losing her grip on the preserver, couldn't feel it anymore. The motor's growl grew in strength, coming closer and closer until its vibration thrummed the water.

The sun flared as she turned her head to the side and let it rest on the life jacket's webbing, all of the world lost in the harsh glare of spring light on water and chrome. The boat was almost to her now, and she reached out for it as the mist thickened, beginning to shut out the sun.

Something tugged at the back of her shirt and darkness claimed her.

47

A hand held her own, warm and tender, while another grasped her arm and squeezed painfully.

Hard, harder still until she was wincing and coming away from a half-lit place where she was watching herself in a chair, watching as her head turned toward her.

"Shhh, hey, you're okay now, hear?" a voice said from beside her, and Mira blinked her eyes open with effort.

She was in a white room with windows gazing out to a cloudless sky. There was a curtain pulled halfway across the room to the right, and a TV hung from the opposite wall. On the other side, a machine's digital face displayed numbers and lines. A tube ran from it to the blood-pressure cuff squeezing her arm. Next to the machine seated in a chair was an older woman with rounded features and mottled hair. She was the one holding Mira's hand. Mira searched for the woman's name and finally unearthed it.

"Nessie." Her voice was a frog's croak.

Nessie nodded and scooted forward on her seat. "See I made an impression on you, dearie. Glad you're awake."

She swallowed, her throat feeling like she'd drank a tumbler of rusted screws. "Where . . ."

"Mercy Memorial," Nessie said. "You're okay."

For a moment, there was nothing, her memory an empty room when she tried recalling how she'd gotten there, then her feet tingled unpleasantly and she experienced a stomach-swooping sensation of falling and saw the pond rushing up at her. "Oh, God," she whispered.

"Yeah, I'll say. Though it didn't look as though he had much to do with you being here now. You're a toughie, as my daddy used to say. Hard as a coffin nail to survive in that water."

"They . . . they were . . ." How did she explain what had happened? How could she begin to describe the nightmare she'd endured?

"Keeping you hostage, I'd wager," Nessie said, finally releasing her hand. Mira felt her pull away and panicked, reaching out again until Nessie squeezed her hand once more. "I'm just getting you some water."

The water in the plastic cup was tepid, but she drank it all even as her stomach turned on itself. When she could speak again, she said, "How long have I been here?"

"A day or so," Nessie said, settling back into her chair. "Gave the doctors a scare a few times, but you pulled out of the nosedive you were in. On the border of losing your toes, but they managed to save them, too."

In response, Mira wiggled them and winced at the swollen tingly feeling but watched the sheet move at the bottom of the bed with a measure of relief. "What happened?"

"You were lucky, is what happened. That and a little nosiness on my part, I suppose you could say." Nessie looked at her strangely then went on. "Back in the fall, something didn't sit right about you. You were a little cagey about going out to that island, and you look—" She paused there. "You look like them, the Wyndclyffes. Especially the daughter, Allison. It was uncanny. I couldn't get it out of my head all winter. Kept looking out there, watching for a boat to bring you back. Kept looking for you in the coffee shop or on the street. That would've put things to rest, but you were never there. Not until yesterday. I was out early, checking downstream to see if a few backwaters were open since fishing season's only a month away, and was coming back when I saw you in the river. Almost a quarter way across, just paddling along. As I was pulling up, here comes their hired hand out of the boathouse, but as soon as he sees me, he turns and pulls right back in. Didn't know what to think of it, and when I got you onboard you were out cold. No pun intended." Nessie smiled a little and sucked at her teeth. "You were blue as Bunyan's ox. Thought you wouldn't make it to shore, but you did. Came in to sit with you a while this morning, and here we are."

Fear pogoed through Mira's center and she managed to sit up. "What about them? The people over there, Eleanor and her daughter, did anyone—"

"Called the police as soon as I got you here. They sent some men out to the island a bit later."

"And?"

"Don't know, but I heard through the grapevine it's a mess over there." Nessie studied her. "Won't go into it now since I don't know anything for sure, but sounds like at least one dead."

Mira could suddenly hear Gael's ragged breathing. Felt the awful weight of his motionless body as life left him.

"There's been a regular armada going back and forth," Nessie continued. "Staties and local PD both. Questioned me, but all I could tell them's what I just told you—had a funny feeling and kept my eyes peeled for you since you went out to that blasted place."

"Thank you. I'm sorry I—"

"Hush that now," Nessie said, waving her hand as if to dismiss a fly. "I was just in the right place at the right time. Don't question a blessing, my daddy used to say."

Mira settled back into the softness of the bed, the hospital bed, not the bed in the manor. She was out. She was free. All at once, she was on the verge of tears but too tired to cry them. She couldn't keep her eyes open any longer.

"You rest now," Nessie said softly.

"Will you stay? Until I'm asleep?" She barely formed the words. "Please, Mom."

Nessie's reply came from a great distance. "Yes. I'll stay."

Mira floated further away and sank into darkness and didn't dream.

The days following her escape were a surreal spasm of time that leapt forward and tangled upon itself in rushed hours and creeping minutes. A nurse by the name of Bellows befriended her only to torture her with exercises and meals she wasn't truly hungry for.

"You'll thank me later," Bellows said one morning two days after Nessie had fished her out of the St. Lawrence as she assisted Mira down the hall with a walker. She was a big, matronly woman with hair tied so tightly back, Mira imagined she could hear it squeak when she turned her head. "Hard as it is now, you'll be glad you moved rather than sat around. Circulation is important for frostbite."

Mira grudgingly did as asked despite the hobbling pain in her toes and feet. She was thankful it wasn't worse—the resident doctor had told her there would be minor tissue damage they might have to remove a month or so down the road, but for now, extra oxygen and light painkillers would do the trick. She would keep all her toes.

A Detective Denbrough from the state police interviewed her on three separate occasions. He was very tall, with bushy eyebrows needing a good trimming, and asked quiet questions while always waiting for her to answer fully. Mira found she needed the space he gave her to relate everything. There was so much that was muddled in a drug-induced haze and so much more she recalled too well.

When she was finished Denbrough stared at a place on the floor between his feet. Mira shifted in bed. When the silence spooled out, she said, "What happened to them?"

Denbrough brought his gaze back up, seeming to weigh something. "We don't know yet. They're gone." Mira's throat tightened and she shifted uncomfortably. "Jeffry Abbot, who has several other aliases and two outstanding warrants, was spotted at a gas station a hundred miles south of here. Looks like he had some cash saved up and lit off with it. We think he's heading toward Mexico. My guess is he'll be brought in soon." Denbrough paused again. "Oliver, Eleanor, and Isabelle are all missing as well. They made it across the river to Canada. We have them on camera in Ottawa, renting a car. From the footage and speaking to witnesses, it appears Isabelle was heavily sedated. Her parents were transporting her in a wheelchair. Given what you said, it seems like the only way they could get her to flee."

Mira looked out the window in the direction of the island, not knowing what to feel. Beneath the rancor at what they'd done, she saw Isabelle's long, desperate struggle. She saw a mother and father trying to help their child no matter the cost.

When Denbrough had gone, she thought of the people on the island. Thought of Gael first and why he'd helped her when he did. She guessed he hadn't been fully aware of the others' plan and had been coerced by the kindness he and his mother had been shown by Oliver and Eleanor. But it had weighed on him when he realized what he'd become a part of. She thought of Isabelle and her own inability to thrive in the world outside the island, how her best friend who might as well have been her sister had been torn from her—partially because of her own actions—and the guilt spawned in the aftermath. Isabelle, who'd lied to Mira. But there'd been truth in the lies, too. A cry for help. She pictured Eleanor and Oliver planning into many long nights, and thought of their desperation to fix the wrongs, to keep their family together no matter what.

And Allison. Scarred so deeply by the violence and loss she'd endured.

Mira thought of them all, and in the sleepless quiet of the nights she wondered, if she were given the chance to change the past and fix the future, how far she would have gone.

On the second interview, Denbrough handed her her phone before settling in beside the bed. Nessie had sent her a small bouquet of flowers, and its scent seemed to magnify the sunlight in the room.

"Figured out why that didn't work so well on the island," Denbrough said, nodding to her device as she turned it over like some alien artifact. "And it wasn't just the poor reception. Investigators found a room on the first floor with something in it called a jammer. It's a device that blocks cellular signals within a certain radius."

Mira tried turning the phone on but it denied her access. "Why's this locked?"

"Because that's not your phone."

"What?"

"It's a copy. A clone, the techs call it. Your phone was cloned in late October."

Mira set the device on a nearby table. "Right after I got to the island."

Denbrough nodded. "I'd wager they drugged you on the first night of your stay, slipped into your room, and cloned your phone so they could access calls, emails, photos, everything from this device. All to manipulate your state of mind. Also found cans of fake dust along with pretty convincing synthetic spiderwebs. You mentioned the room they changed on you—they must have set to work on it as soon as you were out of the manor, dressed it up like no one had been inside for months or years." He paused and shook his head. "We found the photo you mentioned—of the car crash. You were right; it was a picture of your parents' wreck. And the last call you made to your brother's facility was rerouted to a line in the house. Looks like they did everything they could to unhinge you. They studied you for some time before they made their move, got ahold of as much personal information as they could prior to all this."

They were following me. I hadn't been imagining it. They must have been watching her for weeks before Eleanor introduced herself. Everything afterward had been carefully choreographed—all to destabilize her state of mind. To make her believe she was someone else. It made her want to crawl inside herself so deep, the world would fade away.

Denbrough sat back in his chair, looking past her out the window. "I've never seen anything like this. Terrible crimes, murders that would haunt you for a lifetime, but nothing ever like this." He blinked and seemed to come back to the room. "We found some vials of the drug they were slipping into your food and drink in the same room as the jammer. Something our forensic specialist calls Devil's Breath."

"Devil's Breath?"

Denbrough nodded. "Doesn't sound real, does it? Most often comes from a plant in Colombia—borrachero or something like that. Used primarily as a date-rape drug. Nasty stuff when derived correctly. Causes all sorts of symptoms like dry mouth, dizziness, fatigue, headaches, amnesia, and hallucinations."

The lucid dreams she'd had, the feeling of detachment from herself, the derealization. The gray wall in her mind going up and up forever. "Are there any long-term effects?"

"Still looking into that, but if I can speak candidly with you, these people were careful and calculated. They were in it for the long haul. They wouldn't have wanted to shut down one of your organs and lose their little project, so I'd wager there won't be major ramifications."

Mira didn't reply. Couldn't bring herself to tell him about biting back screams in the middle of the night or the sickening see-saw of her thoughts when it came to navigating her waking hours. How could she explain having to constantly reassure yourself you were who you were? Her identity had almost been stolen from her—how could anyone say what the long-term damage would be?

Denbrough cleared his throat. "On another note, we followed up on a couple of leads and contacted a woman named Kirsten Killian. Does that name mean anything to you?"

"No."

"She's an actor, lives in a suburb of Chicago and was on a few of those reality dating shows a while back. She works at a theater company now as a talent coordinator. At first, I had no notion of how she fit into all this, but turns out you and her have quite a bit in common." He took a glossy photo from a file folder and handed it to her. As she looked at it, Mira's fingertips took on the familiar numbness of the days past.

In the picture, Kirsten Killian was sitting on a chair in the middle of a stage with one hand propped under her chin. Dark hair fell in long curls around her shoulders and her lips were quirked in a smile at one corner. "The likeness is uncanny," Denbrough continued quietly. "I spoke to her myself yesterday. She said she was contacted almost a year ago by Eleanor Madsen. Madsen made her an offer of a hundred thousand dollars to play-act as Allison. The contract was to be for an indefinite amount of time. Killian said she considered it but turned the job down in the end."

Mira's breath came in small sips. The photo shook slightly in her hands. "Why?" she heard herself ask.

"She said she got a bad vibe."

Bad vibe. A giggle tried climbing up her throat, and she did her best to suppress it. If she started laughing now, she wouldn't be able to stop. Mira handed the photo back to him, unable to get it away from her fast enough. "I think that's about all I can handle today," she said, glad to see the detective rise on his long legs and head for the door.

"Any word on when you'll be discharged?" he said before disappearing into the hallway.

"Not soon enough," she answered. And then she was alone again.

48

Shay arrived on the fourth day to take her home.

Her friend had been crying; she could see it in the puffiness around her eyes and how she kept fiddling with the cuff of her sweater. Mira had been sitting on her hospital bed, looking at the sneakers she wore—a size too large and loosely tied to accommodate the bandages within. Her toes and feet still ached when she walked, but the pain was getting better. The island-like quality of her mind was improving as well. For the first few days in the hospital, physical objects and people held a strange, removed feel for her. She felt separate from them on some elemental level bordering on suspicion. Like any moment, their veneers would chip and scuff away until what was beneath became visible. And it would be ugly and dark and threatening. She spiraled into panic attacks, which were only aborted by doses of the pills Nurse Bellows brought to her in little plastic cups.

"You'll get through this," Bellows said soothingly to her once in the middle of the night when she'd woken and bolted out of bed, making it all the way into the hall before reality finally reasserted itself. "Time is the great mender if you let it be. It doesn't heal all, but hopefully it'll be enough." Mira clung to the idea that time would also erode the images replaying in her mind, because if she tried moving on too quickly, they would still be inside her, causing a sepsis which would never go away.

Now, with the sight of her friend tugging at the sleeve of her sweater, an apology in the normally set lines of Shay's features, the scale of hope tipped far enough to get her on her feet and across the room. Then she was hugging Shay to her, eyes dry for the first time in days, and it was stoic Shay who was sobbing softly into her hair.

"I told you not to go," Shay finally managed. Mira exhaled a quiet laugh and hugged her tighter. "I'm sorry. You didn't call or text for so long, and then when I finally sent you a pissy email, I got that response back. And I should've known it wasn't you. You wouldn't ever say those things, but—"

"It's okay. I know; I know." For a long time, they stood holding one another in the doorway, then Mira stepped back and wiped Shay's cheeks free of tears. "Sight for sore eyes."

"You're so skinny," Shay said, and coughed out a strangled laugh. Mira laughed too, and it felt like better medicine than any she'd received in the last few days.

"Then let's get out of here and get something to eat. You're buying."

Mira stood at the entrance to Village Gardens and attempted for the third time to step forward and grasp the door handle and go inside. It was as if another barrier besides the steel and glass barred her way, invisible yet stronger than anything man made.

She'd been in the city for two full days and hadn't seen her brother yet. The more time went by, the harder it became. It was like being gradually swept out to sea in a riptide, the shore losing more and more definition while the entire ocean waited behind her.

Her initial impulse had been to have Shay bring her straight here so she could see Aaron before going anywhere else. But as they neared the city limits and the buildings climbed higher, her doubt and anxiety matched them, and she faltered. What had Aaron gone through in the intervening months? What had he felt? What had the staff told him when his sister ceased to visit? No forwarding address, no calls, nothing. The payments had continued to flow from an account set up for his care in her name, so what was there to tell him? That his sister had finally gotten tired of visiting, that she'd chosen to focus on herself and her own life instead of his? That the dreams of a home outside the city would never come true?

She was making herself sick again. Each time she'd tried to overcome the fear and anxiety, she'd gotten so nauseated and dizzy, she'd had to return to her room at Grace Home. Twice, she'd made it to the very spot she stood now, only to hurry away, biting back bile while a burning ember of shame smoldered in her chest. Her fear was that Aaron would be so hurt by her absence—unable to understand why he'd been abandoned—that he would refuse to speak to her.

A nurse coming on shift walked past, and Mira avoided her gaze, pulling her phone out to fiddle with it until the woman was gone. She swallowed a blossoming lump in her throat and glanced around again. She was alone save for a few people moving past on the sidewalk. A light rain had begun falling, forming black dots on the gray asphalt that expanded into dark puddles. She could hear her father telling her to always watch out for Aaron, could see her mother standing in the window, watching them play. Their love had guided her to this point, had been her compass. She'd trusted it, still did.

Now it was telling her it would be all right.

Aaron would forgive her because the same love bound them.

A tear leaked from the corner of her eye, and she reached up and swiped it away. It was activity hour inside Village Gardens, and through the glass doors she could see several staff members handing out puzzles and coloring supplies to the residents in the rec hall. The television on the wall was on, and two people were walking hand in hand down a sunlit beach.

Mira sniffled once, feeling as if she'd stepped back from another ledge. Then she pulled the door open and went inside to see her brother.

ONE YEAR LATER

49

She thought it was raining but couldn't be sure because she hadn't opened her eyes yet.

Mira Caine lay in the queen-sized bed on the second floor of the Tudor-style home, the large dormer spanning over the room pattering with the sound of a light storm. It was April in Connecticut, and that meant she was sleeping with the windows slightly open at night to bring in the fresh air. Through the crack in the window the sound of the ocean came again over the rain. The distant shush of waves rolling up onto rocks cast there since time immemorial. That hush of the ocean sent her off to sleep every night and woke her each morning. There was a steadiness to it more reliable than the ticking of any clock and never failed to calm her when she needed it. And these days, she needed it less and less.

The prior spring, she'd held off for nearly three weeks before traveling back to Yellow Bay. The little house on the end of a southeastern street was tidy, and you could almost believe someone lived there until noticing how all the windows were darkened with drawn curtains along with the For Sale sign tipped on its side near the front walk. Mira had cruised past it once, double-checking the county tax data on her phone before parking in the nearest alley.

The backyard was empty when she hopped the fence, and the back door hadn't resisted too much to the long flat-blade screwdriver she'd brought in her purse. A few seconds and a short screech of wood, and she was inside.

The interior held the long-dead air of an unlived-in home. Here and there were trinkets and touches of personality. The one stopping her longest was a yellow shawl, crocheted and folded lovingly on the back of a well-used chair in the living room.

In the kitchen, everything was in its place. She indulged an image of Gael cooking there for his mother before she passed. Then she went to the stove and took apart the ventilation hood above it.

Four screws and the filter came free. Beyond it was what she'd come for, hoping and not really believing it would be there.

The cash was sealed inside a plastic bag. There were twelve thick stacks, all bound tightly, all hundred-dollar bills. By the time she'd examined the money and set it on the countertop, she was trembling. Soon she was shaking. It took three tries to replace the filter, and when she was done, she had to sit for a spell in one of the kitchen chairs.

Two minutes later, she was out the back door and moving to her car. She saw no one the entire time.

The house and property she'd settled on were located fifty miles over the southern Connecticut border, near a small town named Ulman. An acre with a modest two-bedroom home sitting on a gentle, sloping hill that gave gorgeous views of the sea in the distance.

Of all the places they'd toured, Aaron had fallen completely in love with the Tudor and the view. The frugal part of her, the part her father had handed down through his stories of a childhood growing up in the rural poverty of western Maine, cried out to find something less expensive. They didn't need ocean views (or the taxes that came with them), but seeing the look on Aaron's face when he watched the flow of water course in and out of the rocks, how transfixed he was, and the stillness that fell over him quieted any reservations she had.

She listened now to the rain pattering down without opening her eyes and searched past the sound for the soft snores coming from Aaron's room across the hall. She almost always rose before him and got breakfast started by the time he came downstairs, already telling her about what he hoped to do that day.

It had taken months for a sense of normalcy to return between them. She'd relived the moment, after finally gathering enough courage to go inside Village Gardens after her six-month absence, of stopping at his door, seeing him there, sitting with his back to her as he had before she'd left for the island. How she'd rapped out their knock on the doorjamb, and how his head had come up and half-turned toward her, then stopped. How he'd looked away and hadn't returned his part of the greeting.

Those memories would be with her until the end of her life, scars of another kind layered and hidden where no one could see.

Mira sighed and finally opened her eyes to the whitewashed ceiling, beginning to brighten with morning light. Sometimes, it was hard to believe she was here and this was really their life. It took conscious thought to assure herself it was over, at least as much as it could be.

In the aftermath of the ordeal, she'd found herself edging on an abyss of despair, one that could've easily swallowed her whole, and might have if she hadn't sought help. Shortly after moving, she'd found a therapist and begun seeing her twice a week. With the gradual relief the therapy brought, she'd begun exploring options to get a degree in psychology herself.

Something called to her when it came to helping others. Aaron was obviously at the heart of it, but Isabelle was there too. Despite her betrayal, she'd been reaching out the only way she could, and it had left a mark on Mira. Trauma was a chain stretching into the past, and sometimes it couldn't be broken without help—Leland was proof of that, given how badly skewed he'd become by his father's apathy and embarrassment of his son's condition. His stigmatization had in turn gone on to affect Allison, then Isabelle, creating the terrible choice for Oliver and Eleanor. She knew some people wouldn't feel sorrow for them, but she did. She couldn't help it. If she'd learned anything on the island, it was that her prior belief was true.

Everyone deserved help.

In the end, she was most thankful for Aaron. She didn't know what she would've done without him. The move from the city had been the closing of one book and the opening of another for them, a new story they were writing each day with one another. In the evenings, they walked along the nearest stretch of beach where Aaron liked to collect shells and bring them home to paint. He had an entire series of watercolors devoted to the shore, and Mira had reached out to a local gallery that was in the process of finding a place in their upcoming schedule for a show featuring his work.

It felt as if they were slowly but surely making their way clear of a shadow cast by some crushing weight and that soon they would emerge into full daylight. And when that happened, it would be—

Her train of thought gradually ground to a halt as she realized something was wrong with her fingers. They felt cramped and tight. Slowly, she realized she recognized the sensation.

Someone was holding her hand.

With a jerk of her head Mira looked to the left into Isabelle's face inches away. "You promised you wouldn't leave me," Isabelle said.

A hoarse cry erupted from Mira, and Isabelle wavered, taking on the appearance of a heat mirage on a highway. Then she was gone and Mira was rubbing her hand, trying to massage away the feeling of the woman's fingers intertwined with her own.

When she felt strong enough to sit up, Mira swung her feet over the edge of the bed but kept them from hanging low enough for someone hiding beneath to reach out and grasp her ankle. She settled her face into her hands and waited until the rampaging panic ebbed.

A waking nightmare. One of dozens she'd had since escaping the island. Intrusive memories—the past inserting itself into the present—powerful and frightening but unable to hurt her. Nonetheless, that didn't stop her from performing certain ritual compulsions in her day-to-day life.

She'd gotten rid of all her wall clocks during the move and now relied solely on her phone and the display on the microwave, making sure their times always matched. Before going to sleep, she checked under all the beds and behind doors in the house and had taken to marking the corners of furniture and decorations on the floor with a piece of chalk to make sure they hadn't been moved while she wasn't looking. Then there was the feeling of being watched whenever they went shopping or to a movie in Ulman, the instinct to glance over her shoulder incessantly while always expecting to see Eleanor or Jeff a few steps behind.

Mira rose and went to the attached bath, and laved water across her face. Over a year, and there still had been no news of their whereabouts. Detective Denbrough kept in touch, giving her a few updates on leads, but nothing came of them. Mira didn't expect anything to. If money could become camouflage, the authorities might never find any of them. Still, the idea they would come seeking revenge stalked her at times even though she knew it wasn't logical.

Of course, logic didn't always outweigh fear, so for the meantime, she would continue to check beneath the bed and look over her shoulder. She would keep going to therapy and striving to help others. Maybe someday it would be different, and she held tightly to that hope.

She dressed and made her way silently into the hall, pausing by Aaron's door. He was beginning to stir. He'd taken a particular liking to a recipe for banana walnut pancakes, and she thought she'd make them for him when he woke.

Mira moved down the stairs into the kitchen that was filled with the light particular to spring mornings. She paused by the small table where she and Aaron ate most their meals to look at the photo hanging above it. It was a shot of her and Aaron and their parents in front of their old house. They were all smiling, and she could almost feel her mother's hands on her shoulders as they were in the picture. She'd placed the photo prominently on purpose, because it twisted her heart with a beautiful ache each time she looked at it.

And because it was a reminder there was no going back, no changing what had happened. There was only the sweet heartbreak of memory, of time and its passage giving way to something new. Hopefully something better.

Mira touched the photo once, then fixed herself a cup of coffee that she took onto the front porch, where the air held the sound of the sea's heartbeat, and in it sang the single word of home.

AUTHOR'S NOTE

While the characters and situations in *Wyndclyffe* are completely fictitious, sadly, many of the struggles depicted are not. An estimated one in four US adults suffer with some form of mental illness, while over 54 percent of them do not receive treatment.

As common as mental illness is, it is still tragically stigmatized, but there are many organizations dedicated to treatment and education when it comes to mental health—two of which are listed below. If you or anyone you know is suffering and in need of help, please don't hesitate to reach out.

You are not alone.

NAMI (National Alliance on Mental Illness): www.nami.org or 1-800-950-6264

The National Suicide Prevention Lifeline is a national network of local crisis centers that provides free and confidential emotional support to people in suicidal crisis or emotional distress twenty-four hours a day, seven days a week. They are committed to improving crisis services and advancing suicide prevention by empowering individuals, advancing professional best practices, and building awareness.

Call 1-800-273-8255 or visit https://suicidepreventionlifeline.org/

ACKNOWLEDGMENTS

As always, I'm beyond grateful to my family for their love and patience since I couldn't do any of this without them. Huge thank you to my agent, Laura Rennert—I'm so fortunate to have your unwavering support and guidance. Many thanks to Jacque Ben-Zekry for helping mold the initial shape of the book into something so much better—your insight is beyond valuable. Thanks to Jessica MacLeish for the excellent developmental edit. Thank you to the entire team at Podium whose enthusiasm and championing of this book is most appreciated. And eternal thanks to the readers who keep making what I do possible; I am forever in your debt.

ABOUT THE AUTHOR

Joe Hart is the Edgar Award–winning and *Wall Street Journal*–bestselling author of seventeen novels, including *Wyndclyffe*, *The River Is Dark*, *Obscura*, *The Last Girl*, and *Or Else*. His work has been translated into eight languages and been optioned for film. Hart lives with his family in Minnesota.